Further Praise for

BUSY
MONSTERS

"The prose is electric. . . . Genius." —*Poets & Writers*

"*Busy Monsters* may be the best literary present you could bring to a brainy guy's bachelor party. It boasts lots of gonzo adventure, wacky sex and an endorsement by Harold Bloom. . . . William Giraldi's cocky first novel is a romance for real men—real nerdy men willing to fight for a woman's heart. . . . These busy antics are awfully funny. . . . Hijinks keep spiking through this screwball narrative, but what really keeps pumping it alive is that impossibly odd and self-conscious voice, a mixture of 19th-century gentility and modern hipster. . . . It's irresistibly strange. . . . One of the weirdest comic novels of the year. And it has a delicate sweetness that shows through at just the right moments in what is, after all, a very old, romantic story." —Ron Charles, *Washington Post*

"A certain kind of reader, weary of contemporary fiction's polished 'craft' being mistaken for distinctive style, will not be able to stop reading when teased with [Giraldi's] sentences. Although Giraldi admires (and has been obviously influenced by) the late Barry Hannah . . . he is the bastard literary son of Evelyn Waugh. The title of *Busy Monsters* is not the only way

D0051565

in which Giraldi's novel resembles *Vile Bodies*, Waugh's second novel. Both are hilarious; both satirize the unruliness and overindulgence of their characters' lives and yet revel in every minute of it; both are terrified of boredom. . . . And beneath the facetiousness and verbal hijinks, there is a seriousness of Christian purpose to *Busy Monsters*. . . . Giraldi's model is the 'antithetical fusion' of high and low, superb and uncouth, which Erich Auerbach describes in *Mimesis* as the 'mixed style' of Christian rhetoric. Giraldi resorts to it to suggest the need for something that is missing in most postmodern lives."

—D. G. Myers, *Commentary*

"At the heart of *Busy Monsters* is Homar's brilliance, humanity, and understanding. . . . Homar is a giant in his multifariousness, a gushing-blood romantic whose longing infiltrates every sentence. . . . What makes Giraldi's enormous characters so fascinating are their complexities and contradictions. You've never met these people. But then again, you've met all of them."   —David Holub, *American Book Review*

"William Giraldi . . . achieves a sort of poetic lunacy in this debut novel. . . . Giraldi's prose throughout is enveloping but it's also intimate, reading almost like the lovesick diary entries of Franz Kafka. But beneath the surreal, there's substance: The encounters with fantastical creatures and lampooning of famous epics (like *The Odyssey*) are merely set pieces in his Gen-Y ruminations on relationships and mortality. . . . The fun here is not in the destination, but in the journey itself. And with monsters like these, what fun it is."

—Jeremy Medina, *Time Out New York*, Critics' Pick

"Wacky as it is, *Busy Monsters* has a lot to say about literature with its off-kilter meditations on literary conventions, including strained father-son relationships, love stories, quest narratives and the contemporary phenomenon of the made-up memoir. *Busy Monsters* is hilarious, ridiculous, brimming with energy, and makes a promising debut for Giraldi, a writer with a strange and appealing mind." —*Dallas Morning News*

"Skewering the false bravado of the aughties memoir craze, *Busy Monsters* also reads a bit like the type of screenplay Wes Anderson might write in the midst of a roid rage. . . . The whole fun of *Busy Monsters* is in Giraldi's sentences, which manage to be both parodic and wholly original."
—Jonathan Messinger, *Time Out Chicago*

"In his riotous debut novel—up there with, say, James Wilcox's *Modern Baptists*—Giraldi tells the story of Charles Homar, a jilted fiancé who embarks on a hilariously ill-advised odyssey to win back his beloved. . . . Charles's journey—filled with offbeat characters, seen through a perfectly skewed worldview, and related in an idiosyncratic voice—might remind readers of the one taken by the equally wrong-headed Ray Midge in Charles Portis's comic masterpiece, *The Dog of the South*." —*Publishers Weekly*, starred review

"Here we have a seriocomic picaresque that references everything from the *Odyssey* to medieval romances to *Don Quixote* and *Moby-Dick*. A brilliant first novel that may well be in the running for 2011's literary awards." —*Library Journal*, starred review

"In this very funny first novel, Giraldi launches his loquacious narrator on an absurd quest that is touching as well as comical. . . . Erudite, salacious, and frequently hilarious, *Busy Monsters* heralds the emergence of a prodigiously talented comic writer onto the literary scene." —*Booklist*

"As unpalatable as the fictional [Charles] Homar would be as a real live person, he's an absolutely delicious character, making a series of hilariously nearsighted (and outright bad) decisions to propel himself through this far-fetched (and downright funny) narrative. . . . The voice [Giraldi] has given Charles is singular and arresting . . . and filled with quirky turns of phrase, unexpected literary and cultural allusions, self-aware asides, and highfalutin word choices that would make Roget swell with pride. The plot, too, is an exciting yet masterfully managed hodgepodge." —*Salon*

"Much of the joy of *Busy Monsters* comes from watching the protagonist bumble his way from one misadventure to the next, all the while maintaining an impressively detailed first-person monologue. . . . An absurdist jaunt, a particularly fanciful picaresque . . . governed by its own peculiar internal logic." —*Bookforum*

"William Giraldi is one of those writers for whom every sentence matters. He commands language like Kingsley Amis or Peter Carey. *Busy Monsters* is . . . a postmodern quest that riffs on every epic story in Western literature, yet never takes itself too seriously." —*Powell's Books*

"The book's antics are entertaining, but the real treat is how much fun Giraldi seems to be having with language. It's a contagious passion that makes *Busy Monsters* a promising debut."   —Samantha Nelson, *The Onion*

"Readers will be swept along in breathless, disbelieving glee."
                                        —Chris Barsanti, *PopMatters*

"Riotous . . . part Don Quixote, part Jack Kerouac."
                        —*Washington Independent Review of Books*

"A bold, satirical debut."   —*Times* (London)

"Populated by extraterrestrials, Asiatic sex slaves and beasts of the deep, William Giraldi's first novel is not a debut that enters the literary scene blushing. This book shouts: it's linguistically playful to the point of hyperactivity, yet self-consciously attempts to place itself in the American canon. . . . Beneath the surface of this extrovert book is a story of bewildered masculinity and neurosis. The result in places makes Gary Shteyngart look restrained."   —*Financial Times*

"Henry Fielding's *Tom Jones*, Cervantes's *Don Quixote*, Voltaire's *Candide*, and Vonnegut's *Breakfast of Champions* comprise the club of picaresque that William Giraldi's lively *Busy Monsters* aspires to join. . . . Bold, propulsive prose and hilarious, thought-inducing cultural references. . . . A compelling work of literary merrymaking."
                                        —*Daily Beast*

BUSY MONSTERS

BUSY MONSTERS

a novel

WILLIAM GIRALDI

W. W. NORTON & COMPANY   NEW YORK   LONDON

Excerpt from *High Lonesome*, copyright © 1996 by Barry Hannah.
Used by permission of Grove/Atlantic, Inc.

For information about permission to reproduce selections from this
book, write to Permissions, W. W. Norton & Company, Inc.,
500 Fifth Avenue, New York, NY 10110

For information about special discounts for bulk purchases,
please contact W. W. Norton Special Sales at
specialsales@wwnorton.com or 800-233-4830

Manufacturing by Courier Westford
Book design by Ellen Cipriano
Production manager: Devon Zahn

Library of Congress Cataloging-in-Publication Data

Giraldi, William.
Busy monsters : a novel / William Giraldi. — 1st ed.
p. cm.
ISBN 978-0-393-07962-3 (hardcover)
I. Title.
PS3607.I469B87 2011
813'.6—dc22

2011007710

ISBN 978-0-393-34293-2 pbk.

W. W. Norton & Company, Inc.
500 Fifth Avenue, New York, N.Y. 10110
www.wwnorton.com

W. W. Norton & Company Ltd.
Castle House, 75/76 Wells Street, London W1T 3QT

1 2 3 4 5 6 7 8 9 0

For Ethan Jacob,
my busy little monster,
and his mother,
Katie Lin,
who accepts
the monster in me.

Ask the locals how sweet the wreckage of damned
near everybody was around that little pube-rioting
Juliet and her moon-whelp Romeo.

—BARRY HANNAH

We hunt the wind, we worship the statue,
cry aloud to the desert.

—*DON QUIXOTE*

What is your beast?

—CHARLES OTIS WHITMAN

BUSY MONSTERS

1. ANTIHERO AGONISTES

STUNNED BY LOVE and some would say stupid from too much sex, I decided I had to drive down South to kill a man. Gillian and I were about to be married and her ex-beau of four years, Marvin Gluck—Virginia state trooper, boots and all—was heaving his psychosis our way, sending bow-tied packages, soilsome letters, and text messages to the bestial effect of, *If you marry that baboon I'll end all our lives.*

I, Charles Homar, memoirist of mediocre fame, a baboon?

Coercing him into kindness, Christian or otherwise, had already failed—large. For more than a year we had implored him to leave us be, appealed to the protector-of-the-peace in him, filed complaints with not-caring police here in our Connecticut town, suggested religion, yoga, even herbs as antidote to his crocodilian stance, his swamp of a heart: nothing worked. His threats were usually followed by some truly treacly pleas for forgiveness, a smattering of *I'm sorrys* all in a row. Regret is an acid; it pecked at his innards. Good. He wanted to be a better "humany person." I wanted him dead. Seven thousand citizens die each day in our America—why couldn't he be one of them? Traffic calamity, aneurism, lightning bolt: anything would have done, anything to keep me from doing this deed I wasn't keen on doing and didn't know whether I could do or not.

"I think he's only bluffing," Gillian said on the afternoon we received one of his murderous notes. "I know he can be really kind when he wants to."

"Kind? Darling, that memo there says he'd like to impose trauma upon my person. He has the manners of a microbe."

"I'm really sure he's bluffing, honey. Let's ignore him. He'll go away," she told me, but I could see that she was frightened, that all with her was not groovy. "Anyway, why don't you write about it in your column?"

"Gillian, love, I don't need extra material for my memoirs. They're already depraved enough to warp the mind of any adolescent."

"He'll go away, Charlie."

From Gillian's pictures and videos I knew this vulgarian was a colossus of a gent whose voice and testicular presence could hush the human flotsam in any riled-up room. Furthermore, he had a face so uglified by his parents' DNA that it recalled a clay-shaping exercise gone heinously wrong. Left eye like the oblong knot in a plank of pine. The kind of guy who eats a tomato like an apple. A disposition downright redneck. I've known fevered men like Marvin: they get a certain idea in their noggins or, worse yet, a funny feeling in their hearts, and nothing on earth can deter them from their channel. They go agog with havoc, get off on outlawry. Quite frankly, I was frightened, too.

Here's the other end of it, and I have no shame: I couldn't live with knowing there was a man out there who loved Gillian the way I did, who had swum in her sweet-scented flesh, who had eased apart her thighs, delved into her special center. Also, the bedlamite had her name tattooed across his pectorals, from one fifty-inch side to the other, in large red Gothic letters, too. If her name were *Jennifer* or *Michelle* it might not have vexed me so; but *Gillian* is a rarity, and those letters on his chest could mean only her, always. It caused all the amino acids in me to swirl, swirl.

Insecure or homicidal: the adjectives don't bother me one bit. Having to silence a single man for the sake of solace does not make one homicidal. Of course I am a Christian and know the program, but love and sex have their own sacred creeds and they burn every bit as much as the ten laws of the Lord. I've perused the *Kama Sutra*. Listen: I was not proud of what I had to do, but I had to do it just the same. Some will understand, and those who don't know yet one day will.

All I have to offer in my defense is the mathematical truth: I wanted to love my bride in peace and tranquillity but Marvin Gluck was not going to let that happen. The way I see it, he made the decision, not I. He just had to go and pledge an undying love to Gillian and couldn't grab hold of the fact that such pledges are made every day and most don't mean a damn. I'll give him that: he makes a pledge and sticks to it. Still, his pledge was crowding mine. What a man feels for his woman can be all-out unholy. When Gillian tried on her organza wedding dress for me, I wept with the joy of the resurrected.

I met her on the Ferris wheel at the local bazaar held to raise money for a children's hospital. I had volunteered to run the wheel because when I was a teenager, my kid brother Bartholomew was chewed up by leukemia, plus I thought I could add the charity-giving experience to my weekly memoir column for *New Nation Weekly*—circulation a hearty six hundred thousand—and thus come across as a guy who cares, a balladeer with heart to spare. It rained that night and hardly anybody came, but then in floated Gillian under a green umbrella, a tantric Mary Poppins, handed me a ticket, and said she wanted to ride the wheel 'round and 'round. This dazzling babe alone on a Friday night? I couldn't even speak; her odd beauty was the injurious kind, radioactive—it had physical effects on me, my anatomy in quake—lovely hawkish nose, straight black mane dyed with streaks of red henna, flat-teated and thickish through the bottom, symmetrical toes showing through her sandals. She was as if the word *gustatory* had grown legs and got a dress.

For twenty minutes she rode the wheel, and I watched her with her head thrown back and eyes peeled on the sky, patches of light aglisten behind evil gray clouds. And then, horrors: the rusty wheel stopped turning—the organizer of the bazaar had saved a wad by renting only semifunctional equipment—trapping my lady at the top, and this despite my frantic punching of buttons and yanking of levers, consulting with the bazaar electrician and other bewildered passersby. Can you imagine? The damsel a hostage sixty-some feet up there? Well, I in my valor and Levi's jeans could not very well let her stew in the drizzle, and so, with very little pause and a showy casting-off of my rainwear, I began climbing, lemur-like, up the steel links and bars of the Ferris wheel.

"You're gonna break your skull, fella," the gal kept shouting down to me, to which I replied, "I'd break that and many a more in the name of your safety." She stressed to me that she'd just as well wait for the fire department—those valiant buccaneers of Ladder Company Number 5, skirt-chasers and wannabe samurai, all of them—rather than risk bodily damage straddled across my back. I'd hear nothing of that.

"That is not romantic," I told her. When I reached her in the cage I thrust out my strong grip just as I had seen numerous movie heroes do—Errol Flynn and the like—and then, reassuring her of my brawn, flexed a bicep. I was in excellent physical condition, it's true, and could have modeled for one of those home gym systems with all the pulleys and wires and whatnot. Likewise, my hair had Vitalis shine, was not thinning.

She appeared incredulous and who could blame her? "Just hold on," I said, "and put some trust in me, Charles Homar. Others have done so and not been badly disappointed."

"I'd rather not die, thanks."

"Not a chance. I am neither bogus nor brash, just a citizen out doing his duty. Look into my eyes, miss. What do you see there? That's right: I was a Templar Knight a few lives ago. Let's meet the earth."

"Why do you speak that way?"

"What way?"

"That weirdo way."

"*No comprende, chica.*"

"Oh, Christ," she said. "Are we really going to do this?"

And I said, "Really."

Light as a bag of foam packing peanuts—I had once toiled

for a shipping firm—she held on as I descended that metal mess Mr. Ferris would have disowned had he seen it. This feat of heroism came breezily and without much sweat, so jazzed was I on her pheromonal scent, the elements of lust just then coalescing into love, a single-celled splotch becoming a giraffe. Onlookers cheered, some clapped; one obese popcorn-eater, spellbound by the scene, had a swift back-slap for me and then mumbled something incoherent, though it sounded faintly congratulatory.

Soon the fireworks were done; boredom ensued and people dispersed. Gillian and I stood there, hands in pockets, not five feet apart, her breath still the nervous kind of the almost-harmed. Me: I was sweating now, but not from the climb.

"Thanks for saving my life, fella," she said. "I guess you're a hero."

"It's just a job, madam," I said.

"But we could have waited for the fire department, you know."

Where did her lips get their collagen pink puff? The last time I had seen lips like those in person was when unwise nuns had hired me to teach autobiography to a classroom stocked with teenage Catholic females. In my head now was a violin and organ ditty circa 1850. Something German.

"Local firefighters would have accidentally grabbed your breast while helping you down, believe me."

"I see," she said. "And your touching my breast was accidental?"

The record playing my dreamy German ditty scratched to a halt: you know the sound. "What? I touched your breast? No. I'm a gentleman. Really. No, I didn't. Did I? What?"

"I'm kidding," she said, and her teeth were so white! "Not touched. More like brushed."

"Oh, shit, I'm sorry, really, this is an abomination, a breast-brushing abomination, I didn't mean to, I mean, I was just, you know, saving you, and—"

"I'm just fooling with you. But I *am* grateful for your gallantry, so thank you. Tell me your name again."

"Charles Homar," and I proffered her my hand, a-tremble.

"Not the writer? *New Nation Weekly*?"

"The one and only, madam," and I bowed here like a squire or some-such. Someone who owns property, fights criminals, admires estrogen.

"I like your columns. I don't read them every issue, actually. But the ones I've read I like a lot. That silly one about how you almost burned down your house trying to kill the squirrel in your attic?"

"Oh, yes, that squirrel," and I feigned modesty, looked bashful.

"They make squirrel traps, you know. Or you could have called an exterminator. You didn't have to build your own flamethrower."

"Right," I said, her splendor slapping me sideways. "That makes more sense."

The end of rain, some orange sky aglow, and the carnival got hopping again. All around us families and teenage kids—some on skateboards, some smoking, some with arm tattoos in advertisement of their parents' bungling (even the girls! so unladylike and pubic)—scudded to and fro and fro again, clutching popcorn and cotton candy and the kind of acidic soda that makes lead vanish, all of them unaware of the enchantment happening right there in front of me, what the orange sky meant above.

Gillian said, "Is everything you write true, though? Sometimes I have a feeling you're making things up."

I must have been staring in silence, owlish, at those diamonds below her brows because she said, "Mr. Homar?"

"Yes, yes. I mean, no, no, everything's true, one hundred percent, absolutely."

"But why is a, umm, kind of famous magazine writer working a Ferris wheel?"

Kind of?

"Charity," I said. "Goodness. You know, Christian values. Hey, you don't sound like you're from around here. What brings you to the democratic state of Connecticut?"

"A job, what else? And I had to get away from my boyfriend."

The overeager wolf in me, all woof and wow, couldn't keep his jaw shut.

"So you don't have a boyfriend still?"

She only shook her head ever so wanly and glanced down at my sneakers, new Nikes that made me feel younger by three or four wrinkles. Of course, what followed was an awkward, sweat-inducing pause, me trying to summon a sentence devoid of degeneracy.

"Well, thank you again, Mr. Homar. I look forward to reading more of your memoirs."

She touched my shoulder just then before turning away, and I watched her leave, all the centimeters of me paralyzed in a way I had not felt before. But inside me: think Vesuvius. For many minutes I felt her hand still there on my deltoid, her scent lingering as if smoke from a much-needed flame.

Okay: I am not a deluded man—right?—nor barmy. My life was not lucky; beauteous females with a slight Virginia drawl did not often accept my offers. Past girlfriends had told me I was just a pinch shy of handsome, which I did not mind. And so I let Gillian stroll away that night, a dark cavern beneath my breastplate, all the bats slapping their wings wildly. Ten minutes later, the Ferris wheel now defunct, I went to grab my raincoat and saw her green umbrella hooked there on the entrance gate.

Opportunity! Did she leave it on purpose? I turned over that entire village-in-a-parking-lot—including back alleyways where grotesque carnival creatures transgressed against God with absinthe and inquired about my mission—and couldn't find her anywhere. She was gone.

You should have seen me sprinting to my car through the carnival crowd, knocking into elbows and pocketbooks, pieces of popcorn flying in one direction, Coca-Cola spraying in another, multiple mouths cussing directions about where I could go and how fast I should get there. I hurried off the grounds and started down a vacant Main Street, a suburban boulevard so cosmetically altered since my childhood that sometimes I'd wake from a nap and feel like Rip Van Winkle molested.

Here's a limbic liberal outburst, a knee-jerk obligation (when my knee works): the acres of green in my town had been bought by cloven-hoofed condo developers and strip malls; the piss-colored McDonald's arches and the mom-and-pop-killing Walmart smoldered on the horizon like Chernobyl; the twenty-screen theater and the A&P so gargantuan you have to take a break in the produce aisle both replaced a baseball field where children like me went to dream and dream again. Let's not forget the sixteen new roads paved to accommodate the SUVs tanking to it all, which they have algebraic difficulty doing: just try driving through town around four forty-five p.m. on a weekday. You better bring a book, and I don't mean an audio one.

There, in front of Vinny's Pizzeria—the very place where I had been clogging my arteries since I was a freckled boy on a BMX bike, one of the only businesses in town with the Sicilian ardor to stay—there was Gillian! I recognized her distinctive walk right away and veered to the curb.

Stretched across the seat, I said through the passenger's window, "Excuse me, miss. You forgot your umbrella."

"Who's that?" she said, coming closer.

"It's me, Charlie Homar? Remember me, I saved your life? Back there on the Ferris wheel? Just now, before?"

She said into the open window, "You're stalking me now, Mr. Homar?"

Just as my viscera were about to go topsy-turvy from dejection and being made a fool of—the word *crestfallen* occurred to me—her cushioned mouth stretched into a grin and I nearly sighed with relief.

"Oh, you're joking," I said. "Thank God. No, I just wanted to return your umbrella. It looks like a good one."

"And I suppose you're going to offer to drive me home, too? On account of the weather?"

Well, of course I was.

"Tell me, Mr. Homar, why would a girl want to get into a car with a complete stranger?"

"Well . . . because I'm not a complete stranger? Because I

saved your life? Oh, and because you've read my memoirs?" Long pause, during which I tried to recall the name of the saint who protects the half-faithful. "And, well," I ventured, "because you're lonely like me?"

"Interesting," she said, tongue jabbed into cheek to reveal a thinking gal. "What makes you think I'm lonely?"

"A man can only hope."

After a short pause, she said, "The door is locked, Charles."

"Oh, shit, sorry," and I hit the button and then jumped out to race around and open the door for her, chivalrous and suave, I thought, something to remember. "Wait here," I told her, "I'm getting our dinner," and I did more racing into the pizzeria.

"Vinny," I said, "how long have I been coming here?"

From behind the counter, next to the one-ton, fifty-year-old oven that was the secret to his ambrosial pies, Vinny said, "Since you a kid, a-maybe like, who knows, a-twenny year."

"That's right, Vin. Twenty years or more. And I need you right now to give birth to a delicious cheese pie, the kind that double-whammies: first the taste buds, then the heart. My nights from now on depend on it. Do you accept this mission? Because, if so, I need this godly pie in, like, five minutes," and I thumbed out the window to Gillian waiting in my Ford hybrid.

"Ahh, okay, Vinny see. You a-got it, Charlie," and he clapped his red-and-white-striped helots into action with a Sicilian tantrum.

Now, imagine this, if you will: me at the pizzeria window looking through my reflection at Gillian, who was at the passenger's window looking through her reflection at me. Get it?

Proust would give you sixty pages about those reflections but this is Connecticut and I've got to move on here.

No beer in a bar, much less sex in my car, but just the two of us perched on the top step outside her one-bedroom prefab townhouse with a cheese pie so succulent it rendered us speechless for minutes at a time. She had said that, lifesaver though I was, if I attempted anything wacky or even suggestively satanic, she'd go succubus on my ass—she had studied ninjutsu and Descartes and knew how one enhances the other—"so don't get snaky," she said—and I warmed with admiration. Here was a gal with gumption, sangfroid, with a Virginia voice that might melt wrought iron. In the driveway slept her yellow Volkswagen Beetle, the face of a whopping flower painted on the hood and testifying to goodness.

We talked and ate till midnight, the familiar chatter about childhood, siblings, and what we would buy if we won the lottery. I said, "I'd donate half the money to the children's hospital and use the other half to build a house with no other houses in view. Privacy matters."

She hinted that she was unmoved by my soppy wish to play Robin Hood for a hospital, and that if I was trying to win her approval with stories of sick kids, the donkey in me could forget it. She said she'd spend all the money on a curvy boat and a team of scientists and fishermen, trying to be the first-ever person to capture a giant squid, which no modern human has ever seen alive but about which tales abound. Astonishing! Gillian collected giant squid curiosa and could hold court with any ocean-loving dweeb in thick glasses.

"It lives," she said. "I know it. Ancient seafarers have seen it and written about it. The problem is, we think it lives at such great depths it's nearly impossible to find. Some carcasses have washed up onshore, but we need it *alive*. There are only a handful of scientists who have dedicated themselves to finding it. Sadly, the really big funding is scarce for the giant squid."

"Giant squid, huh? How'd you become interested in that?"

"In childhood, Charles. Always in childhood."

"A monster?"

"No, not a monster," she confirmed. "A beautiful animal."

And I thought, *Yes, a beautiful animal indeed*. When I drove home that night—her number already entered in my cell phone, me jittery with a teenage thrill, alive again after what seemed bubonic eons, the lunar light pulling at my water—I was certain that if I switched on the news in my living room I'd find that the cosmos had been washed of brutality and outrage. Remember the stimulating incipience of romance, the excitement of possibility, of being rescued from the abscess of lonesomeness and having someone to share your hydrogen with? Recall the glee? It meant your little life was worth something, your personality, yes, have-able. It meant sex for your now-laudable seed, and dinnertime conversation, too. Go grab your lovers, people, hold them close, feel the validation. You're barely carbon-based without them.

So that was our beginning in the Garden of Connecticut. The bog in me had ceased its bubble.

HERE'S ANOTHER CONFESSION while I'm hard at it: I dislike cops. You give a man that kind of authority and just like that his cock swells six inches. What it does to female cops I'm not qualified to say, but it can't be good, though each one may be maternally erotic in her own way. Marvin's being a Virginia state trooper could have had some influence on my decision to shepherd him henceforth, seeing as how state troopers can be more crooked than the common cop. More important, he'd always be able to find us, no matter how we tried to elude him. I've heard those troopers have access to supercomputers that will let them locate anyone anywhere, which was how he had managed to remain in contact with Gillian even though she had fled Virginia and started over in suburban Connecticut. His being Southern had zero to do with it; as a Democrat and New Englander I harbor no prejudice and do not care for the Neil Young song that claims the Southern man is a louse. In addition, I readily admit that Robert Lee was the most honorable individual ever to mount a steed, his photographs boasting integrity incarnate. My side won the war and I had nothing at all to prove, but I won't budge on this one point: NASCAR is not a sport.

Now, to the business of killing a man: plenty of books and movies are filled with it, and kids today get batty with their sadistic video games, but the truth is that the standard person has never committed murder and never will, nor is he likely to know anyone who has or will. I suppose I don't fit into the standard category because I don't believe every human life is precious, Christian though I am. Mankind would be a prettier lot without certain sons of bitches. So I've always felt myself capable of killing but was grateful I never had cause, not till hobgoblin Gluck presented himself to me as a pesky root that needed plucking. The cycle of his threats and slobbering apologies gave me digestive trouble or else caused me to urp unkindly.

One Wednesday when Gillian was at work I consulted my friend and confidant Groot, an old high school chum who just happens to be a Navy SEAL and has murdered many men— in Iraq, Afghanistan, the former Yugoslavia—some of whom didn't even know they were in the same room with him. He can cleave an apple with a knife from twenty feet away; I've seen him do it. My favorite story is how he and his unit were flown to a mosque in a city north of Baghdad. Insurgents were headquartered inside; it was after midnight in the stygian heat of July. Groot told me the Navy has secret helicopters that make no sound; they can hover six feet above your hair and you'd never know they were there. (UFO technology, he told me, from Roswell. His imagination has a child's beauty.) So one of these choppers clipped in close over the mosque and Groot and his pals rappelled down to the rooftop, dropped themselves just below the ceiling wearing night-vision goggles. Then, with silent carbine assault rifles, they proceeded to shoot every insurgent while he slept. The whole thing sounded very Mohican to me.

Groot's parents still live in town; several times a year he returns home to visit them and that's when we get together to yak. After I called he came to our place, and as we perched at the kitchen table with perspiring glasses of iced tea, I told him my unkind Marvin dilemma while looking crossly at the cowboy hat I had cautioned him never to wear in daylight.

"Charlie," he said, "you aren't Josey Wales. Killing a man is not what it looks like on TV. At least not at first. Maybe I should just fly down there and have a talking-to with him. You know, make him see things our way."

"Groot," I said, "this Marvin Gluck is not the talking-to

kind. Believe me. We've tried. I have letters and emails here that look as if they were scribbled by an eighth century psychopath with Manichean tendencies."

"Ahh, yes, I know the kind."

Looking through the sliding glass door into our meek backyard, I saw what work needed doing: Tom Sawyer the fence, hang a new clothesline, replace the cracked patio, all less viperous than planning homicide, which I was still uncertain whether or not I could carry out. But I had at least to *seem* firm, fed up and stalwart, lest Groot think me gutless and easily plodded upon, opinions I know he had held in the past when I was too yellow to defend myself: Back in high school, for instance, when a lacrosse-playing orangutan falsely accused me of attempting to look up his girlfriend's denim skirt at a keg party, never mind that her legs were barely mammalian. He smacked the spittle from my mouth and I was too frightened to fight back. When Groot saw this across the yard from his vodka vantage point, he charged over and chopped the goon across the throat, at which point said goon gagged himself red and nearly fainted from air loss. Other lacrosse-playing thugs attempted retribution but Groot slid out a chilling combat knife from somewhere inside his jacket. And then—I couldn't believe it—he licked the blade. Didn't talk. Just licked the blade. Those thugs halted and then dawdled away carrying their throat-crushed comrade. After that, we retreated to Vinny's Pizzeria and Groot gave me pointers on how to disable an assailant with bare knuckles or else garden tools if they're handy. We had been pals since kindergarten but never before had I felt that kind of love for him.

"Are you going to write about this Marvin Gluck adventure in your memoirs?" Groot asked.

"And implicate myself? Negative."

"Charlie," he said, "as your trusty compadre, I'll do it for you if you can't manage. Really. I don't think I want you to do this. You're not made for it, Charlie. I am."

"That's sweet. But I have to do this myself. Is it really that difficult?"

"Honestly, no, not at all. The human being is flawed with frailty. And the quality of mercy is *so* strained"—that a bit of Shakespeare I'd have to look up.

He slid out a seven-inch blade from inside his cowboy boot—by what means he had acquired his high regard for that babble clucked out by Garth Brooks, I cannot say—and handed it across the table to me. It was, by golly, the same knife that nearly filleted those lacrosse bullies fifteen years earlier. The rubber and metal of the thing felt so . . . balanced. And clean. It seemed a great shame to dirty it with Gluck.

"Use this," he said.

"A knife, eh? Not a gun? Or, uhh, poison, maybe?"

"No, a gun's too messy, too many potential problems. The noise, ballistics, powder residue, and all that. Poison is hard to get, besides too traceable."

"This is all new to me, Groot. You kill with a knife, and I kill with my words. Ahem."

"That blade is serrated on one side, a razor on the other. When you exit the body you pull up on the serrated side. You know the vital areas?"

Of course I did: I myself was mostly vital areas.

"The Southern man," he said, refilling his iced tea at the table, "is one sick dude. Some of the sickest dudes I've ever met in the military are Southern. Hostility left over from the Civil War. They're good soldiers, so use caution."

"I shall," I said, and held up the knife to the sunlight jabbing in through open blinds.

And then we didn't speak for a stretch; we just stared at the sun reflecting off the blade, Groot no doubt convinced I had snapped my cap, I wondering about the repulsive mess the knife would make when it found Marvin Gluck's jugular.

"Frankly, Charlie, I'm worried about you. You've always been the artsy kind, peace-loving and all that. I never understood it myself, but I esteemed the idiot in you. Now I feel as if you might be crossing a line into a whole new mode of existence."

"Groot," I said, "understand: this must be done. He'll stalk and kill her one day, I can feel it. Or firebomb our wedding. He already said he would. We told the cops; they don't give a damn. Bastards protect their own. So what kind of man would I be to do nothing, to let my lady live in fear?"

"Syrupy Miss Gillian really has a vise grip on the heart of my pal Charles. It makes me proud to see you all grown up," and he winked at me. "When we were in college I was worried that you might become a loner and misanthrope, a stranger to the flesh of others."

"Likewise, loyal Groot. You make me proud, too."

"Just call me if you have a problem, Charlie. And whatever you do, don't turn yourself in if you get to feeling guilty."

This was an allusion to the robbery we'd pulled off our senior year of high school: Each Christmastime, a local sporting goods store rented a warehouse in an industrial park to sell all overstock items at discounted prices. Groot recruited me for "the job," as he kept calling it: at eleven one night—the start of "the witching hour," he found it necessary to inform me—he scaled the wall with a grappling hook and rope, unscrewed the skylight directly above the warehouse, dropped the rope, and zipped down inside. He then unlocked the door to let me in— no alarm and no security guard, which he knew because he had "cased the joint." We loaded six gigantic outdoor garbage bags with so many coats, watches, sneakers, and boots that they almost didn't fit in the backseat and trunk of my car. We had purchased the bags at Food World before we went; they were called Steel Bags, and Groot thought it a comedy beyond Mel Brooks that we were using them to *steal*.

Two days later, a front-page article in our local paper proclaimed the theft, and right there next to the piece blared a color photo of a crying woman: the owner. She and her husband were the kind of distraught that occurs in the Congo. I felt so wretched about what we had done that I brought back all the loot—still in my car because Groot's mother had a habit of turning over his room in search of armaments—directly to the owners themselves. Mine were the apologies of a reformed swindler—I believe I uttered the word *exculpation* and made a reference to Hammurabi—and they were so grateful for the missing merchandise that they let me drive away without calling for handcuffs.

Why had I committed the crime in the first place if I knew I wasn't of the crime-committing mold? Boys, let me share a bit of wisdom I've picked up along the way: males want mostly the esteem of other males, even when in earshot of the pom-

pom swish and rah-rah chants belted out by a bevy of disrobed cheerleaders. If you ask me, this male want is absolute Neo-lithic, which just goes to show how far we've come.

But I was not yet a grown man in love when we pulled off "the sporting goods massacre," as we—he—titled that legend-ary thrill.

No, a grown man in love is a different critter altogether.

A MAN CHERISHES his lady and he owes nobody an explana-tion, but in my case I have a whole catalogue of reasons why Gil-lian is worth protecting, some of which I'll share. First, she's the only woman I've ever met who hasn't asked me to adjust my per-sona, enlarge my heart, tweak my ideas, or alter my language, and this from a lady with Opinions. Second, she cradles me at night and hymns Nina Simone softly in my ear—that in itself is worth the price of murder. Only the thane of a prosperous land receives that kind of cuddling. Third, her lovemaking is as close as I'll ever get to being a spaceman, and every man wants to strut on the moon. (In the past—I'm ashamed to admit—before I had met Gillian, tenderness, compassion, and concern had always strangled my otherwise meaty libido. I had to dislike the gal in order to climax. Shrews, bozos, those with shrunken cerebellum—they were the only ones I found alluring. Sex with a generous and beautiful woman felt a little like pissing on a flower.) Fourth, she has no annoying emotional complications, wasn't neglected or abused by Big Daddy when she was six years old, pigtails bouncing as she hopped. Fifth, she cares for my ail-ing father when she can, visits him every week, brings him pres-ents, and giggles at his not-funny jokes. If you knew my father you'd be mightily impressed by this: a killjoy with half a dozen heart-related maladies, he's no prince to be around. And lastly, Gillian and I have never had a single argument (although, yes, there was that one time we agreed to disagree about having children: she said two sounded nice and I said they sounded like smallpox). You might call this unnatural, unhealthy, or untrue, but I call it a nice fit.

And I remembered what my layabout life was like before her, nothing even vaguely kinetic in my breast and limbs, me a somber piece of animal in gym shorts and a sweatshirt far from the gym and not sweating. See me chopsticking dinner alone at the House of Wong on a Friday night; or scrolling up and down an Internet dating site on a Saturday afternoon, and then in bed by nine with an unannotated copy of *Psychopathia Sexualis*; or visiting my blasé parents on a Sunday because I had no one else to call on, my college pals dispersed across two continents and my only boyhood friend constantly in goggles and a wetsuit in some other hemisphere.

How many times did I travel around New England and beyond to conduct research for an essay and wish I had had a devoted lover to share the scenery with, someone who admired what I wrote and liked me a lot to boot? For instance, several months before I met Gillian I drove to the woods of Maine, to my maternal grandmother's cottage on a lake, the locale of my childhood summers, a place planted at my hub, in order to ignite my memory and write an essay about those bucolic days and what they meant to the Wordsworth I am. I brought along a woman I had gone to high school with, someone I had remet at the pharmacy in town after twenty-odd years: divorced, two kids, the face of a cover girl on a cloud but the mind of an amoeba, couldn't tell the difference between *hearsay* and *heresy*. I kept saying, "Look there, that's where I swam! And over there, that's where I caught a five-pound bass! And there, I chased a moose through the brush! And see, that window in the cottage there, that was my room!" But it didn't matter because she didn't care; we weren't invested in one another; she and her indifference wrecked the weekend for me, and I never wrote the piece about my youthful summers in the pine scent of Maine.

Gillian entered my world with all the force of a javelin hurled by Schwarzenegger in his prime—*Pumping Iron*, say— and nothing I saw was ever the same after that first night with her at the bazaar. You can read in various greeting cards courtesy of those saccharine quasi-scribes at Hallmark, or hear in the melodic yeah-yeah-yeah on an early Beatles record, about how love heightens, enhances, makes a home for misfits like you and me, but I never believed the baloney until I hit thirty-one head-on and discovered myself solitary. My being alone seemed a great crime, a slur against my humble good looks and the fame I had—minuscule, sure, but verifiable. One month I went on twelve dinner dates, nearly every one a tour de force of discomfort. Two or three were very effective exercises in pessimism and soul rape. Only after too many encounters with the fraudulent can one recognize the authentic. Gillian the javelin, my dream.

That lopsided bastard Marvin knew what he'd had, all right, but it's not my fault he couldn't accept defeat and welcome himself to the cruel world—women will leave you, cold and hard and all of a sudden; brothers and parents will die, some horribly. Gillian left him because he got too pushy; she had difficulty breathing within sight of his face. He wanted her sex three times a day, said he couldn't function without it, said it was like meth for a junkie. He needed to stuff his face between her thighs and keep it there for half an hour or more, inhaling deeply the soggy scent of her. Sometimes he insisted on watching her pee, his face above her lap. Other times, à la Napoleon and his queen, he demanded she not shower for days at a time so he could—yes, you're hearing me right—lick her clean. There are certain words a man cannot use with a woman, *demand* and *insist* being just two. If you are a male imbecile, jot that down.

Is it any wonder she fell for me? Among my more commendable traits are these: a belief in equality across the human tribe and the opinion that gals should be allowed to use the toilet in privacy. This took a lot of getting used to for Gillian during the inaugural months of our love fest: she wondered aloud why I wasn't suspicious or jealous, probing into her erotic past or inquiring into her whereabouts, where she went and with whom she went there and what clothes she had on in the process, times of arrival and departure and the number of gents in the vicinity. What really tossed her for a loop was the afternoon I handed her a hammer in the garage and asked for help in nailing together a new bookshelf. Apparently Marvin Gluck held the certain knowledge that women shouldn't handle hammers, for their own safety and the safety of others.

That afternoon in the garage she asked me, "Why don't you call me sixteen times a day? And why doesn't it bother you if I don't call back right away?"

"Darling," I said, "I've waited my entire life for you and along the way have learned the patience of Buddha."

Gillian no doubt expected to wake one morning soon and see Marvin's sultan face staring down at her. He'd say something like, "I've finally found you; we'll never be apart again," right before plunging a Civil War sword between her ribs. And how many times had I witnessed her twitch awake in the center of the night, startled by bad dreams of Pleistocene proportion? I'd clasp her humid body and wipe the tears with my T-shirt, asking her about the dream, knowing full well it was Marvin Gluck the vagrant hounding her through a Southern glade oozing with alligators, and my Gillian, wanting not to alarm me, saying it was simply stress from work. It was on one of these nights, at the black magic hour of three in the morn, that I understood, with every wisp of my brain and groin, that Marvin Gluck must be abolished.

But I ran into a mental snag a few days before I planned to leave for the South. I went for my yearly dentist appointment and as I sat waiting, I picked up a student's left-behind tattered copy of *Macbeth*. It belonged to one Amanda Jove, tenth grade, Alexander Hamilton High School. Her handwriting was exquisite, her name the stuff of chivalrous love songs. The play was familiar to me: once, as a sophomore at Central Connecticut State U, in between bouts of Hegel and some nutter named Marx—neither of whom could write a cogent sentence—I had puzzled through its pages and thoughtfully vandalized them, though Amanda Jove's made my marginalia look like the feral scratchings of Cro-Magnon's cousin. I started reading and for some reason could not stop; the thing made my upper lip wet. When that sorry man saw the dagger float before him, leading him down the corridor to his snoring victim, I looked up from the pages and will testify that I, too, there in my dentist's waiting room decorated like every dentist's waiting room in North America, saw a dagger before me, though it was actually Groot's knife. Amanda Jove had written in the margin, *Important: guilt madness*, and by her mere suggestion I thought I felt a scintilla of my own guilt and madness. She will no doubt go on to be a great scholar, heralded in headlines, heaped upon with medals and awards, glasses lifted in NYC.

The bard's story caused a tremor in me: was I really marching pell-mell into my own mess-up? Nothing admirable, it seemed, could come from murderous ambitions, though I realized that my predicament was really a kind of self-defense, a preemptive strike against someone with a talent for menace and rout. Nevertheless, the floating dagger had me doubting my whole personality, which was uncomfortable since I am not the type who changes his mind unless scientific proofs are presented. Resolve is important. That night indigestion forced me to swallow a chalky pink antacid; a low hum of anxiety had infested my guts like a gang of bees. As we lay in bed I continued to feel my gizzard clench from what resembled fright; at one point I caught my hand trembling and my whisper on the verge of prayer.

Gillian looked up from her new book on the giant squid and asked what was wrong. I said, "Your beauty boondoggles me," and that pleased her quite a bit.

"Listen to this," she said. *"The giant squid can weigh as much as two thousand pounds and grow to over seventy feet in length.* Seventy feet! *It's the largest of all aquatic invertebrates, and lives at depths of two thousand feet.* No wonder we can't get at him. But I can smell him, Charlie. I know he's down there."

And I found these facts perplexing; I could not fathom two

thousand feet or, at that moment, two steps. Facts about the giant squid make my lover damp—I encouraged her pre-bed reading—and we indulged in each other's bodies for nearly an hour. Twice I thought I would hyperventilate or else have cardiac arrest.

My dreams that night were made by Lovecraft. I woke disturbed and canceled my writing work for the day. After pacing through our apartment all morning, I called on a priest at my boyhood church, Christ the King, because, let's face it, no man can outpace his childhood, how he was harangued by those in positions of authority. A lapsed Catholic is the most devout Catholic of all; you have to experience this virus for yourself really to get my gist, though in the meantime just trust me. A Gothic-looking structure of brownstone, Christ the King Church is flanked by wide rectangles of green lawn and canopied by olden oak trees. As a kid I always wondered who cut the grass; as an adult I know it's a kiss-ass congregant volunteering to push a mower in hope of earning a bed in heaven. It was noon this day, not the usual time for sinners to divulge their crimes, but I told the priest I wouldn't speak unless we were in that confessional booth, the crimson velvet curtain like a blanket between us. This priest had NBA limbs; something about him looked tubercular. His face was pockmarked, his dimples deep enough to hide marbles.

"What troubles your soul?" he said.

"Well, Father, you might not get this, but I have a burning love for my lady."

"My child, I as well have a burning love for Christ our Lord."

"Right," I said. "So you know what I mean."

"I do."

"Good. And when a man has this burning love, nothing at all can keep him from it."

"Not all the demons in Satan's service," he said.

"Right, all the demons in Satan's service. Exactly. A man has the right to defend his happiness."

"To defend his faith."

"Yes, his faith in his happiness, and in his love, his lady."

"His Lord."

I said, "That, too, sure."

"Then go, my child, and defend your happiness. Be a soldier."

"Really?" I asked.

"Really," he said.

"Precisely, then. I shall. Thank you."

We both left the confessional booth at the same time, standing there eyeball to eyeball. He had half a sandwich in one hand and an entertainment magazine in the other—at least it wasn't porn—the cover of which advertised the sexual abandon of some Beverly Hills starlet eighteen seconds to anorexia. Bits of tuna fish, I believe, were tucked into the corners of his mouth. We shrugged in confused unison, and then I left.

Or attempted to leave. On my way out I brushed coats with Father Henry, the pastor-in-chief of Christ the King, he who had pestered me with constant pleas to become an altar boy, to forsake bombast and ballyhoo, to tinkle more substantive change in the offering basket each Sunday, and other spiritual what-have-you. I had thought or tried to think that he had perished or retired decades ago, perhaps been arrested and incarcerated for what you see on the news, but there he was now, in stargazing eyeglasses, pumping my arm up and down like he was trying to get well water to spring from my throat.

"Charles," he said, "what a pleasant surprise."

"Hello, Father Henry," I said. "Nice to see you."

"What brings you here today? It's been years. But I've been reading your memoirs every week in that magazine. Not so Christian, I must say. Especially the one about how your routine rectal exam prompted you to investigate the origins of Catamites in ancient Greece."

"I know, Father. I apologize."

"But you have a certain, uhh, certain, *strained* way with words, Charles. It gets dizzy."

"I've been dizzy since I was a teen, Father."

"Still, I admire your . . . is it success you have?"

He had shrunk a few feet since I'd last seen him, sometime during my senior year of high school. The cancer stamp on his blanched scalp looked a little like Siberia.

"Thank you, Father. I'm sorry about the Catamites. But I came today because I was seeking some spiritual counsel. I saw that other fellow there, the tall one. I didn't know you were still here."

"Spiritual counsel, I see. What is the problem, Charles?"

He guided me a few feet backward and we sat in the last pew, precisely where I had hidden as a youth so as not to be noticed dozing or else thumbing through the pages of an X-rated periodical. You'd think a gruesome seven-foot crucifix hanging behind the altar—an aggravated Christ with his head up and back in the why-hast-thou-forsaken-me pose, plenty of blood leaking from beneath that crown of thorns and the spear wound in his rib—not to mention a fifty-foot cathedral ceiling with skylights to let in lanes of God's spy-shine—would be sufficient to dissuade me from photos of girls with such handsomely haired genitalia. But what youth is not visited by hullabaloo, cyclonic inside him? Exactly.

"Father," I said, "I've made a mondo decision and I was just looking for some advice that might indicate that I've chosen correctly."

"Ah, yes, your parents tell me you're getting married. Many congratulations, Charles. I hope Christ the King will be conducting the ceremony."

"That's kind of you, but Gillian is Jewish, Father."

"I see. Well . . . that's okay. Our Savior was a Jew, as well, remember. She can always convert, though. No one would have to know about her . . . past. Perhaps talk to her about that. Now, about this dilemma of yours."

I asked if I had his confidence, if he was cloud-bound by the Lord to stay mute about whatever I spilled to him, and when he confirmed, I belched out the Marvin Gluck saga front to back.

When I finished, he felt the blubber above a collar cranked too tight and said, "Sounds like an atheist, this Marvin. Strychnine in society."

Ahh, strychnine in society: so he *was* a fan of my verbiage after all.

"Father," I said, "he's an atheist through and through. I hear he has a sculpture of Percy Shelley and Bertrand Russell doing a French kiss and ball-sack grab."

"Scandalous. All these atheists everywhere all of a sudden. Writing books—bestsellers!—giving interviews on television, having conferences. Call themselves the New Atheism. Nothing new about devil worship, Charles, believe me. I've been around quite a while."

I nodded emphatically, dunce-like.

"And so you say you'll murder him, Charles?"

"Well, I think so. I mean, that's what I've been telling people. You know, pump up my image as a man's man."

"I see," he said. "Makes a good story, murder. Murder sells."

"Right. Agatha Christie and so forth."

"Charles," he said, "you have my blessing," and he patted my forearm and breathed heavily to his feet. "Society could use one less atheist. Don't get caught."

I stood, too, and we shook hands in the back pew. "Many thanks, Father. I knew you'd understand. What with the Church's history of conspiracy and gore."

"And see about conversion for Gillian," he said, hobbling down the red-rugged center aisle of the church, like Yoda.

ON A FRIDAY afternoon Gillian left work and went to visit her vegan cousin, Sheri, in Vermont for the weekend while I went online and got detailed directions right to Marvin's awful doorstep. Just the day before we had received another menacing package from him; it was a bundle of blackish, withered roses with a greeting tag that read simply, *Death*. Gillian pretended not to be bothered but I could see that she was shaken right through to her spine. After she left, Groot called me from deep in South America, where he said he was liquidating cocaine growers and setting fire to their crops. He had been thinking about my "mission" and had some further tips for me:

"Wait till he's asleep so there's no struggle. Wear gloves, naturally. A state trooper is bound to have security on his house, so don't break in, don't risk an alarm. Hide behind a tree or something, wait for him to get home, and when he goes to take the garbage out, try to sneak in. Park a mile away, at least, so no one sees your ride at the scene. Wear shoes one size too big, in case you leave a footprint. Remember, pull up on the serrated end of the blade. Enter through the bottom of the windpipe, drag up to the chin, and then over the jugular. That way, if he doesn't die right away at least he can't scream and wake up the neighbors."

All this I appreciated. But I wouldn't have to worry about sneaking in after Marvin got home because Gillian had a key to his house. And I wasn't much concerned with an alarm because I figured a guy who owns an arsenal of firearms would feel protected aplenty.

The whole way down to Virginia, I listened to Nina Simone to comfort the shebang inside me. If I were a man given to the depth of philosophy, this would have been the time: more than eight hours in my cushioned car, a killer's knife tucked into my boot, on my way to commit a capital crime, all for the love of a woman and, sure, an uninterrupted existence. Of course I considered the law and my soul, but neither seemed very vital just then. I had thought about sad Macbeth and his dagger since I had spoken with the priest, but the story had stopped spooking me. Actually, I remembered some of the lines Amanda Jove had highlighted; the demented king was actually allowing me some courage:

"I have supped full with horrors. Direness, familiar to my slaughterous thoughts, cannot once start me."

Indeed.

"I am in blood stepped so far."

What a boast.

"Things bad begun make strong themselves by ill."

Couldn't have said it better myself.

Still, my palms would not stop sweating; I had to slip on leather gloves just to grip the steering wheel. Then, an hour or so from Marvin's house, I spotted a billboard off the highway: SEE THE GIANT SQUID. I slowed and made a mental note of the exit: 43. There was a painting of the red beast that made it look profligate, guilty of crimes greater than mine. Gillian would not have approved of this artistic rendition. The giant squid exhibit was a sign—right?—but of what I could not say. I don't make my way in the world in accordance with signs, though I'm sure the deities sometimes function that way, just not with me. One needs to be a pretty special person to receive a sign from on high, and despite some scant evidence to the contrary, Charles Homar is just not that special.

Darkness started and I did as Groot had instructed: drove a mile from the mailbox, parked at the far end of a recently built strip mall with the requisite drugstore, pizza place, and Chinese food joint. The frosty March night showed my breath to me; the emotions at my center were an assortment of the reptilian and numinous: you know, fear of the practical combined with spiritual certainty. What would a man like me think about walking a mile on that empty stretch of wilderness road, going to do the dastardly deed I had in mind? I tell you, insofar as it is possible for a person's cranium to be a void, mine was. There's no telling what the noises were in the empty cockpit of my mind. If I quivered, it was not solely from the chill of that strange Virginia gloaming, trees everywhere thick and spooky.

But I was not confused. Another man walking that isolated road might have paused to wonder how he had arrived there; he might have contemplated the various factors that had added up to this moment, perhaps regretful that his circumstances were not different, that he was not living on a different dome, by the light of some other ordinary star. The most sensible of men might even have had the good humor to laugh at his own cocksure silliness, unfurled *ad absurdum*, and excused himself from this John Wayne drama. But that man would not have had Gillian and the gut-tingling pleasure of her. Plus: a morsel in me still harbored the dullest hope that I could somehow talk some sense into this monstrosity, Marvin Gluck.

His one-story house was not impressive—a shack, really— renovations were in order, cleanup was needed, though I was relieved that the massive pine trees allowed ample cover from the road and any Confederate-flagged vigilante looking to upset a Yankee. A new Ford pickup was parked around back by the single-car garage; no lamps shone in the rooms. I crept in the wooded darkness for some minutes, in between the pines, feeling the brass key in my pocket. Having punished my bladder for the past half an hour, I pissed furiously onto the pine needles, wondering if this would be the way I was appre- hended: DNA samples from my urine, collected by some savvy officer of the peace. I was glad I had not recently eaten because vomit felt possible. Again I crept in the darkness, waiting for an orange lamp to light up the kitchen that probably had no modern appliances. And then it occurred to me, a bit tardily, true: this mission might be knavery and not its rhyme. But just consider how close *tardy* is to *retarded* and you'll start to get an idea about who you're dealing with here.

No lamp ever switched on inside and I guessed that Marvin was not home. Perhaps a reject-sibling had picked him up for a meal; perhaps he was in his police cruiser, foisting tickets unto the workingman who could ill afford them. At the front door I searched for signs of an alarm system, a colorful sticker on the glass meant to inform the dubious likes of me. I tried the key in the deadbolt and the knob; when it would not fit in either I experienced light-headedness and then drudgery; air moved noisily in my stomach. To have made it this far. Why would he have changed the locks on his door? I stood gawking at it as if I could, by psychokinesis or Christian incantation, make the thing swing open.

I tried the knob anyway to see if it would turn, and just like that I was standing inside Marvin's snug kitchen. Either the boob had neglected to lock the house upon leaving or else he was here napping with dreams of my Gillian.

I stifled my breath and listened hard, my hand still on the knob. That day-old odor? Cat food, no doubt clumped like mud in a dish somewhere. (Something else I admired about Gillian: unlike so many of my past girlfriends, she did not require cats in her life, and so my furniture and clothes were saved from assault by hair.) A creature meowed somewhere in Marvin's living room; from my back pocket I pulled a slim flashlight—Groot had instructed me to bring a slim flashlight—and when I aimed it through the doorway . . .

There was Marvin, lounged back in an armchair, looking at me with yawning eyes. The gray cat was arched on his

shoulder, licking the bullet hole nestled in the side of his skull.
I aimed the flashlight at the carpet near the chair and spotted
the handgun. On the baby-blue curtains behind him, his blood
was splattered better than a Jackson Pollock.

I had to instruct myself to breathe and then to breathe
some more; my ribs groaned and creaked around a ghoulish
heart. Marvin sat bare-chested, Gillian's name tattooed across
his pecs. Except now the word FOREVER was blazoned on his
mushy abdomen, and as I stepped closer I saw that he had
recently carved it there himself with a razor or steak knife.
And then I knew: the roses we had received the day before
with the message *Death* were not meant for Gillian or me, but
for Marvin himself.

Witness, all ye nonbelievers, the thunderous power of my
lover.

"Marvin," I said, giddy. "You shouldn't have."

The place, in fact, was a paragon of filth, stained clothes
dropped on the carpet, crusty dishes in every room, crooked
framed photos of Gillian grinning from the walls. Outside, I
paused there in his dirt driveway to weep.

"Goodbye, Marvin," I said through my tears—I cry when I
can—"and thank you."

Then I remembered the cat. I couldn't just leave it there to
mope and starve, so I retrieved it from behind the door, saying,
as you know I did, "Here kitty kitty," and it was delighted to
come with me, no doubt having had its share of one Marvin
Gluck. On my lap it sat with love, made cat sounds. At a pay
phone in the parking lot of the strip mall, I fanned through the
tethered directory for the closest animal shelter, and when I

got there twenty minutes later, I said to the T-shirted teenage girl at the front desk, her mouth a mutiny of metal, "Find this feline a loving home. And remember always the difference between s-o-r-e and s-o-a-r."

My next stop was the giant squid exhibit off the highway. Yes, it would be a mere twenty feet long and made clumsily of rubber, suspended from the rafters of some lonely farmer's barn. But he would take a Polaroid photo of me in front of it, and I would smile wide for the camera, and have this photo to give to Gillian upon my return. And I would make a pledge to her, now that we were unencumbered, that I would soon dive to the bottom of the sea and drag back her beloved squid, kicking and screaming, so that she could hold it, and smell it, and measure its abundance, all the days of her life.

2. WITCHY WOMAN

GILLIAN LEFT ME in a lurch two months before our wedding and turned me into another lovesick numbskull with a hacked-up heart. I arrived home from the library one immaculate afternoon and as soon as I walked through the door I could smell her absence: dusty and metallic, like a warehouse. In all matters love, the baser senses are heightened; I could sometimes smell her panties tucked away in the top drawer across our bedroom, her athletic socks in the laundry basket downstairs. Bears and wolves know what I mean.

My eyes were no great help that day; nothing much looked amiss. It was only upon inspecting her closet that I found the spot where her suitcase had been, her favorite pair of leather boots removed, a few choice sweaters, pants, and books missing, too. Teetering was the wire hanger that once held her checkered wool jacket. I might have said, "Hmmm," and searched about some more and then dialed her cell phone. When she didn't answer I might have felt my stubbled chin as the confused are known to do. Suddenly, more things were missing: a duffel bag, toiletries, multivitamins, a special note-book. Then I sat at the kitchen table, novocained through the knees, my hands folded as if in prayer. And I stared. For many minutes. And wondered. For many more. And knew. For sure.

Panic lodged itself in my chest and soon I got antsy, pacing a rut in the living room rug, nightmaring from room to room to room. That's me: calling her phone again and then calling a few more times. Valves began shutting, hoses hissing, and somewhere in my torso a drip-drip-drip. I wanted to find a cushioned seat, but before I could look I was already on the floor, facedown and panting. Men, it's true, are not made well. Who was it who said that grief feels like fear? Give that bard a plant as a prize for insight.

Most poets blather on about the darkness and cold, but I tell you, for an entire day all I felt were flame and light. She never called back. My temperature rose and rose. I left an uptight voice message for her vegan cousin, Sheri, something about phosphorus in my arteries, a hootenanny in my head. *Malignant*, *medieval*, *medication*: those were the words that occurred to me. What could I do? Baffled, I dipped pita bread into my hubris and then declared that hummus was the fatal flaw that got Agamemnon stabbed in his bathtub. I thought about carving Gillian's name across my pecs with a not-sharp steak knife, like Marvin Gluck. So this was what that maniac had been raving about.

But perhaps this was a misapprehension? Perhaps soon I'd be saying silly me?

'Round about nightfall, I began sniffing for clues, as any animal would. Gillian of course had left me nary a note; that would have been too typical, and my lady revolted against the typical. "Uniqueness in every act" could have been her motto. Raiding her desk, it didn't take me long to discover that the giant squid was at the bottom of this heartwreck. Gillian's obsession for the elusive fiend was consummate—never before had reliable human eyes ever fixed themselves upon a breathing giant squid—*Architeuthis*, pronounced, so I gather, Arki-tooth-iss. The ugly bastard was a mystery to the scientific community and laymen alike. If you find this obsession goofy, you are not alone.

Books about the beast lay open and closed in her home office; posters decorated the walls and a little plastic model terrorized the citizens of her fish tank. I recalled that Gillian had been in correspondence with a big-shot squid hunter named Jacob Jacobi, some ocean yahoo affiliated with the Smithsonian Institution and the University of New Hampshire. The guy had his own boat and called it *The Kraken*, which was what ancient peoples had named the giant squid. Every year Jacobi spent three straight months out at sea in pursuit of the thing. His book: *How the Squid Lives*, two pounds of obscurantist dross typed in an almost-English academics and scientists seem proud of. The imprudent photo on the back of this book showed a mustache looping over his top lip, dangling from either side like a hawser, as if at any moment a miniature person might appear from his nostril and climb down to safety. And how to describe those eyebrows? Stalinesque.

Mind you, I'm no beauty fit for TV, but anyone with macroscopic vision could see that I was handsomer than this rollicking jerk-off.

I ransacked Gillian's desk to locate the missives and printed emails sure to be there (a sentimentalist and conspiracy theorist regarding Bill Gates, she printed every important email ever received). When I found them beneath binders in the middle drawer, my breathing went wild and then nearly halted. Certain cogs crucial to my existence would not turn; a hailstorm appeared between my ears. My lady had been trading affections with this worm; nothing sexual, I'll admit, but still the lines were catastrophic to my napalmed heart. They had never met, but with letters, emails, phone calls, and photos, they had developed a fondness for each other. My lady spoke of having a crush, which might sound innocuous to your ears, but my own ears had different ideas.

Think about how that word now applied to me: our wedding was crushed, my heart crushed, I must crush Jacob Jacobi, perhaps crush him beneath my car, after which my future would be crushed as I decomposed in prison for the murder of a giant squid hunter respected the world over. My world, over. How could I go back to being alone or dating knuckle-headed post-nymphs? All that noisy steam broke free from my pipes—and I moaned, sprite enough to haunt a house.

At first Jacobi's letters were all about the giant squid, but with each new one the monster was mentioned less and less. I was treated to his whole life story: a childhood in Cincinnati, of all places; a brief stint in the Coast Guard; and the fact that—I was near vomiting—he slept in the nude. The thought of this hirsute tug brushing up against the milky smoothness of my Gillian caused my lungs to ignite; somewhere in the center of my sternum lay a fissure leaking acid and bile. All my major organs were now rethinking their purpose and contemplating a strike. The last letter was dated just a week ago. They were to set off on a three-month voyage in search of the kraken in the bottomless waters near New Zealand, and were scheduled to depart from a port in southern Maine in just, horrors, one day—tomorrow.

How to relay the upset tearing through me?

When I was a child of ten, I flipped over my handlebars on Brooks Boulevard and flew headfirst into the plate-glass window of Kline's Liquor Store. This was a time before parents got sued for not outfitting their kids in bicycle helmets and other regalia, and the impact knocked me just this side of Saturn or a ring thereof, all stars and diaphanous clouds and other deep-space holy-moly I could not name. And then the dark, and I was gone, dropping through unconsciousness until, long seconds or minutes later, Christ-loving pedestrians shook and petted me back to the light.

I've never forgotten the heaviness in my tiny body, the distant sound of adult voices not one foot from my face, the world blurred and drained of color, a sepia shot of who-knows-what in God-knows-where. A sirenless ambulance arrived, bulbs twirling on top in shocked silence. Where had it come from so quickly? White-clad rescue workers, man and woman, floated over to me not as angels descending from paradise, but as two practiced in sorcery, prepared to mend or mash, I couldn't tell which. They lifted me onto a gurney and strapped me down, and through my fogbound vision I tried to spot my mother and father rushing to my side to quash this theft of me. Being taken by these strangers felt like being zapped up to a flying saucer by smut-fed aliens.

My parents didn't come, not for many hours. I lay in a hospital bed with more heebie-jeebies than I could control, concussed and crying, and when I saw them come through the door, my trickling tears turned to weeping, and not because I was grateful that they had finally shown up to save me, but because I knew that they had betrayed me by setting me loose and reckless on a bicycle and then not arriving before I could be stolen by stranger-medics in an ambulance.

I had lost a whole day being nearly incinerated by surprise; Gillian and Jacobi's departure date was the next morning. Gillian must have wanted to arrive in Maine early in order to—hmm, what? Oh, gods on Olympus, if you're there, save my mind from fancies of lust and lubricity! Aside from some innocent flirting with Jesus, I had never placed much stock in the supernatural, but now was the time. I was prepared to consult witches and magicians, or any lunatic on the street with a vacant stare. These being in short supply, I again called on Groot; his instructions on how to rub out Marvin Gluck had been miracles of imagination.

When I got him on his cell phone after a dozen rings he said, "I read 'Antihero Agonistes' a few weeks ago in *New Nation Weekly*. You said you weren't going to write about it."

"But did you like it?"

"You've always dabbled in hyperbole, Charlie. I just hope the cops don't show up at your door."

"People think all memoir is fiction. Plus cops don't read. But Groot," I said, "listen. I am afflicted again."

I told him the sordid details of my dilemma, the tussle and upsurge of it. Hearing myself give the details, it all sounded so Seussian. A red-and-white-striped top hat would not have looked that absurd on me.

He said, "Giant squid hunter, eh?"

"Correct."

"Is liquidation in order?"

"You mean more murder?"

"That I do."

"I don't know what's in order, Groot. I'm trembling here. Where are you now?"

And—luck—he told me he was home, reclining on his parents' sofa, summoned by his mother to celebrate his father's sixtieth birthday.

"About this giant squid hunter," he said, chewing something squishy. "He could be, more than Marvin, a formidable opponent."

"I'm going to get Gillian back. I need to know how to proceed."

"Are you armed?"

"With impulsiveness and grief only."

"Useful as they are, they will not do now. He probably has a big harpoon. I'll be there momentarily with a plan. Stand by."

I studied Gillian's prismatic poster of the giant squid and puzzled over its lidless eyes, dead-black and bigger than hubcaps; the underside of its eight rubbery arms outfitted with razor-like sucking circles; the two long whippy tentacles employed to entangle its hapless prey; a pointed tail Satan must envy; and a creepy bird-like beak that nature had placed in an unlikely spot: between its arms. The son of a bitch doesn't have a head; it's a mess of engineering, unintelligently designed, unsightly and wrong. My lady loved it.

Groot arrived and declined my offer of a beer, choosing instead a glass of iced tea, and looking as he had always looked, sans cowboy hat and boots, thank God: tallish and lean with that Navy buzz cut and face that defied aging. After a whole day in my skivvies, I was now fully dressed, Nikes and all, tapping my fingers on the kitchen table. Groot wouldn't talk until he had finished the entire glass of tea. I whistled and kept glancing at the digital time on the microwave oven.

"Charlie," he said, "Miss Gillian is an awful lot of trouble for you."

What was the meaning of that statement? My face didn't know what to do.

He said, "Have you ever thought about just getting a new girlfriend? Maybe?"

"Groot," I told him, "that would be like having the greatest name in history, Cassius Clay, and then changing it to some common abomination."

A moment of facial expressions from the both of us.

"I see," he said, but clearly he did not.

"How is this helpful right now, Groot?"

"I'm just saying, Charlie. If she left you, she left you. Have you ever tried to change a woman's mind? You need abracadabra to do it."

"The plan, Groot. Please get out of practical mode and get into military killer mode. Please?"

But the truth was that he had never cared for Gillian. Too much of a gentleman and pal ever to say anything, he nevertheless had made it known over the years with the subtlest facial tics and changes of tone. Something inside him had detected something afoul inside her. Although, true, the only human female Groot thought incapable of double-cross was his Latvian mama, plump and proud of her single boy. She still wears his diaper pin as a brooch, and I mean every day, on every outfit.

Deep inhale, deep exhale. The rolling of his eyes. And
then: "Time," he said, "is of the essence. My data tells me they
depart tomorrow morning from a port in Maine. I estimate the
target will have four to five henchmen. Three months at sea is
a perilous task for just a man and his new lover."

"Ouch, don't say *lover*, Groot. Christ, man."

"Sorry," he said, and flipped open a notepad on the kitchen
table, licked a pencil, and began drawing diagrams. "Option
One A: you lay in wait at the vessel and once the adversaries
board, you eliminate with either pistol or blade or close-quarters
assault rifle, at which point you may retrieve your bride. Option
One B: you lay in wait on a rooftop with an adequate rifle and
snipe the enemy as they board, at which point you descend to
retrieve your bride. Option One C: you rig the vessel with explosives and once the enemy boards you blow them all to hell, in
which case you will not retrieve your bride."

His artwork consisted of preschool scrapings that were
supposed to be a boat, a knife, a rifle, and a mushroom cloud.
He spun the notepad around for me to see. The boat, for some
reason, had oars.

"Groot," I said, "your bloody mind is a beauty, but I really just
need to get Gillian back. The less dismemberment the better."

"Okay, then," and he spun the notepad back around.
"Option Two: you find the pair and talk to them of decency
and creed, convincing your gal that she has erred in judgment.
Then you convince the squid hunter that he really doesn't
want to covet your bride. Your gal gives up her lifelong passion
for the giant squid and her unique opportunity to capture it.
The hunter goes his way, you and your bride go yours. Perhaps
there's a handshake."

This diagram tried to show two hands shaking, except they looked more like claws than hands. One had on a wedding ring.

I said, "Hmm. I see. About those firearms and explosives."

"Precisely. Let's convene at the trunk of my car. I've come prepared for such possibilities."

"Perfect," I said, and we rose from the kitchen table like Boy Scouts about to get filthy. But then Groot stopped me in the foyer to add an aside, asking me if I was certain that Gillian had never read "Antihero Agonistes."

"No," I said. "I don't think so. When that week's issue of *New Nation Weekly* hit the stands I went to Food World in town and bought up every copy so Gillian wouldn't see it when she went shopping."

"She could have seen it online."

"They don't post my memoirs online, Groot. Only excerpts."

"Someone could have told her about it, then."

"Not that many people read my stuff, Groot. What are you getting at, please?"

"I was just thinking: she might have flown the coop when she realized you were a murderous bastard who knows the ins and outs of immoderate behavior. And pardon me for saying so, buddy, but your bent mind is just like Marvin's."

"She wouldn't have been flattered, then?"

"Negative. Women are a breed unto themselves. You know that or else you wouldn't have bought all the copies at the food store. Now, to my car."

"Right. Pull into the garage so the neighbors don't see us with a rifle and call the very bored police."

When Groot's car was safely inside, I shut the garage door and clicked on the fluorescent row of bulbs above my work area. The sight of the rifle felt like being plugged into the nearest socket: amps or watts or volts hummed through me. Its matte-black prettiness beckoned a man to touch it, and I, in my man-weakness and curiosity, did so. It cradled so naturally and comfortably in my arms I understood immediately why human beings so enjoy firing them at one another.

"That's a DSA Gas-Trap Carbine, .223-caliber, a feisty girl, fully auto, though loyal. She can get out of hand at times, but stroke her tender, don't squeeze her rough, and she'll spit the way you want her to. The .223-caliber is the way you want to go. All your standard Army-issue M16s are .223, as is the civilian AR-15."

"Is this what I need to kill forever a man and thief?"

"Any old john, or the squid hunter?"

"Yes, Groot, the squid hunter. Jesus."

I was trying to aim through the scope at the basketball on a shelf, left eye squinted, but I couldn't see anything.

"At close range or from afar?" he asked.

"I don't know, Groot. How about from medium range?"

"Indeed. That will do. She spits fire, so be careful. I've got thirty- and forty-round magazines. You'll need ten of each. When the heat comes you don't want to stop every five minutes to reload a clip. When we were going door-to-door in Baghdad half of our equipment was loaded clips."

I asked about destroying the boat but we forwent the possibility of C4 explosives because Groot said I'd no doubt blow myself jihadist-like to Jupiter. He was all patience and compassion when showing me how to operate the rifle, said I held the weapon lovingly, like a musician with his fiddle, and that this was a pleasing indication. Of what I did not inquire; I just took the compliment. He said the laser sight was idiot-proof: press the trigger halfway and the red dot would find the target. I couldn't miss. Then he added that my garage required a grease-stained calendar of naked women in possession of tools.

But: my tentative plan was not to murder Jacob Jacobi, only show him that I was a man aflame. He needed to hear that awful grinding of my inner machinery. And then naturally I'd perforate his vessel so it would plunge to the floor of the harbor, where seaweed and starfish would call it home. Perhaps I'd snip off strands of his enormous mustachio, too. In any case, I wanted to be feared. I wanted to be taken seriously, and few sights in life are more fearsome than a refugee with an automatic weapon. Just click on the television if you want to know how men are supposed to behave in America.

"Are you sure about this?" Groot asked before leaving.

"Do I have a choice?"

"Every man has a choice."

"That's movie dialogue," I said. "And not true."

"But true enough," he said. "And it would make a great movie. Just think—"

"Yes, I have thought of it."

"Just scare him, Charlie. Teach him to stay away from another man's gal. Don't kill anyone."

MY PARENTS' HOUSE: nearly unchanged from the time of my youth, New England suburban, a Cape with lawns front and back, two-car garage with electric opener. Inside: pointless brica-brac aplenty. I had learned to crawl there on that pukey 1970s rug. My first car at seventeen, a white Buick Regal, was allowed to take up one-third of that macadam driveway, beneath the basketball hoop, which for some reason was still there. The neighborhood had a watch program, concerned Christians with one eye on the imminence of felonies, which usually meant any poor black guy who happened to wander down our streets, impressed by the towering trees and Crayola-green front yards. God forbid *two* black guys happened to wander by: a cop would be there in four minutes flat with menacing stares and maybe a torch. Why had I not made my own home farther than ten minutes from my parents', Paris or Barcelona, say?

Sunk in their sofa now, creased down the middle, staring up through the skylight and beguiled by cumulus clouds, I was nothing but jetsam to my Cleopatra. My father and mother sat on the sofa across from me, both of them soaking in what I had just told them, looking over at me with a mishmash of sympathy and disgust—although my father, career curmudgeon since the death of my brother twenty-some years earlier, was more disgust than sympathy.

Two sixty-year-olds sitting a cushion apart: one who looked twenty years younger in jeans and running shoes and hair that was not a blue Brillo pad, and another who looked twenty years older in checkered pajamas and a bathrobe, grayer than the soot piled in the fireplace, a battalion of pill bottles beside him on the end table. *This* was what I had to look forward to without Gillian? Married to someone I merely settled for and liked only a little if at all? Ulcerous, every bit of it.

My mother said, handkerchief by her mouth as if she'd soon be sick, "Where did she go, again, dear?"

And I told her again: Jacobi, the squid, the letters I had found. I couldn't lower my head from the skylight or seem to feel my feet. My voice, I heard, was born as a whisper.

"I'm not surprised," my father said, a wool blanket across his lap—the very wool blanket Gillian had knitted for him the previous Christmas. "This Jacobi sounds like he has a real job. Doesn't make up stories for a living."

"Thanks, Dad. I'm not making up anything."

"Even that name is a lie. *Homar*. What's that? The last name I gave you isn't good enough? You embarrassed by your name?"

I had to tell him about pen names, etc. The grandfather clock, older and more erect than me, tolled the arrival of five p.m. Whole precincts inside me shuddered.

My father said, "I'd like to know how you pay your bills. That's one essay I'd want to read, actually: 'How I Pay My Bills,' by Charles Homar. I'd read that one."

"Bernie," my mother told him, "*pretend* to be understanding."

He said, "How does a guy almost burn down his house trying to get rid of a squirrel? Answer me that. You have to be some kind of dummy."

If he kept on this way, his breath coming out in lunges, my mother was going to have to retrieve the oxygen tank and slap the mask across his mouth. Yes, this was middle-class melodrama, folks. Just think how much *melodrama* sounds like *melanoma* and you'll begin to get the picture.

"And who writes about a rectal exam and Socrates?" he asked. "Who would do something like that? Embarrass his old father like that."

I nearly asked him to be human, have opposable thumbs.

He was looking at me as if he yearned to leap across the carpet and asphyxiate me almost to death. And it occurred to me then, for the first time in my life: You know who my father looked like? Dennis Hopper. In *Blue Velvet*. Does that explain anything?

"I sit before you now no better than ejecta," I said, "a discarded pipsqueak with a whole gaggle of hurt within him."

"Don't talk to me that way," he said. "Who talks like that? I'm not Groot, degenerate that he is. That doesn't even mean anything, *a whole gaggle of hurt*. This is America, Charlie."

I said, "Groot fights for our country."

"He's a mercenary. I never liked that boy. The two of you speaking like weirdos all the time. You should both get real jobs."

"Bernie," she implored, "Charles needs our *understanding* right now." And then to me, "What about the wedding? I bought my dress."

"Our understanding?" he asked. "He needs a brain in his head is what he needs. Your mother showed me your last little story, about going down to Virginia to murder that trooper. Is this how we raised you? To tell lies and pass them off as truth?"

I was still too exhausted to sit up straight on the sofa and look my father in his brown marbles. But I could see him leaning forward, getting more excited by the minute, and I thought: *If you have a heart attack right now I wouldn't move half a centimeter to help you.*

"You're lucky you're not in jail, pal. And what about the dig you gave me in that piece? You want to explain that to me?"

I must have had a look on me that pronounced confusion or any one of its synonyms, because he said, "Don't play dumb, you know goddamn well what dig. You said that Gillian really cares about me and this is a mystery to you because I'm a no-good bastard, or something to that effect."

"I didn't say that."

"You very well goddamn did."

"Now, that's a sentence," I told him. "*You very well goddamn did.*"

The day was dying; through the skylight I could see the navy blue going black. My mother had so many color patterns going on—from the shag rugs to the fake art on the walls to the flamingo couches and blue throw pillows—a contract was needed to help coordinate them. But if you had searched with Sherlock Holmes himself you wouldn't have found a film of dust or cobweb or food smudge anywhere in that house. My mother subscribed to the view that cleanliness is next door to godliness, heaven being a bleached-clean abode.

He said, "Gillian is the best thing that's ever happened to me, and this horse's ass had to screw it up. He's stupid, I think."

"Charles isn't stupid, Bernie. You know, he's a literary man, like Mark Twain. Please calm down."

"Ha, Mark Twain," he spat at her. "You soil the good man's honor. There was a man who told the truth and wasn't ashamed of his name, the great Twain family from Connecticut."

"Twain," I said, "is a pen name, Dad. And he was from Missouri."

"Don't tell me where he was from. I went to his house in Hartford, moron. What, you ashamed of your home state now, too? Connecticut not good enough for you?"

Listening to him speak was like watching a leper scratch his scabs.

"If he writes like Twain, then I golf like Jack Nicklaus."

And my mother said, "You don't golf at all anymore, Bernie."

Golf: there you have it—officially suburban.

We three endured several minutes of pathetic silence as my mother dabbed her eye corners and my father attempted to bridle his breathing. And I remembered something, sitting there: a tableau from my childhood when I wasn't more than waist-high, maybe five or six years old, my brother Bart still in diapers and goo-gooing around the house. My mother dropped me at the elementary school one roasting summer morn to attend a puppet show. She left me there to wait in line outside in a summer heat trying to make wax from asphalt. When I realized I was alone, a whippersnapper without guide or guardian, the fear in me a barbed thing, I began crying as any dumped-off child would.

An Indian man—Indian as in Pakistan, not Pocahontas—and his boy my age tried to soothe me and then offered to drive me home, if I could remember how to get there. Although I wasn't tall enough to see over the dashboard of his beige car—an Oldsmobile, I'm half sure—I somehow navigated him to our house ten blocks away. They stayed put behind the wheel; I bounded out, and when I did, I saw my mother at the front storm door, Windexing the glass, wearing a blue bandanna to rope back her pile of vanilla mane. She cracked opened the door and jabbed out her arm to wave, either to me or to the Indian savior behind me, a wave of either hello or goodbye, it wasn't clear. And all those years later, sunk in my parents' sofa, I still didn't know.

"Okay, Charlie," my father said finally. "Look—your mother and I want to help you. We'll get Gillian back. Who else talks to me once a week, brings me things, shows interest? Who else cares?"

My mother ignored that. "Charlie," she said, "we should consult Father Henry. He always gave advice to you when you were a kid."

What an unorthodox definition of *advice* she had. I said, "When I saw Father Henry a few weeks ago he knew about the wedding but didn't seem to know Gillian is Jewish."

"Yes, we read that in the magazine, dear."

My father said, "Gillian's a Druid?"

"Jewish," I said.

"What's that mean?"

"Gillian," I said, "is a Jew. Please tell me you knew that. If you'd read my memoirs you *would* know it."

"I don't read that trash. Your mother reads it. I only skim it looking for foul references to me."

"Thanks."

"Gillian's a Jew? Since when?"

"Oh, Christ, I'm leaving," and I tried to find the muscle to move.

"No, stay, Charlie," my mother said. "You hungry?"

"It's fine," he said, "it's fine. I just didn't know . . . I mean she doesn't *seem* . . . And I don't know how you could expect people to believe that a *priest* gave you his blessing to kill someone. That's what I mean—it's all lies."

Several more minutes of silence ensued and when I began sobbing—a meager sob that nevertheless owned the potential to shift into a howl—my father said, "Oh, Lord," and my mother rose to pass me her handkerchief. And they just let

me sob—I no more than an aquarium exhibit whose glass they
saw the pointlessness of tapping on.

Now that night had fully come, the neighbors behind us
began turning on lights, and over my father's shoulder I could
see the illuminated upstairs window of what was once Emma
Bishop's bedroom, exactly even with my own from across the
modest width of two backyards. Several years older than me
and boilerplate-beautiful, blond Emma was the reason I asked
for binoculars for my fourteenth birthday, to watch her prom-
enade back and forth unclothed on the telephone, she unaware
of Newton's light laws that said I in the dark could see her
but she in her lit-up bedroom could not see me seeing her. She
never shut her shades.

This was the year Bartholomew's leukemia grew fangs and
bit hard, bruises on him like stigmata, his decade-old body a
dartboard for doctors with no hope but plenty of pins. You've
seen the after-school specials about saintly sick kids, termi-
nal and uncomplaining, who enjoy affirmations about how
fortunate they are, about God's great plan, etc. That wasn't
Bart. Angry overmuch, he had the bitterness of an Apache
circa 1875, and who could blame him? On an arctic Decem-
ber night before bed, as I watched Emma Bishop model her
nipples for my binoculars, I heard Bart's faint cough behind
me in the dark, and when I turned, I saw his sallow, vaporous self standing in a boulevard of moonlight just inside my
bedroom.

I said his name, and although I couldn't see tears, I knew
he was crying, and not because his brother was a voyeuristic
pervert all packed for hell, but because he could see Emma

too, and his ten-year-old heart and brain—already howitzered by what life is—must have suspected that her radiant nakedness was the very incarnation of a man's happiness, a happiness he would never have the chance to hold. Three weeks later he was dead, just in time for Christmas.

When I left my parents' house that evening, my father tried to slip me fifty bucks, as if that would lighten the half ton on my heart.

NOW: I HAD the name of the port in southern Maine from one of Jacobi's emails to Gillian, and after a dozen phone calls and some clicking on the Net, I also had detailed directions: a two-hour ride. Groot said he would join me but his mother had given him firm orders to retrieve an ice-cream cake for his father's birthday bash. I understood, and with his blessing over the phone I set off, the loyal rifle and clips under a blanket on my backseat. Geronimo.

I was fully aware that history was repeating itself, sort of, life being marked by panic and patterns: another car ride to kill in the name of Gillian, Interstate 95, north this time. Think about the dejection I felt driving to this harbor in Maine: it was a whack to the temple and then the aorta. Still, I was almost certain I would not be able to massacre Jacobi and his underlings. I'd probably just discharge some rounds into the air, cause a disturbance, scatter robins. And then— what? I didn't know; my ribs were closing quick around the anguished drum my heart had become. Opposites and contraries were hard at work: the hours hopped side to side on one leg; my wrinkled brain numbed and sharpened; always was fast becoming never. And there was the persistent question, the tiny word I saw all along the highway in New Hampshire, on green road signs, personalized license plates—one read FO SHO, the ghetto equivalent of FOR SURE (I checked)—and along the trailers of eighteen-wheelers hell-bent on destination and pollution: *Why? Why had she done this?*

Several times I had to stop driving, park at darkened rest stops with overfull trash cans, because I was being barraged by what felt like the menopausal hot flashes of a disappointed woman. Gillian was quite possibly, just then, sharing with Jacob Jacobi the riches I thought belonged to me alone. Imagine if your child were to call another man Father, another gal Mom; what descends upon you is not just betrayal and hurt, but a disorientation most impure. I was not fit for the highway. The car horns of oil-gurgling SUVs and tiny hybrids alike were blasting at me left, right, and rear. I yelled through my window, "I'm armed. I'll shoot your Honda full of holes and write a haiku about it."

As it always does when I flail about blind, poetry spoke to me. Gillian had collected every piece of literature that made mention of the giant squid, and in an effort to impress her with my interest, to mesh or meld, I took it upon myself to read these verses and stories, committing many of them to memory. Mr. Tennyson devoted a poem to the beast, and when he wrote the first few lines, he had my sorry state in mind:

> *Below the thunders of the upper deep,*
> *Far, far beneath the abysmal sea,*
> *His ancient, dreamless, uninvaded sleep*
> *The Kraken sleepeth.*

As you can see, that was me: *thunders*, *abysmal*, *ancient*, and *dreamless*, as in the destruction of my dreams. The creature and I were kin; we were hunted by Jacobi the Slayer. Some prayers to Poseidon were in order; I needed, people, all the help I could get.

The effects of shock and dehydration, in concert with my hungry woe, were beginning to make themselves known to me: throbbing forehead, a mouth like drying cement, intestines pretzeled into artwork, and jagged thoughts that aspired to destruction and deliverance both. Part of my floating brain wanted to imagine Gillian and our relationship, how we met and what she meant. But a private under fire does not stop to consider the history of the projectiles whirling by his limbs; he soldiers on until he is either out of death's path or else perforated in a ravine. Man liveth after the Fall. Axl Rose, that rock-n-roll maniac from the late 1980s, once screamed, "Welcome to the jungle," and we've all heard that higher-seeking seer Jim Morrison warning us, "No one here gets out alive." Yes. It hadn't occurred to me to click on the radio.

The two hours were up and I couldn't find this harbor anywhere; I wasn't even sure I was on the East Coast anymore. North and south no longer made sense; a compass would have come in handy. A giant Mainer gas station attendant, six feet six inches of meat descended from the Visigoths, gave me succor, but not before tipping back his cap and looking at me askance. We were leaned against the trunk of my car, beneath the bug-frenzied fluorescent lights. As I could tell from the stitching on his shirt, his name was Thud, and apparently, before asking for directions, I had mumbled something cryptic about the kraken and prelapsarian bliss.

"You need a soda pop, fella?"

"That I do, Thud."

"I'd get you some water but the pump don't work 'cause the vandals took the handle."

Wha . . . ? Did he just . . . ? Did I hear him . . . ? My ears were all tricks.

He handed me a Fresca free of charge and the chill of the thing nearly pushed out my tears. Imagine if I had allowed myself to weep in the grizzly grip of Thud: all would have been lost, my mission squashed. One can't let loose with an automatic rifle after coming nose to nose with the fact that all human kindness has not gone the way of the plesiosaur.

The neon OPEN sign in the window blinked on and off at odd intervals as if trying to make up its mind. Eviscerated autos all around this Exxon had opened up and were saying *Ahh*. In the woods nearby rotted all types of rusted-orange auto pieces, a carbuncle of a sight to my seen-too-much self. Untold tons of junk on the earth. I like my nature living and very close to God, my gas stations clean enough to lick in. Thud pointed at my map with a black fingernail and said, "Go there, then here, then there, then back this way, then around, then around again, and then you're there . . . mostly," and I knew I wouldn't remember a word of it.

"Thud," I said, "I feel as if I'm hunting the fair-haired child who used to be me. Does that English make any sense?"

"Be thy own son," he said, me not knowing if he meant *sun* or *Son*, or even if I had heard right and he actually said, "Fee-fi-fo-fum."

We shook hands like passing travelers on our way to and from the Land of Nod. I said, "Thank you, Thud. May you find the spot we call paradise."

He muttered, "Never heard of it," and I left that odd place.

Hours later, after many wrong turns and another gas station attendant who appeared to share a mother with Thud, I was there, in a parking lot at the harbor, among all the GMC trucks and trailers, gazing at the wet planking of the piers and the bright boats bobbing in dark water. A horror-film thunderstorm gathered out there on the horizon; swirls of gray and black were no doubt coming closer as if intent on more midnight. Directly in front of me, wanting to taunt or chide, was *The Kraken*, Jacobi's multimillion-dollar laboratory-at-sea. My headlights showed me that an artist-for-hire had painted my brother, the giant squid, on the fiberglass hull. We were hideous twins, neither of this world nor any other.

I had all night to wait before marauding, and I considered driving through town to see if I could locate Gillian's car but was sure I wouldn't be able to find my way back. Raindrops began bursting on my windshield and soon I was so sleepy I couldn't keep my eyelids from slamming shut. I crawled onto the backseat, placed Groot's rifle and magazines on the floor, curled up beneath a beach blanket, listened to the lulling rain, and trembled like a man with malaria until a wrecking-ball slumber shut me down. With what dreams would a person in my situation be visited? I tell you, that night I had none. Dreams are for those who have not yet passed under the sign ABANDON ALL HOPE YE WHO ENTER HERE. Yes, that dirty word, *hope*. Admit it: things did not look good for me.

With what visions would you be visited for those few moments before slumber? A child's funeral in the snow? A mother and father savaged by grief but too spent to weep? Or a teenager's trembling in half-light, terrified the genetic spade that scooped a ditch through his kid brother would come for him next? An acned freshman in high school, his hormones in hee-haw, is supposed to grasp what *genetic* means? He knows only that it means *family*, that it means *him*. That would make two of us never holding an Emma Bishop . . . a Gillian.

Sleep clobbered my body for nine hours uninterrupted, and I woke in the morning to chattering, well-rested voices eager for something. I had to remind myself where I was, and why I had come. My windows were fogged but I could tell that the rain had ceased and that the sun was trying its best to bust through a velvet mantle of clouds. When I pushed open the back door and fell to the graveled pavement, I looked yonder, and there on the pier boarding *The Kraken* were Jacobi, Gillian, and the henchmen Groot knew would be in attendance. I was able to get to my feet with about as much suavity as an epileptic under seize. Then I was running—or jogging, I suppose—toward the ship, yelling her name and trying not to slip on the wet planks. The sight of her, my Lord.

They stopped boarding and turned to squint at me as if I were the squid himself. I said my lady's name, and she said mine: Charlie.

Let's face it: movies and television have programmed us like the empty heads we were born to be, so I admit that my first sentence will win no points for originality. I said, "How could you do this to me?"

"Charlie," she said, "Jesus, what are you doing here?"

I believe I ogled and ogled and could not speak.

"You shouldn't have come here, Charlie. I was going to send you a letter. Why did you come?"

"Why?" I asked. "Oh, I don't know. Maybe to put an end to this flim-flam?"

"We don't want any trouble here," Jacobi cooed, "just relax," and his mustachio lifted in the breeze.

He was built like a two-hundred-pound lunch box, and what's worse, he wore a navy-blue New York Yankees sweatshirt and not the proud red and white of the Boston Red Sox, which is, as any New Englander can tell you, sacrilege on par with what the Achaeans did to the temples at Troy. The guy had dandruff in his *eyebrows*.

"Trouble," I said. "Speaking of which, wait here. I have a rifle."

He said, "A what?"

"A rifle."

"Charlie, stop," Gillian said. "You're not a gun person. You're smarter than that. Don't be rash."

Huh? What? What kind of person was or was I not? The denim jacket she wore had been a present from me on her last birthday; this seemed a great upset to my generosity as a gift-giver.

"I don't think you understand," I said to Jacobi and his cohort. "Let me be clear: I have a rifle. Automatic, very arresting. This woman is my kraken and there will be many maimed humans on the dock before I let you take her from me." I pointed at the mustache. "You, sir, are a thief and scoundrel, and the sea, from what I know of it, peddles karma and vengeance. Your voyage is doomed."

"Perhaps you two should talk this out," he said.

To which I retorted, "Perhaps you should remember that *desperado* and *desperate* share a root."

He ascended onto the ship, his ass-kissing graduate students in tow, all of them dressed in Communist clothing, a few of whom eyed me evilly and enjoyed it. Gillian came closer and I almost instinctively reached out to embrace her. If only I could suckle at her swollen breasts I was sure we could arrive at some kind of agreement, one that involved her coming back with me and forsaking her squid-related dream. But as we stood there staring at each other I was overcome with an incredible dread, one that clamped right onto my guts. I had always been afraid of her, it seemed, because all *Homo sapiens* live in fear of the mighty who strike with lightning.

"Gillian," I said.

"Oh, Charlie. Just go. Okay? There's nothing I can say to you that will make you understand this. That's why I just left without saying anything. I need to do this. Please go, Charlie."

This? I thought. *What's under discussion here?* Was now the time to talk of sacrifice, the debts we owe as organisms on the earth?

"This is insane, Gillian. You're just leaving? Nixing the wedding? Two great years? I'm a shish kabob."

"Sit here with me," she said, and we parked ourselves on a wooden bench many a fisherman had used to contemplate the various faces of ocean ferocity. "I love you, Charlie, I do. But I've never loved you more than I love the squid."

That sounded to me so intensely aberrant I considered using two pinkies to clean out my ears. When I looked at my ankles I saw that one sock was green, the other brown.

"Please understand," she said. "I watched my mother

give up her dreams of being a scientist"—her mother had dreams of being a scientist?—"so she could marry and have children and basically support my father's career. And she did, and she never complained about it, but I could tell that it was always a regret for her. And I won't be that woman, Charlie."

"Maybe you could have told me this a while ago? Like when we first met? Like before we moved in together? Or maybe when I asked you to marry me? Or how about when we put the deposit down on the wedding? Any of those times would have been good, Gill."

Really—this realism was too much for me. The wind off the water mistreated her hair and then carried the familiar scent of her shampoo straight into my face: a hint of coconut, a splash of mint. Loss, I thought, has a smell, and you can purchase it for about twelve bucks at your neighborhood drugstore. Seagulls said something not far from my feet; one aired out its armpits and, I think, spat.

"I've done a lot of waking up over the last few weeks, Charlie."

"I have too, Gill, every morning, right next to you in our four-post bed, and it would have been real nice if you had shared this shit with me much sooner than now."

I bent toward her slightly in emphasis and dyspepsia.

"And Charlie . . . did you really go down to Virginia to kill Marvin?"

"You read that, huh?"

"Yes, I read it. Did you really think you could hide it from me?"

"I bought all the copies at Food World so you wouldn't see it."

"I have a subscription at work, Charlie. And my God, Food World, I despise that place. See, that's what I'm talking about. I never want to walk into another Food World for as long as I live."

Despise Food World? With its mom-and-pop owners and chicken rotisseried fresh each evening, and only the choicest meats from Connecticut farms, to say nothing of their customer service, so caring and true?

"That reminds me," I said, "what are you doing about work? You'll just quit your job so you can go fishing for a while? Lose all your health care and pension?"

"They gave me a leave of absence. And I don't want to live my life in deference to *health care*. Don't change the subject, Charlie. I don't care one bit that Marvin is dead, but it scares me a little that you were willing to murder him."

"I just wanted to talk to him, Gill, that's all. Tell him to quit harassing us. I wasn't really going to kill him. That was just macho talk for Groot. I did it for you."

"And then hid it from me."

Wait a minute: *She* was the angry one here? *She* had been double-crossed, duped, deceived? You should have seen the look on her face, her pursed lips pissed off.

"Ms. Lee," a henchman called from the boat's railing, "Professor Jacobi asked me to get you now."

"I'm coming," she said. "I have to go, Charlie."

We stood and faced each other, a welter in me.

"When are you coming back, Gill?"

"I can't say. Three months, maybe more. Time doesn't really exist for me right now."

I had a watch on my wrist to prove otherwise; it was there, ticking and turning—I almost showed her.

"But our wedding," I mumbled. "My parents."

She shook her hair, solemn, and told me the diamond engagement ring was in her underwear drawer, on top of her black thongs. The mention of her panties caused a jig through my inner parts. I looked up and spotted Jacobi in the porthole, his expression that of a convict half bored with his crimes. Apparently I would not be killing him this day.

She waved goodbye from the deck with neither sadness nor joy, and I thought I could read her lips: *Wait for me, Charlie*. As I stood there, I imagined myself with patience: I'd wait at the harbor and sleep in my car, a man with a gun surviving on fast-food burgers and his own capacity for psychic mutilation. I would not consider the overdue bills piling up in my mailbox, nor the fact that I'd most likely get fired from a magazine job it had taken me a decade to acquire. I'd become an observer of seagulls, a bearded seer, a from-the-pier fisherman with a cheap rod and reel I'd always be mending with duct tape. I'd watch the boats come in and go out, by sun and by moon, knowing that *The Kraken* and my lady were due to land sooner or later, in weeks or in months, or, okay, if you insist, years.

But ultimately, I had to admit, I was not the waiting type. A maternal aunt, educated and obese, had once told me that I was three parts impulse and one part woebegone. I stomped back to my car, smashed a clip into the rifle, stuffed another into a back pocket, sprang the first round into the chamber, and then stomped back down to the boat. And I did this partly because I was aware that if you put a loaded firearm in reach of the afflicted, said firearm will sooner or later discharge. The Russian doctor Chekhov said that or something else close to it. Who was I to haggle with Chekhov?

Gillian and the sailors had gone belowdecks to . . . I didn't know—make a toast? I dropped to one knee, aimed the rifle at where the hull met the water, and squeezed the trigger, only half surprised when nothing happened. No discharge. I examined the gun with what must have been the most quizzical look on my face, and it took me a minute or more to realize that the safety latch was on. I hoped nobody was looking at me and laughing; Groot hadn't told me about a safety latch; for this I would scold him. But soon I was unloading. I had expected an intrusive *rat-atat-tat,* but what came out of the barrel was more akin to a rapid *thump-thump-thump*, like a—what else?—a heartbeat. Empty shell casings spit from the chamber and clanged onto the dock near my feet. I nearly fainted from adrenaline.

The rounds pierced the fiberglass with loud knocks and made the lapping water go splash, though I couldn't have been firing for more than twenty seconds before the clip was empty. Overalled fishermen dove for cover; a car in the parking lot sped away. It didn't occur to me that I might be hitting human beings inside the boat. The only human that mattered was Gillian, and at that moment I felt certain she was armadilloed, impervious to gunfire.

I unloaded the other clip in the same fashion; then it became clear to me that the boat would not sink. A rocket launcher or its equivalent would have been ideal. Still, I had a duffel bag full of loaded magazines in my car, and I once again stomped to it, the butt of the rifle resting on my right hip bone as I had seen in photos of various masked militants.

Waiting for me in the parking lot was a vigilante fisherman, an old-timer named Bart or Sid, who had taken it upon himself to patrol the dock in the name of all things lawful. When I reached my car, there he was, crouched down near the front tire of his dented pickup, charged with the initiative of a Vandal, shooting his cap gun in my direction without asking me to drop my weapon or mend my sinful ways. His was a philosophy primal and much like my own: shoot now, worry later. Bart or Sid the Fisherman had me perplexed; if he hadn't been firing his tiny-caliber pistol at me I would have wanted to sit down swami-style and get all Hindu, ask him questions about the cosmos and my uncertain place in it. Here was an old man with the dance still in his bones. Instead, I ducked and ran, dropping Groot's gun to the wet pavement.

Little bullets were whapping into the things around me but, thankfully, not into any of my moving parts, because Bart or Sid the Fisherman was an awful shot, probably three-quarters blind and having flashbacks to the beachheads of Normandy. I was running now at full sprint in the direction of the water at the end of the pier. As I ran past the boat I saw— imagine this—Gillian's dismayed face in the porthole.

And then . . . I was in the sea, almost frozen in time—that daffy fifth dimension Einstein was certain of, said could be warped—cold-swimming in slow motion as if through sludge, suspended in blesséd silence full of bubbles, the dim light at the surface my only clue of heaven. In another twenty minutes, I would find myself handcuffed aboard a police boat, accused of profanation and peccadillo alike, crimes not conducive to society. I had once promised Gillian, at the apex of our love, that I would dive to unknown depths to capture her prize and drag it back for her to hold. Now, swimming, I felt determined to find that wretched kraken, yes, but not to kiss it, no—I would choke the bitch to death, damn its every breath.

See the last words of Mr. Tennyson's poem about me: "In roaring he shall rise and on the surface die."

Dying is a ball; it's the roaring that hurts.

3. THEM PRISON BLUES

MY MISSION SHAT upon by the Miocene logic and cruel outcomes afflicting all those with pluck but no punctilio, with hearts that run on gasoline: okay, I overreacted, I admit it. Today in our America you can't discharge an automatic weapon and not go to prison for it, and so I crouched for three months and change in a no-security state facility, mostly for men with wily checkbooks, after crouching the first two weeks in a not-bad county lockup, jinxed and well read because neither I nor kin could or would produce the bail bond to spring me. I told the detectives in charge—not a single one reminiscent of cops you've seen in *Dirty Harry* flicks but rather collegiate types with good hair—that Davy Crockett was a distant uncle on my mother's side and Daniel Boone on my dad's, but they did not care, not a whit. "Life is about the living," one said, and I pondered that aphorism for about seventeen minutes straight.

Also: prosecutors, cops, and their kind were on the phone to some lawmen in Virginia who were trying to tether me to attempted murder charges as a result of my memoir "Antihero

Agonistes," but my appointed lawyer, Deidre Jenkins, was young and feisty, a lukewarm fan of my modest yarns. I looked forward to my daily meetings with Deidre the way a Svengali looks forward to duplicity. She waved a wand and some charges went poof—she knew everyone in Maine with a law degree or part of one; as it turns out, many Mainers are related by blood or by moose—plus she took advantage of the current blurred line between fiction and non and convinced apathetic judges that my essays were purely imaginative, as far from fact as skinheads are from Elvis Presley's pompadour. Still, I had to squat behind bars for a while, hissed at and hooted on by certain family members. Deidre mailed me a study of the USA and its many guns by a bearded scholar: without a Detroit automobile and a firearm an American is just a Frenchman.

Once they transferred me from county lockup to the detention that was to be my dwelling for the duration of my sentence, I discovered that most of what one learns about prison from Ted Turner is really not all that true for the gross majority of offenders. By which I mean that my jail—in the untouched middle of Maine, our nearest neighbor an elk with Epicurean inclinations (I spent many an afternoon watching it from my cell when I couldn't slap two sentences together with spittle)—was no more than a onetime factory of some kind with bars bolted on the windows: spacious unlocked rooms instead of cells fit for spiders, weaponless guards with nicknames such as Snowball and Grandpa. No aggrieved sentries in towers with cannons, or razor wire coiling atop chain fences. No groups of stunted Latino hooligans bellyaching about the tattooed KKK-sympathetic trailer trash, or dancing a bloody hootchy-koo with a steroided rabble of blacks fond of ditties by the rappers N.W.A and the metaphysics found therein. No, we were a forested outpost of middle-class white dudes, essentially nonviolent and semi-educated, with mothers in civilization (not mine) who sent us baked goods and wool socks, as well as a vest or two sporting multiple pockets. If you're skeptical that such a prison could exist, I've beat you to it: I spent three months there and I'm skeptical still. But Maine is a special place: there's something about untold acres of natural beauty in concert with an underachieving public school system that leads to deviations from the customary and commonsensical.

Anyone who's ever tried prison food, raise your hand. That's what I thought, and I'm here to tell you: don't believe the lies. For three months I chowed down like the guest of a flourishing nation: grilled chicken, prime rib, red potatoes, and, I swear, the occasional lobster. The chef was an obese fellow who went around by the name of Dinner, and if there's one segment of society schooled in the minutiae of cooking and eating, it's the diabetical obese. The inmates were fond of speaking about Dinner as if he were the governor himself, or else someone quite close to Christ and His penchant for messianic magic tricks. His meals could make you feel almost home again. A native Mainer, Dinner said he could have been a chef in Paris if only there had been an escape route from the wilderness west of Portland. Instead, he ate much and drank more, and despite his flab could aim a fishing pole or rifle with the best of them.

Once, while strolling around dispersing hot buns to the men on Floor the First, Dinner said to me, "Charlie, you should have approached your Gillian with a just-made croissant instead of an automatic rifle and right now you'd be coddled in her arms."

"Dinner," I said, "you underestimate the ardent fettle of a woman with means. Thanks for the bun."

The mere mention of Gillian's name caused a wobble in me, a holler that forced my heart into a game of peek-a-boo with my brain. I think Tom Eliot from Missouri once asked, "Where is the Life we have lost in living?" and I thought: *Exactly*.

My cellmate Paul Fuss was a native Mainer, too, nearsighted and stringy, decidedly nonathletic, pale beyond apparition standards, a computer whiz who had defrauded his company of two mil and then spent the loot on seventeen-year-old massage specialists from the Orient. Fuss was part wanton, part rigmarole, with just a splash of Baptist decorum. He spent most days inspecting the jail's ample library as if in those aisles stood Relief and supermodels to split it with. This I didn't much mind except that he returned to our room each evening with a racket of facts stuffed up above his brow and the very eager need to quiz me. Did I know the name of the bone disease that bothered our darling President Lincoln? Isn't it astounding that Newton was born on the very day Galileo died, a coincidence more beguiling than Jefferson and Adams dying only hours apart? Why did William James, otherwise so cerebral, put such stock in that charlatan spiritualist Maggie Fox? True or false: Edgar Allan Poe slept at the grave of his young cousin-bride, drunk beyond locomotion. And the most insistent: Did I know that Loch Ness mightn't have the food supply to support a monster for a single day, never mind millennia?

"Fuss," I said one evening, "I have had my fill at the moment of deep sea creatures and the like. The topic incites me to parlous pondering."

At opposite ends of the room Fuss was at his desk and I was at mine, our heads down—not seeing each other and not wanting to. The notepad before me sat blanker than a list of Fuss's willing girlfriends, the pencil sharp enough to slay.

"But Charlie," he said, "I've just read four books on Loch Ness. This is a subject that binds us: your passion for the giant squid and mine for the Loch Ness Monster."

His voice came out prepubescently, a grating squeak with hardly a note of manliness.

"Correction," I said, "the passion is not mine but my lady's. Also, I don't see why we need a subject in common, Fuss."

"*Your* lady? You sure about that?"

He was a button-pusher atop his other talents; several times a week it took all my muster not to suffocate him.

"Careful, now, Fuss," I said, my eyes stretching over my left shoulder. "Very, very careful, now."

"You can talk to me about it, Charlie. I want you to know that. If you need to talk, I'm here for you."

I spun around in my wheeled Staples chair to face the back of him; his hair was aslant his skull like a cap that can't fit, his face so close to the pages of a magazine he could have licked the pictures.

"Fuss," I told him, "I will not have my grief autopsied by the likes of you. My malady is beautiful, to paraphrase Mr. Tom Waits, folk balladeer, and I shalln't have its beauty despoiled by a man barely brachiate."

"Hmm. Barely brachiate. I didn't know it was an adjective, too, pronounced that way. Are you writing something now?"

I swiveled around 360 degrees and on the way glanced at the blank, bewitched pages of my notebook. When I had been in county lockup for those few weeks, I had a cell to myself and thus was able to scrawl orgasm-like until all of "Witchy Woman" squirted out wet and clumpy. I mailed the ink- and pencil-smeared pages to my editor at *New Nation Weekly*— who spoke with a faux-British accent, like William F. Buckley, conservative Kimosabe: he pronounced "helicopter" *hee*licopter even though his mum squeezed him out and brought him up in Brooklyn, New York—and in response he clicked me an angry email about the costly time it would take his assistant to type out such an overlong and barely legible confession. *You ass*, I replied, *I AM IN JAIL*, which led to abject apologies and a fetid fruitcake via FedEx.

"Actually, Fuss," I said, "I'm trying to, but a noise is coming from the direction of your neck."

"You know, Charlie, I was a pretty good writer in high school. Got A's in English. And I've always wanted to write a book. Maybe I will."

"I've always wanted to perform a bone marrow transplant. Maybe I will."

"Or journalism," he said, "like what you do. I might want to move to Boston when I get out of here. Maybe write for the *Boston Globe* and the *Boston Herald*."

"Fuss," I said, "numbskull. Wanting to write for the *Globe* and the *Herald* is like wanting to fight for the Austrians *and* the French."

Through the bars of our window I could see the Epicurean elk and his antlers brushing by the branches of pine trees, his quiet pleasure consummate and the cause of my envy. Oh, to be an elk and not give a damn except about elk-related issues.

"Or I'd like to be a cryptozoologist," Fuss said. "Track the Loch Ness Monster and other supposedly extinct creatures. I have big plans for myself, Charlie."

"Right, Fuss. Cryptozoologist. You know what you need in order to qualify as a cryptozoologist? A mouth that can say: I am a cryptozoologist. It's barely a job title, one for the uneducated or socially unlucky, and one step down from porn star. So good luck with that."

A passage of silence here as Fuss mulled over his options on the earth. The elk moved on out of sight and I returned to my desk to sulk.

"Well," he said, "I can't stop thinking that there's something in that loch, Charlie. Are you telling me that all those eyewitnesses over the decades have been mistaken?"

I heard him using Scotch tape on something.

Deep inhale, deep exhale.

"Fuss," I said, "I am telling you nothing. But if you must know, then yes: eyewitnesses at Loch Ness are hokum-makers trying to sandbag you and lonely others like you. If your lizard lives in that lake, then I hope you go fish it out one day and then smile for the camera. All I'm saying is this: I don't care either way."

"You should."

"And why should I, Fuss?"

"Because the monster hunters of the world must unite. Marx said that."

"Fuss," I rejoined, "the giant squid is the business of science, while that lizard in Loch Ness is the business of bartenders. I find you hidebound and homespun, more spunk than smarts. Please refrain from talking to me."

"We should ask Dinner about this."

"We should not. Please quiet your strange self lest harm come to you."

So instead of prattle he taped to our walls nineteen photos of the Loch Ness Monster and then began making little newspaper-and-glue models to situate here and there and there around us. Other times he used his Internet hours to research up-to-date info on Nessie and the mushroom-eaters who swam after her, very often leaving on my pillow black-and-white printouts of blurs supposed to be a monster. I had my own fata morgana to brood on—Gillian cavorting I knew not where, my thoughts in agony—and tried to ignore Fuss's growing fascination with a creature he himself admitted did not have the food supply to subsist a single day. I wished he would reacquire his lust for teenage Cambodians.

Among Fuss's other singularities of character was one I had never before encountered in a fellow humanoid and shall not soon forget: his dislike of music. And I don't mean his dislike of a certain kind of music, but of *all music*, any la-di-da produced with an instrument. For example, I myself do not care for the nitwit twangy platitudes and silly hats of country-western—and this despite the Garth Brooks always on rotation in Groot's vehicle—but I'd suffer welts and lesions without certain R&B singers and, say, David Bowie circa Ziggy Stardust. Who does not require Bruce Springsteen—they don't call him the Boss for nothing—snarling about a road called Thunder

and how to get to where it goes? Or Dylan gargling, bringin'
it all back home? Neil Young and his thrasher? But my cellmate: the mutant nearly had a conniption when I'd tune our
radio in to the folk station to sing along with love-torn acoustic
guitars. You tell me: what kind of person doesn't appreciate a
salty piano ballad with lyrics sung through smoke? Precisely
my point: a mutated one.

"Fuss," I said, "your dislike of music makes you part pos-
sum. I believe you shall die from it, in which case I wish you'd
hurry up. This is the exact reason we need a matriarchy, a god-
dess culture of fertility instead of this Yahweh, warrior-god
culture currently in fashion. Because women can dance, are in
touch with their Wicca insides."

"I miss the earth," he said, and did not elaborate.

DEIDRE JENKINS, my erstwhile attorney, had been all along
mailing me packages and semi-amorous missives, which I
thought half strange, since her public-defending of me was finished—genuine billets-doux that mentioned the "sheen" of my
locks, the "bite" of my prose, my love-life alternatives now that
Gillian was "lost" to the squid, what I would do upon my "glori-
ous" release—make a home in Maine, maybe?—and I replied
with many thanks and a gentleman's Christian naïveté, since
indeed I was intensely grateful that her weeks of exertion had
won me only three months in the slammer and not, as some had
been smacked with, three years. There hadn't been a trial, only
my admitted wrong, a courtroom meeting with glasses of cold
water and a pile of paper to scribble signatures on. Then she
began visiting me when I was transferred from county lockup:

once under the pretense of various stray documents that awaited my Hancock, once to deliver me a pizza pie with pepperoni even though Dinner was serving prime rib that day. (Have you ever been forced by gratitude to eat pepperoni when others in the area are having prime rib? It's a truly demoralizing adventure.) I found out later that Margaret Welsh, wardeness of our prison—our prison had a wardeness—had been Deidre's one-time elementary schoolmarm and was now a trusted ally of the Jenkins familia, the mother and father of which were medium-powered Maine attorneys themselves and the grandfather a still-sitting judge with cataracts and a dour disposition on the human spectacle.

Yes, sometime soon after we had met, several weeks earlier, Deidre had begun to fancy me, titillated by my offhand reactions to loss and love, tickled by my willingness to be berserk in service of the heart, made moist by my memoirs she called art but others mostly called crap, the exact point at which mumbo meets jumbo. Apparently the men she had known weren't in the habit of ricocheting through their own lives; they were dullards with nothing to wrestle for, no bonfire in them, not even a flint. A Maine lady needs impulse and oratorio, loathes the lymphatic and lame. So you see, my labors were admired after all—albeit by the wrong woman. But Deidre's want of my man parts and desire to make herself my spanking new muse were the reasons she had pulled all the pullable strings with her parents, her granddaddy judge, Wardeness Margaret Welsh, and the devil knows who else. Couldn't I return a little lovey-dovey, if only by mail?

I tried. And maybe I tried with too much mettle—my lines might have mentioned the "Latin gusto" of her calves and hips in motion, and how the small blond hairs of her nape quelled my fear of becoming a "noncrooning castrato"—because not four days after I posted the letter she arrived at the prison wearing an orange autumn dress, the strapless kind that could reverse a vasectomy. The tubby guard Grandpa appeared at our cell with sweat all over him and a look that said something was about as up as you can get.

"You have a visitor, Charlie," he told me, his breathing that of a fat man terrified. The whole way to the visiting room, his waddle the wonder child of cheeseburgers, he kept glancing at me like I was just then on the converse of death row, and when I saw Deidre—in that fabric aglow, standing next to the Coke machine, her toenails a shade identical to the dress, and in her handbag no doubt a rose-petal net to ensnare me in—I knew the name of death row's opposite: sex row.

"Good God in the morning," I muttered, and Grandpa said, "God got nothing to do with this. Have fun, Charlie," and he left us alone in the visiting room, the sofas a summons for limbs akimbo.

"Umm, hello there, Deidre," I think I said. "You're looking very . . . orange today."

She embraced me, her fruity earrings and necklace in a clatter, and I could smell the citrus perfume. She was a multisensory advertisement for Tropicana.

"I got your letter, Charlie," she said, holding me at arm's length, searching my face, including, I guess, my eyes, which would not lift from the over-round bosoms painstakingly packed into the top of that elastic dress.

"Oh," I said. "That."

Her own eyes announced: *I'm here. I've come for you.*

I said, "Where is everyone else today? Why is the visiting room empty?"

"I had Margaret arrange a private visit for us," and here her brows bounced once as if to say, *Oh, yeah!*

Our wardeness privy to this seduction, a coconspirator in my sullying? Through the barless windows I thought I could see the Epicurean elk mocking me from the pine scrub, wanting to say, *Do not mail letters you do not mean.*

"Is it true what you wrote?" she asked.

Her hands were still clutching my deltoids, her eyes still doing that buggy thing.

"True what? True how?"

"You wrote—I have it memorized—*your gorgeous galore gives insomnia to the dead.*"

"Hmm. I wrote that? Just like that? With *gorgeous* as a noun?"

"Just like that," she confirmed. "Here, let's move to the couch," and she slipped out of her sandals, then unbunned her hair the way porno librarians like to do, all the while grasping my hand as if the helium in me might cause liftoff.

"Listen, Deidre, about that letter," I began.

"Plus," she said, "I thought you could use some real cheering up today."

Plunging backward into the sofa, I asked, "Why? What's today?"

Those were her panties, yes: white with tangerine polka dots, a plumpish mound at the center of them. South of my navel some long-clogged gears creaked to life.

Deidre eyeballed me with doubt. "Today's May eleventh," she said. "Your wedding day. You forgot?"

Those words vacuumed all the air out of me; I could feel my face go white, my tongue like sawdust. Next to the Coke machine across from us someone had tacked up a "Welcome to Maine" calendar; in the photo two impossibly beautiful lovers were water-skiing on a blue lake, a snowcapped mountain behind them. I went to it slowly, weedy through the knees, and examined the tiny square for May 11. How could such a small space on paper be responsible for this magnitude of shatter? How could I have forgotten? And what could those two lovers on water skis be thinking behind their smiles? I had not been keeping track of the days and weeks; Fuss and I had agreed not to hang a calendar in the room, convinced it would make our time lug along. During one of our initial meetings, Deidre must have asked me about the wedding date, and the trap in her head had held on to the info these many weeks. Behind me I could hear her saying, "Well, that's a good thing you didn't remember, right? It means you're over her and the whole thing. Right?"

But I couldn't speak just then, couldn't turn around to look at her. The door to the hallway was right there to my left, and in another few seconds, with vision slightly blurred and the breath still smacked out of me, I opened it and moped away back to my cell—my legs moving I knew not how—leaving Deidre Jenkins open-thighed and astonished on the couch in her orange dress.

I'd spend the next twelve hours curled on my bed, abandonable.

. . .

ONE MORNING ABOUT two-thirds into my sentence, Grandpa came into our cell to nap on Fuss's bed, and I asked him why my cellmate hadn't returned from the library the night before.

He said, "Fuss walked into town and got lost coming back. The fella went for a Snickers bar candy. Snowball took his bicycle to go find him."

"Grandpa," I asked, "are you saying that the front door to this place is unlocked?"

"Well, not exactly, but sometimes," he said, pondering the lights overhead. "Ain't no man gonna run away, Charlie. Most of you don't have homes to run back to. And Dinner has lobster here, though only on occasion, as you know. That man can cook."

I was at my desk trying to write sentences not altogether debauched.

He said, "I've been thinking about that fine little gal in the orange dress. She ain't been back to visit you, though, Charlie. What'd you do wrong?"

"The same thing men have been doing wrong since those cave paintings at Lascaux: emotional mendacity in service of a pitiful ego."

"Not sure what that means," he said, his bulbous eyes closed now. "Just say you're sorry. An orange dress like that don't come around twice in a lifetime."

Indeed I had mailed Deidre Jenkins a handwritten apology in the sanest, most Presbyterian English I could muster, but she never replied. I expected to hear from her exactly never again, which was just as I deserved. Some of us need to dig the wax from our ears before that message will come through: we get what we deserve in this world.

"What's your next plan to win back Gillian? Trying to sink that boat didn't work out too well for ya," and he giggled through his Santa beard.

He lay on Fuss's bed backward, his black Kmart sneakers smashed into the pillow. With me in my chair and Grandpa there on the bed, we looked like Sigmund and his subject.

"Well, Grandpa," I said, "I don't actually have a new plan as of yet. I'm kind of just waiting for an idea to fall through the top of my skull," and for some reason I pointed to my head.

"Well, my wife's a fan of your little stories and wants to see you young folks reunite. She has a pool going with her lady friends. Everyone else in her bridge club thinks you'll fail big time and maybe get dismembered, but my wife believes you'll get back together, and so does one other lady, too, Mrs. Kellog. She's ninety-eight years old, has had dementia for a decade. She's pulling for you, Charlie."

"Grandpa," I said, "you tell your lovely wife and Mrs. Kellog that Charles Homar treasures their support. If either of them has a plan for winning back Gillian that doesn't involve firearms or prison time, I'd be glad to hear it."

"They're eager for a new story. This detention has halted your narration, Charlie. You can't very well write anything exciting about sitting in this room with Paul Fuss. Unless you write about that sweet girl in the orange dress."

Grandpa cracked open his swollen eyes and turned to me. "Maybe a prison break would spice things up. A great escape. You know, like Steve McQueen."

"Yeah," I said, and spun in my swivel chair, "or I was thinking of creating a prison-wide uprising of some sort. That could be interesting to write about. Right?"

Grandpa seemed to consider this a moment. "Well, nah," he said. "You better just wait to be released next month."

And so I waited: the days and weeks of being surrounded by all that menacing male folly, yearning for Gillian's flesh and the salty spot inside it, hour after hour of reading and day-tripping, contemplating all the bad news a man can bear, wondering what my next design should be, sleeping much in hope of dreaming, feeling awful about Deidre Jenkins, and trying to stay, stay the fingernails from screeching down the blackboard in my brain.

Grandpa had given me a cell phone to use during my three-month incarceration but I had been too mortified to dial my parents or Groot or anyone else who might have resembled a friend. But during my last week locked up, while Fuss was in either the library or the computer room, I called my folks hoping to get my mother on the line.

"Charlie," my father said, "Jesus, why haven't you called?"

"How are you, Dad?"

"How am *I*, how are *you*?"

His voice wheezed, emphysemic and scuffed by a youth among cigarettes.

"I'm good," I said. "I'm fine."

"You're good, you're fine? You're in prison. We read about you in the paper, Charlie. And your story in that magazine, about going to shoot the boat. Your mother bawled her eyes out all night."

"I'm sorry about this, Dad."

My mother was in the background, asking questions and no doubt trying to wrench the phone from him.

"Jesus, Charlie," he said, "it's been months. When are you being released?"

"This week," I said.

"We would have bailed you out, but . . ."

"It's fine, Dad. I know you guys aren't rich."

"We're not rich, Charlie. And to be honest, I told your mother a little prison time would do you good. I hope you'll listen to me now. That Groot is a no-good bastard. They should have arrested *him* for giving you that gun."

"Is Mom there, Dad? Can I talk to her?"

Both my mother and I began weeping then—we're a weepy outfit—she for raising a cuckold and dolt, I for disappointing her—again.

"How is it there?" she asked.

"It's fine, Mom. I leave this week."

I had no tissues to wipe my snot with—Fuss had used a whole box in the creation of his miniature Loch Ness Monsters—so I used the bottom of my T-shirt.

"I've been sending you packages. I got the address from your lawyer up there. Did you get my packages?"

"Yes, thanks, Mom," I told her, even though I hadn't received a single thing: not a card, not a cookie. "How Dad's health?" I asked.

"He's okay. He's fine. Don't worry about us."

"Good. That's good."

A long, strange pause here, as awkward as a first date, and then I said, "Day and night I think about what she told me at the harbor. She said she never loved me more than she loved the squid. Day and night: I just can't figure it out. How can that be, Ma? It defies everything I know to be true."

"Oh, Charlie," she said.

Yes, oh, Charlie indeed.

"I've got to go now, Mom. I'll see you soon."

"But Charlie," she said. "Promise me something. No more of this. No more of this madness."

4. SASQUATCH LOVE SONG

UPON MY RELEASE from three months of concrete ennui, it took me half a day just to free my car from the impound lot. Then, bestirred to action, I flipped open a national newspaper in a coffee shop called Java Man and felt the bolts and belts in me shiver and snap. Gillian and Jacobi had fished out their giant squid in the dark-deep Antarctic Ocean—*alive*. The adult female mass of slime and stink measured forty-five feet and weighed nearly a ton; there was its picture beneath a headline boasting, "World's Largest Invertebrate Captured." Gillian grinned, as if at me, from the photograph; her eyes said *satisfaction* and *sated*. My kidneys were making a noise like *chunkchunk-chunk* but I read on: they had trawled for the squid with deep sea lines two thousand meters long, each one equipped with some ten thousand baited hooks. Belowdecks sat a hulking tank designed to house the beast till landfall. A hatted henchman wielded a pump-action twelve-gauge in case the monster began snatching seamen and flinging them toward its snapping beak.

The species of giant squid, I learned, remains so rare it wasn't identified till 1925, though Jules Verne, effeminate Frenchman, had much to say about the goo and gas it is. Zealous experts the world over, especially some squid humper from the Earth and Oceanic Research Institute at the Auckland University of Technology, were right now in the process of hailing Jacobi and my Gillian as heroes akin to Achilles or perhaps Indiana Jones. Breakthrough for science. Words like *wonder* and *imagine* and *deification*. I was, I think, sweating blood.

During one of our balmy postcoital nights now so long ago, Gillian told me that most of what was known about the giant squid had been learned from the cavernous bellies of sperm whales beached off the coast of New Zealand. Or from the ludicrous tales of ancient mariners too long above liquid. No more. Now Gillian had video footage of the one-ton kraken writhing in the foamy waves just off the stern of Jacobi's vessel. Pinkish red and gelatinous, the squid and my heart: we were the both of us just calamari for Gillian and the other predators of earth. I swiped the newspaper aside and thought of Yeshua from Nazareth; I heard this shepherd, too, was crucified for love. My coffee tasted like copper.

The slow and lonely drive home on Interstate 95 south— what was my hurry exactly?—a philosopheress on the radio singing about her hang-around ex-beau who wouldn't beat it, the sunshine mocking my inner nor'easter. Mom had been keeping some watch over my townhouse during my imprisonment, and I returned home to find operating utilities, a barrel of mail, and fish that were not dead. Gillian's absence pummeled me this way and that; she had left in a hurry to join Jacobi, so our place was pungent with her aroma, her doodads and knick-knacks placed left, right, and center. Womanless, formerly incarcerated for unwise discharge of an automatic weapon, I sat in the foyer of our townhouse for perhaps seven hours, unable to move, staring at my knuckles, thinking about the derivation of *melancholic*. Somebody Greek had known my name.

I snoozed on the sofa that night because entering our bedroom would have forced a multitude of tears, each one an icicle. My dreams were callous, squid-filled; the fiend had me in his jelly grip, trying to choke the breath from my ribs. A bikinied Gillian had the thing in a bridle and was riding it like a rodeo steed, wearing cowgirl hat and boots, with spurs, I believe. If I had clicked on the TV and scrolled to CNN I would have no doubt seen Gillian and Jacobi at the other end of Anderson Cooper, and this I could not abide. Indecisive, I sat in the sun out back for hours and tried to will the beams into a healing heat, Vitamin D and whatnot. The grass needed mowing but mowing was just then beyond my abilities. Then I called my friend, you know who, the Navy SEAL whose name I can no longer declare in my yarns—he says it's bad for his military career.

"Friend," I said, after the opening whys and wheretofores, "I am released, and in need of further counsel."

"Christ, Charlie, more trouble?"

"Christ indeed. Trouble for sure."

He told me my essay "Them Prison Blues" was short on emotion, didn't delve into how I was really *feeling*, and then accused me of retreating from emotion in all of my work. I think I held the phone away from my ear and looked at it. Everyone a critic.

He said, "Paul Fuss sounds like a talented pain in the ass. I would have gotten another prison term for dispatching that bastard henceforth."

"Friend," I said, "that's in the past. Our concern is the future. When can you come over?"

"Give me five minutes flat," and he was there in four and a half.

We perched at the kitchen table for many minutes in silence—he no doubt wondering how I had gone from the semi-standard boy he once knew to the blotch now before him; I wondering the name of the witch doctor he had consulted in order to ward off aging—and then he wanted to know what went wrong when I took his rifle to the dock. He admitted that my memoirs "Witchy Woman" and "Them Prison Blues" were cheap on details, not nearly as thorough as they could have been were I blessed with quote Jamesian interiority and the plotting proficiency of Wilkie Collins unquote. Plus he added that rock star über-ego Don Henley wouldn't be tickled if he knew I stole his title "Witchy Woman," even though the Eagles were "the dullest band ever to cause a musical note." Furthermore, my prose was just then "making Misters Fowler and Waugh scoff in their graves." Groot uses his English degree whenever he is able, especially when it has zero bearing upon the matter at hand. His life was almost about books until the U.S. Navy rang his bell with offers of killing certain desert-dwelling Arabs who boast ill-gotten Kalashnikovs.

"Well, I'm a little fuzzy," I said, tasting the bad breath I had from lack of sanitary care. "I tried to perform as you advised, but once I arrived there and found them about to shove off in that boat, I think I just started shooting what was in front of me."

"Not a bad strategy: when in doubt, start shooting. Where's my gun?"

"They took it when they arrested me."

"No matter. They can't trace it. Sorry your mission failed. I feel shitty about all this. Especially since your father hates my guts. I've always known it, I guess, but to read it in your essay and know for sure was a little upsetting to me."

Sensitive Friend.

"Don't think twice about my father," I said. "We need a new mission. One that does not involve fury or frazzle and the possibility of further imprisonment. By the way, why do you have a beard? I haven't seen a beard on you since we were in high school and you were trying to look like John the Baptist for some reason."

"The beard is because I'm off to Afghanistan this week. Undercover shit. Don't ask."

"I won't ask," I said, and felt weepable.

Friend examined his fingernails—they looked manicured by Korean expertise—and said, "I saw her on the news. The both of them. They're still in New Zealand, displaying the sloppy beast for the excited and prying eyes of science."

"Yes. That's what I was going to ask you. Do you think I should go there?"

"To New Zealand? And then what? Coerce her back with poetic lines and perhaps a daffodil? Negative. You need a vacation, Charlie."

A vacation? Huh?

"How can I holiday with this bile loose in my sternum? Here, feel my hand. It's putty. The rest of me, too."

Friend sighed in either irritation or empathy, I couldn't tell which.

"I'm off to Kabul this week, Charlie. I don't know when I'll be back. My wisdom to you now is vacation."

"But where do I vacation? How? You really don't want me to get Gillian back, do you?"

He rolled his eyes in that way he does, the way that means I'm a hopeless jackass for thinking such rubbish, and then I could see him pondering, staring at the wall as if a non-English sentence were scribbled there and he the linguist who would decipher it. Then he rose and sauntered down the hall to the latrine while I looked bleary-eyed at my meaty fingers, all of them marvels of movement.

When Friend returned he said, "Charlie, what do you know of the legendary Sasquatch?"

"Friend," I said, "I appreciate the sentiment, but this is no time for a woman's genitalia. Plus I'm hurt internally."

"You boob, Sasquatch is Bigfoot," he said, and sat, taking up notepad and pencil. "Half man, half ape. Eight feet tall, six hundred pounds. Undiscovered primate in the Pacific Northwest, Washington State."

His drawing was a blur of hair that didn't have anatomy.

I said, "Washington State. An old girlfriend of mine relocated to Seattle or thereabouts. Sandy McDougal. Very nice gal."

"Charlie," he said, scratching his new beard, "please stay focused."

"In that case, Friend, I do not follow."

And so he described: Before he was called to arms earlier in the week by the U.S. Navy, he had planned an excursion to the state of Washington with a compatriot called Romp—the unimprovable tag would soon make sense—in order to uproot all varieties of flora and fauna and bag a Bigfoot. It was his idea of vacation: the purity of unhurt wilderness along with the possibility of shooting a primate unknown to science. As I listened to him pour forth about *Gigantopithecus*—the extinct thing Bigfoot supposedly is—I wondered how much aspirin and whiskey were stowed away in the kitchen cabinets, and how much of them I would need to consume in order to know what life was like in Andromeda.

When he stopped I said, "Pray tell, Friend, why would I want to fly to the West Coast to hunt a Sasquatch? Especially after I recently mocked a man with a soft spot for the monster of Loch Ness."

"Charlie," he said, "you are dull, made of links rusted and out of date. Why? Because if you nab an unknown primate you, too, will be a hero to science and civilization alike, perhaps noteworthy to a folklorist or fabulist, and, more important, once again in the affections of Miss Gillian. The capture of a giant human-like monkey will dwarf by many yards the capture of that giant squid. CNN will summon you. Plus it makes for a good story. See now?"

His language was for me just then akin to what apish *Homo erectus* felt on the African savanna when he tamed the first fire, the flame hip-hopping at the end of a log. After a stretched moment of my thoughts lining up in both alphabetical and chronological order, I said slowly, "Indeed I do," and felt the soda-like fizzing of thrill move up my guts, all those tubes and pipes rotted by loss. This here was possibility for a poo-bah like me. Providence was once again proclaiming: *Move*.

"You are," I said, "genius and messiah both. I'm certain I can find a race of giants in the woods. I mean, they're *giants*. Must be about as hard to find as a Ricardo in Juárez."

Friend passed me Romp's card—Romp had a card—and instructed me to converse with him about the expedition. The card stated simply, *ROMP: I BRING IT BACK DEAD*, with a telephone number beneath that promise. Friend then advised me to search online or else trek to the county library for Sasquatch understanding so I wouldn't seem like such a luckless ass when I dialed Romp.

"What should I know about this fella?" I asked.

"Hunter. Scholar. Priest. Negro. Prophet. Man of jazz and all items sacrosanct. Shaves with obsidian. Has razzle and the necessary dazzle to mix it with. Also copulated with Florence Ballard in 1974. He wrestled Bigfoot in 1980 at Bluff Creek in Northern Cal, in the same creek bed where the famous Patterson footage was shot. He lost that bout, but just barely, and managed to chomp off the hominid's ear. Then he tried to fire his rifle or his camera before he passed out, but, sadly, could not."

I asked who Florence Ballard was and he said, "Idiot. She was the second Supreme of *the* Supremes."

"Oh. He couldn't get Diana Ross?"

"Focus, Charlie. Sasquatch."

But wasn't focus for those farther away from the web-footed than I just then felt? Finally I asked, "How do you know all of this about Romp?"

"He told me. Plus he wears the severed ear around his neck. He's been hunting Bigfoot ever since they grappled that day. Says it insulted his mother in words reminiscent of Aramaic."

I could see that I would need to proceed with gravitas, with doo-wop and pomp. Already in my cranium was a delirious slideshow of my detaining the celebrated North American ape man, of my blesséd reunion with Gillian, and of Jacobi's hot dishonor in the face of my achievement. The ceremonies, awards, and millions were ancillary but welcome and I would show the proper meekness and thanks. Christ, too, was meek, and this people appreciated. He has done well for Himself, and so, I thought, shall I. Far from those bilked fatalists who condemn mankind as automatically snakebit, light-years away from God's polish, I was a real go-getter, found my own bur-nish on this blue dome of commotion. Watch me work.

Upon leaving my condo that day, Friend said, "Onward, and make sonnets of your sins."

"I shall. You as well. And keep your blood on the inside."

"Oh, and Charlie," he said at my door, "don't write about this one, okay? You promised your mother no more mad-ness, remember? And believe me when I tell you that Romp is ninety-eight percent madness and two percent pilgrim."

Well, how bad could he be?

THUS BEGAN MY Bigfoot research. I viewed online the infa-mous 1967 Patterson footage; the brawn and bulk of that beast swashbuckling across the creek bed caused lengths of electricity to hum over my bones. My Lord, it lived; that was no man in a monkey getup: the height and weight, the muscles stretching beneath sun-soaked fur, the mellifluous locomotion, the creepy turn of its head in a distinctly nonhuman style. White-haired professorial experts with many letters after their names—Dr.

Grover Krantz at the front of the pack—spewed forth with the
facts of the case and presented an arsenal of evidence to choke
all naysayers: footprints, hair and scat samples, sixty years of
eyewitness reports by undrunk citizens, and the holy grail of
Bigfoot fandom, this Patterson film, all of which could not be
indisputably disproved, not even by those Mickey Mouse computer maestros at Disney. Why, I thought, would any maver-
ick scientist plumb the seas for a giant squid when this hirsute
beauty lay in wait out there in the Pacific Northwest? And as
for those multitudinous naysayers: each one had a slum for an
imagination. Most men are not bold, never mind valiant; they
find safety in the status quo. Magellan would not nod.

After nearly six hours of absorbing Bigfoot factoids—you
wouldn't believe the kooks out there who think he came from
outer space—I rummaged through Gillian's library because I
remembered a hefty book on Bigfoot that once adorned her
bottom shelf. Although it had a publication date of 1980, the
photos were colorful and the diagrams informative. I felt ready
to dial Romp; ours would be the repartee shared between those
intergalactic explorers digitized into being by George Lucas
or that sane scientist Spielberg. I hadn't really studied figures
and available lore since college—unless you count the tutelage
I endured under Gillian's giant squid blitzkrieg of info—and
so I was proud of my scholar's efforts.

Romp answered his cell with a bass-tone, *"Yasss?"*

I said, "Romp, I am Charlie. Friend has put us in touch and
I believe you could use my primate skills, also my proficiency
in speaking to trees both ancient and new. Let's talk."

And Romp said, "I've been watching you for the past six
hours, Charlie."

Come again? Huh? He'd been doing what?

"Across the street, in your neighbor's treetop," he said. "I've been spying you."

"What's that?"

"Come look."

As I sauntered my way through the dining room to stand at the bay windows, I said, "Sir, this causes me fear and the contemplation of space-time. Are you kidding?"

"Romp don't kid. You're at the window now. Looky here, see the glow of my celly phone."

By Jove, there it was, across the street, atop Mrs. Ruby's sycamore, the small blue-green burn of cellular communicato.

"As I said, I am now afraid, and a fearful man is a danger-ous man, so please explain your strange self."

"Friend called me when he left your place this afternoon and relayed your chart. I needed to execute binocular surveil-lance before you contacted me. My partner on this expedition cannot be among the undeservéd. You should close your cur-tains, Charlie."

"Well. Is it true about Florence Ballard?"

"Affirmative. Plus I have others. Famous sisters you've heard on radio waves. I once built an altar to Negress Aphro-dite and made sacrifices of the Inca sort."

"You couldn't get Diana Ross?".

Silence.

"Hello?"

He said, "Friend tells me you've been to prison and know how to handle a rifle. He adds that you're impulsive and reli-able both, a hunter in your own right who embraces beatitude and has no qualms about homicide. You were prepared to massacre in the name of love. That's sweet."

Was there a correct response to that?

"I'm not exactly proud of these facts, Mr. Romp."

"Plus I've read your stories in that magazine and know the score. You speak Shakespeare and have a fondness for sharp objects. You are, I think, ready for voodoo. Wait one. I'll be at your door."

What would you feel for that minute or more while a stranger named Romp descended from a treetop and made his leisurely way to your doorstep? Would you say to yourself: *Self, your little life has reached a peculiar crossroads, à la Robert Johnson and the devil, and perhaps prudence is now in order.* Or: *Self, stop obsessing over a long-gone gal, giant squids, and Bigfeet; stop your communion with shady fellows of the night; perhaps rediscover Jehovah and his only boy, Yeshua the Nazarene.* Maybe you would; but I, on the other hand, for that minute or more it took Romp to appear on my porch, was an alien to that much-lauded tool, introspection. Rather, I was reduced to a primitive, cold-blooded gadget capable of feeling only, and what I felt warned me of fright and then of freedom. *Gillian*, my many synapses shouted, every one like a downed power line on asphalt. *Gillian*.

Romp stood six and a half feet tall, was equipped with the build of a boxer or prison guard villain, his blackness the inky Congo kind, emphasizing all teeth and eyeballs, his smooth crown sporting the gloss of a Tootsie Pop. When we greeted one another like men of civilized spheres, his grip swallowed my hand and threatened to detach it. The diver's watch weighing down his wrist had abstruse functions unnecessary in central Connecticut. Those were the diamond calves of a sprinter. Two pockets on his camouflage cargo shorts were filled with things that rattled. And there, yes, there around his trunk of a neck, just as Friend had said, dangled the bitten-off weatherized ear of some half-deaf miscreant.

"Charlie," he said in that bass tone, "I think better in the bath, and we have plans to draw."

He brushed past me smelling of primeval musk, leaving me at the door, my sweaty hand on the knob.

I turned and said, "That sounds kinky in a way that makes my intestines move. I'd rather you didn't, sir."

"It wasn't a request. Lead the way and do it now. No drivel."

Lord keep me, I thought, and ten minutes later Romp lay soaking in my bathtub, me on the toilet seat with my head in my hands.

"Good heavens," I said, "cover that river monster with a towel. Please. My manhood is threatened."

"Here's how this will work, Charlie. I quiz you on Sasquatch, and if you pass, you're in. If you fail, I am gone and you never hear from me again. You are not part of the glory of capturing the anthropoid eyesore whose ear now adorns my throat."

"But I must. I must net a Bigfoot. Gillian—"

"I know. Gillian the squid woman. But our journey mustn't be one of puppy love rekindling, only enchantment, annihilation, and everything ontological."

I took my face from the safety of my palms and looked at him. A dab of soap bubble stuck to his chin scruff.

"Are you making fun of me?" I asked.

False blank face. "How so?"

"That sounds like something I would have written in a certain mood: *enchantment, annihilation, and everything ontological*. I think you're making fun of me."

"By the way, I love the scene in that one story of yours, where you climb up the Ferris wheel to rescue that gal. But, Charlie, I never heard of a man climbing up *wet* metal bars and not slipping. I mean, it was raining something hard right before that, right? And you didn't *slip*? Come on, man."

Those purple scars on his chest looked as if some starved predator were trying to claw its way out from under his skin— the scars no doubt left by his historic grapple with the Sasquatch who'd insulted his mother.

"Please just continue," I said. "Everyone's a writer, I swear."

"Okay, question one," he said. "Which of these men was not a well-known Sasquatch hunter: A, John Green; B, René Dahinden; or C, Joseph Smith?"

"That would be C, Joseph Smith. I know Smith as the illiterate wannabe sage of a goofy cult called Mormon, plus someone convicted of fraud and other high jinks against his neighbors."

He kept losing the bar of soap beneath his oversized self.

"Correct. Well done. Question two. Why did Roger Patterson film his footage in Bluff Creek: A, he just happened to be camping there; B, there had been reliable sightings there the previous week; or C, he didn't film the Sasquatch in Bluff Creek but rather at the very base of Mount St. Helens?"

"The answer is B, he had got reliable tips from eyewitnesses. He followed the scent."

"Correct. And now the million-dollar question. Are you ready, Charlie?"

"Ready I am, Romp," and I clapped my hands here, once, loud and echoed the way sports people do when the game is on the line.

He was now using a lavish handful of Gillian's thirty-dollar shampoo to wash his hairless head.

"Here goes," he said, eyes closed. "The most convincing aspect of many Sasquatch tracks is: A, the shape, by which I mean length and toe formation; B, the depth of the prints, indicating the weight of the bitch; or C, the dermatological ridges."

"C, the dermatological ridges. Those can't be faked. Only a handful of people in the world know about them."

His face changed to whoopee and gee-whiz.

"Charlie," he said, "you impress me. I can use you on this hunt. Our terminus is far into the abyss of the Pacific North-west; we might not return. Be warned. But nevertheless we leave tomorrow at dawn. Arm yourself with hunger and the be-bop of jazz. Also, bring a crucifix and anything you know about witchcraft."

Romp's whale-black form unfolded from my tub and then, towel in hand, strutted naked and dripping from the bath-room. Martin Luther once chucked his inkwell at Satan, who lurked behind him as he wrote by candlelight; and for a reason unknown to me, as I sat on the toilet lid that night, I had an identical urge. Don't ask me to clarify it; our thoughts are law-less sparks going this way and that.

"Wait a minute," I said, going after him. "Hold on. I don't know about this."

"Don't know about what?"

He turned to face me and let drop the towel, revealing once again the brown baguette that made its home betwixt his thighs. Don't ever let anyone tell you that stereotypes aren't ninety-six percent true.

"This," I said. "You. Bigfoot, the whole thing. I promised my mother no more madness."

"Oh, yeah," he said, pulling on his clothes, "I read that scene. Didn't believe a word of it."

"Huh? Why not? Why the hell not? It's the truth."

We stood by the railing at the top of the stairs, Romp's own big feet wetting my carpet, and I had a very clear vision of him pitching me over the banister to my broken-neck death below.

"Hey," he said, "don't get mad, little partner. I'm just saying. Some scenes are more convincing than others. It being true don't make it convincing. Didn't you learn that in Intro to Creative Writing?"

"What *are* you, man?"

I believe my face was lemon-pinched.

"I'm a whole lot of God-help-us is what I am."

Romp bade his farewell to me and then was gone. But, yes, I would go with him in the morning. Why? I'll let the Ancient Mariner of Sammy T. Coleridge tell you why:

> *Since then, at an uncertain hour,*
> *That agony returns,*
> *And till my ghastly tale is told*
> *This heart within me burns.*

See?

• • •

I WILL SPARE you, listener, all the minutiae involved in packing for such an excursion, the jumbled thoughts in concert with
such packing, the buzz-buzz of sleeplessness, the doubt, how I
decided not to visit my parents to tell them of my hell-for-leather
agenda, how Romp collected me the next morning in the drizzle, the Bigfoot-facts ride to the airport in Romp's spray-painted
tractor pretending to be a jeep, and then a six-hour-plus cross-
country voyage with those false folks at Delta.

Let's ignore the narrative nudge in time and place and suf-
fice it to say, for the sake of yarn efficiency, that eighteen hours
after Romp left my bathtub, the two of us touched down in
Bellingham International Airport in northwest Washington
State, where we were then met by a cloak-and-dagger confederate who had prepared for us a four-by-four SUV swollen with cargo of both the legal and illegal variety, everything
we needed and didn't need for a two-week expedition through
the crushing cataracts and sylvan snares of God-knows-where.
I didn't meet this confederate—Romp wouldn't let me—and
therefore cannot describe for you his anarchic attire or the sinister gleam in his one good eye. In a vision-pained sea of glint-
ing autos in the middle of a parking lot—my sun shades were
at the bottom of my bag—we inspected the SUV, kicking tires
and so forth.

"Umm, is this a hybrid?" I asked.

Romp bent beneath the giant hood to scrutinize oil and
coolant.

"Do it look like a hybrid?"

"*Does* it look like a hybrid? I can't say it does, Romp."

"Ain't no real man drive a hybrid, Charlie."

"I drive a hybrid."

"Like I said."

"Okay, Romp, I'm not going anywhere in this atrocity on wheels," and I crossed my arms to show I meant it.

"Don't give me this holier-than-thou hybrid crap, Charlie. From what I recall in your writing, Gillian drives a Beetle, and that ain't a hybrid, hypocrite."

"How do you remember that?"

"You're so skimpy on details it's not hard to remember the few you have."

He showed me the dripping oil stick, as if to flaunt the glacier-killing goo we'd be burning too much of.

"She sold that Beetle and bought a hybrid when we moved in together!"

He said, "I do not care, Charlie. Get in the truck. Either that or go away and you do not capture a Sasquatch to lure back your woman."

So I pouted in the front seat. Romp's itinerary? From what I could gather, he planned to scout the British Columbia border through North Cascades National Park, Okanogan National Forest, and over to Colville National Forest, all the while stopping at key points along the way to sniff-snort around and perhaps volley a fusillade of ammunition. I didn't recognize any of his termini as Bigfoot hotbeds of activity and made the mistake of telling him so.

"Ignoramus," he said, driving from semi-urban to rural, "we need to avoid the tourists and the infamous locales you see in books, including Willow Creek, the Blue Mountains of Walla Walla, and Skookum Meadows. Why? Because our prey

avoids them. A beast he is, but not a buffoon. Some say he's
Muslim, knows Allah, maybe jujitsu."

"Right," I said. Silly me.

Our SUV was so cramped with gear—guns and ammo,
food and water, blankets and knives, clothes and tents, cameras
and telescopes, one chain saw, and, God help me, a trumpet—
I couldn't recline my seat. Romp's musky cologne was unnecessary and nauseating; he had made it himself and doused his
torso to lure the Sasquatch. Its ingredients were part urine, part
quote Negress menstrual blood unquote, and part apple cider,
not from concentrate. I wondered if Jacob Jacobi and my gal
Gillian had used any scent for lure of the giant squid; snapshots
of them swirled in my gray matter like those faulty fireworks
you see shot off once a year by drunks. Outside my window the
trees-and-valleys landscape grew godlier by the moment.

"Romp," I said, "what do you know of the giant squid and
its many arms?"

And he said, "One monster at a time, please."

The day inched toward the purple gloaming while Romp
navigated and I munched on peanut butter crackers and non-
perishable camping snacks. We were heading to a place Romp
called Bitch Ravine because "the bitch was spotted there" by
his crafty associate within the past ten days. I assumed Romp
could erect a tent at moonless midnight with the same ease
another man finds the bathroom in the dark, and so I said
nothing of the clock. Miles Davis seeped through the SUV's
speakers and the melody performed calming magic on Romp,
who said that after he was finished massacring some Sasquatches in juicy retribution, he would also tame a few and
teach them to tap their feet to R&B.

"I'm like Don Quixote," he said. "I don't trust men with ponytails," and he did not explain.

We drove for well nigh six hours into some serious green guts; Romp was contemplative and at peace. I slept in the bucket seat and my pilot was a gentleman and let me snore. Even in my sleep I could feel the minutes stacking up into hours, the leaky passage of tick-tock, every mile more distance from Gillian. When we finally stopped, I woke with a jolt and took a minute to remember how hurt I was.

We were in the heart of the heart of some massive, man-neglected wilderness; the ravine made its monotonous water-roar down to our left, and I heard interrogative owls off to our right. The scent out there was piney, almost prayerful; a man could get pleasantly high on that untampered-with air; it reinvigorates the lungs and makes one feel born. Romp kept the headlights burning; bugs did a wingéd dance around them. We both were kind to our bladders, and then he began unpacking. I zipped my jeans and joined him at the hatch of the SUV, saying, "I'll take a rifle and be right back."

"Pardon?" he said, stopping to glare at me askance. "Was that English?"

I thought it was and told him so. "I'm gonna walk into the woods now and bring back a Bigfoot. Then we dial Mr. Dan Rather out of retirement for him and his news crew to come see."

"You'll have to excuse me," he said. "That sounded like mathematics or maybe Pekingese. I'll be right here when your words once again make sense," and he resumed preparing the tent for pitching.

"Romp, they are a race of *giants*, not ants. If a race of giants lives here in these woods, right out there"—and I pointed into a wall of black—"then I will nab us a fresh specimen. Provide me with a floodlight and weapon and I will do thy bidding, kind sir."

Here a disgusted sigh reserved for retards. "Charlie," he said, "I'm gonna provide you with an ass-whupping if you don't shut your hole and help me pitch this tent. Let your tomfoolery take leave of you. Have respect for the hairy wild man of this region, he who the Tsimshian natives called Ba'oosh. You are dealing with powers both ancient and Fortean. Here's your sleeping bag," and he whammed the softness of it into my chest.

Romp's fondness for the firmament and hinterlands was about as important to me just then as the ozone is to oligarchs. I, Charles Homar, from a mid-sized Connecticut suburb, had my own mission to accomplish irrespective of the stars or the lunacy loose in another man's blood. But the shine just then in Romp's eye was cannibalistic and crazed; some self-control was in order and so I mustered it. He seemed to me a combatant capable of roasting another man on a spit while considering the finer points of barbecue marinade.

You should have seen the two of us out there in that before-the-fall real estate, under those dime-sized stars, the forest noises like chitchat Adam and his dame Eve first heard, our tents and weapons and various battery-run doohickeys set up like a military HQ. Romp's fire-building talent would have impressed sad Jack London or some career arsonist; the blaze had girth and stature both, cracking into the cool mossy air beneath canopies of colossal trees. We slurped water from canteens and wished we had had the forethought to include marshmallows among our cargo. Romp petted the high-tech scopes, sniper rifles, radios, satellite phones, and GPS tracking devices, and I mostly just sat slumped at the mouth of my tent, feeling opportunity flutter away, visited by the same thoughts that had clobbered me in prison for three months straight: my Gillian in the mitts of that mustachioed scallywag.

Then the dubiousness settled in on me. "Romp," I said, "there's something that bothers me about Bigfoot and his brothers. Why hasn't anyone ever brought back a body? The things must die of old age."

Annoyed, he glanced up from the box of bullets he was counting from. "Nature takes care of decomposition: scavengers and microorganisms. Sasquatches bury their dead Stone Age–style, if you ask me. You could count on one hand the found corpses of black bears or cougars. Don't be a Doubting Thomas, Charlie. Their habitat is a mass the size of Europe. Plus they have cunning, like Huck Finn and the true Nigger hero of that yarn."

Vis-à-vis his word choice, I once again attempted to explain to Romp my moral and demographic coordinates, but it was like talking hermeneutics with a Hun. *Fall asleep*, I thought. *Fall asleep so I can prowl away, arrest the indigenous, infernal furball with my own cunning, and quick call Dan Rather to put me on prime-time television with a new haircut and designer threads from JCPenney.* We two sat silently by the fire and let it transfix us with its searing magic as it had our *Homo* ancestors so long ago. Romp and Charlie, sipping instant coffee not half bad: we were merely denizens of a habitat for those with faulty frontal lobes. What was I *doing* out there with that Abrahamic madman? I thought of the words *happenstantial* and *phenobarbital* and wondered who had had the craftiness to coin them. Vampiric mosquitoes harassed my ear hole and fuzzy bugs crawled across a boot; all around us the forest made its night noises, the temperature tumbling every twenty minutes. Romp commenced razoring a ten-inch bowie knife on an oiled block of stone.

"Listen, Charlie," he said after a while. "In all seriousness. Why is it so important that you get Gillian back? Man, there's *lots* of honeys out there, just waiting for a dude like you. You ain't an ugly dude, got an education. Why you want this one honey back so bad?"

I nearly laughed out loud and then nearly did it again. "Romp, if I have to answer that for you, then you'll never understand."

"Explain it. I want to understand. Seriously."

"I love her."

"So? I love lots of honeys."

"I don't." And I let him stew over those two words for a minute or more until I said, "You get it, Romp? That's the difference. *I don't.*"

"I'm just saying, man, if you can't be with the one you love, you know . . ." and he sipped his coffee.

"Yeah, I know. Thanks, Romp. That means nothing," and I sipped mine.

"Listen, let me tell you this story. This is true, every word of it. Listen, now. After I fucked Florence Ballard that first night—"

"Must you say *fuck*? It's so crass. In my experience women don't appreciate that verb."

"Ain't no women here, Charlie, but all right, fine, fine. After I *made love* to Florence Ballard that first night, she was hard in love with Romp, wanted Romp twenty-four/seven, was willing to forget about her career and all that, all those dreams of making records, everything. You couldn't blame her. I pounded that pussy so hard—"

"All right, that'll do. Women are not walking pussies, Romp. I'm a Democrat from New England and—"

"Now you listen here," and he pointed the sharpened bowie knife at me, my head region, before flinging it into the nearest tree—bingo, point-first, perfect—then stood up for emphasis. "We're *men*, out in the *forest*, sitting around a *fire*, about to go *hunting*. There ain't no women about. I'm getting goddamn tired of your bullshit liberal routine. Because we're *men*, Charlie, get it? And you know what men talk about deep in the forest before the hunt? *Pussy*. So let me tell my story without you interrupting and giving me goddamn pointers on how to talk. If there's one thing I don't need any advice on, it's the ladies."

"Fine," I said, reclining on my camper's pillow, "go ahead. Just know that you're perpetuating the stereotype that the black man is a ravenous sexual predator, King Kong looking for a Fay Wray to ravish."

"No, I'm not, stupid. That's all in your sick head." He knocked on his own head even though he meant *my* head. "I'm talking about pussy because that's what *dudes* talk about. Stop being such a goddamn sissy and start being a regular dude. Your artificial sensitivity isn't fooling anybody. It's like you're constantly talking to a camera. What's so decent about denying yourself pleasure anyway? You've been so brain-scrubbed by ironic feminists at them liberal universities, now you think it's wrong to be a man. I mean, when that honey in the orange dress went to visit you in jail, all ready to do it up, and you *walked away?* Fool, you crazy? A man is not better than biology."

Okay: I had to admit that I indeed felt sissified after Romp's retort. He *did* seem like a chap who scored manifold points with manifold women, but still, I was about to tell him the difference between pleasure and exploitation, a little tirade I had on hand for just such occasions, when he said, "And I won't be perpetuating anything if you don't tell anyone about it. You better not write about this excursion, Charlie. This shit is all top secret. Now, can I finish my story or not?"

"Fine," I said, giving up and about to cry from homesickness. "Sorry. You were saying," and I thought that a cigarette would make a good prop at this point.

"Precisely. Now . . . let me see, where was I? Umm . . ."

"Florence Ballard's pussy."

"Oh, right. So, she was hard in love with Romp. Made that sister see *Gawd*, no joke. Sister got beatified by Romp. She wanted *every day* to feel next to that divinity I showed her. Now, that's real love, Charlie, when you're willing to give up your dreams for another person. But look, look what happened. Romp said no can do, Romp had other pink to plunder, and look what happened."

We stared at each other over the jagged top of the fire, he waiting for an indication that I understood, I waiting for him to clarify his loopy logic.

Finally I had to say, "Romp, I have no idea what you're talking about."

"Romp said no to her love and Florence Ballard loved *me*. And then accomplished great things. You see?"

I tried very, very hard to see, but it was so dark out there.

"No, actually, Romp, I don't see. Didn't Florence Ballard die depressed and alcoholic at the age of thirty-two?"

His face was not pleased with that remark. He said, "You're the thickest white boy I ever met. You can go on to accomplish great things because Gillian said no to your love. Maybe write the Great American Novel—"

"*Memoir*."

"Whatever. Or maybe capture Sasquatch, or maybe meet the real woman of your dreams, the one who will not say no to your love this time. Maybe some sister with sexy green eyes. That's what I'm talking about, my brother," and he yanked his bowie knife from the bark.

Some sister with green eyes? Bless his heart, he was trying to cheer me up, give me perspective, calm the rowdy within me, and I appreciated the effort, said thank you, and yes, smiled, not believing him in the least, but grateful for his sober Christian trying.

"By the way," he said, seated again, "I like your choice of a Jew gal. Jew gals are some fine pussy."

"How is that *by the way*, Romp? How?"

"You know I'm Jew right?"

"Yeah, right," and I had to sit up to see if he was serious. I kept myself from telling him that *Jew* isn't an adjective and takes an indefinite article everywhere beyond the Wiener schnitzel line at a Nuremberg rally.

"Seriously," he said, "Romp is Jew."

I was looking at him in a way that made him say, "Why are you looking at me like that? You don't think a brother can be Jew? Ever heard of Sammy Davis, Jr.?"

"Actually, Romp, I wasn't thinking anything religion-wise."

"Well, that would be a first for you, Charlie. You Catholics can't never stop thinking religion."

"*Lapsed* Catholic," I corrected him.

"I'll tell you this: as for the top four ideas of all time, Jews are four for four. Jesus, Marx, Freud, Einstein. And that's why I converted."

If I had been able to gather the proper incentive I would have reminded Romp that campfires, the wheel, indoor plumbing, and antibiotics were all fair contenders for the top four ideas of all time. What was the point, though? Look at us out there: two cowboys who were no longer boys and who had never owned a cow between them. Besides, I could see that speaking about female genitalia had caused rigmarole within his braincase and rib cage. He was a stranger now to comprehension, as far from good sense as a day off is from an off day. I made like Paul McCartney and let it be.

SHORTLY AFTER OUR hem-and-haw, I crawled annoyed into my tent, wondering about this little war I had chosen with myself, and wondering, too, about soldiers—the soldiers of, say, Alexander, all those Macedonian middling men who trailed him across the known world spreading around the Greekish. But *why*? They marched and marched again for years on end. Why couldn't they simply say, "Alex, listen, babe, we know you want to be king of the universe, but we're tired and hungry here, we miss our families and farms, we're fed up with dying and being maimed, half of us are sick with infection, and so we're just going to lay down our swords and turn around now, see you later, bye-bye." If each of them had said that to the Great, then the Great wouldn't have been so great at all. Forging on in the name of glory and honor should last about twelve hours tops, and when fatigue and starvation and the cold wet weather bite into them, and when missing the brides and kids clamps down hard around their hearts, then those men should have said no more, said to hell with the knife wounds, arrow holes, and ubiquitous scent of horse shit. But they didn't.

If you want to know what had forced thoughts of Alexander and then of how women are fundamentally the stronger sex because they give birth through that minuscule rictus, you'll have to ask a critic with her nose in the air of academe.

I drifted into a weighted sleep of the sort every insomniac yearns for, the sleep that feels as if some benevolent force is pressing you down into the mattress, a generous paralysis. I snoozed that way for several hours and then was joggled awake by semi-human noises I could not identify. Romp was performing some tribal, shamanistic boogie between the fire and my tent; his shadow gyrated on the fabric and had me worried. I emerged to find him day-one naked, pythonic phallus whacking against his sprinter's thighs, his face adorned with crimson war paint the origin of which I could not guess, and in his grip a sharpened spear made from a surprisingly straight tree branch. Around the blaze he danced the dance of some almost-noble savage; from his throat emanated the primal hoots and howls you hear so clearly on the Discovery Channel.

I think I wiped the sleep from my eyes. "Romp," I said, "pray tell, what are you doing?" And when he didn't respond I repeated the question.

"Out there," he said, in a slow growling whisper, "past those trees. I see you!"

He released a formidable shriek into the night, and, I swear on my own seed, a formidable shriek was returned.

"He's there! He's there!" Romp said. "Not pleased we've invaded his sanctuary."

Pay attention, stranger; from this point on events unfolded speedily, as they are wont to do when courted by crisis and uproar. Just as I was about to glance around for a gun, fist-sized rocks began bombarding us from inside the dense bush.

"Incoming! Take cover," Romp yelled, and we both dived into the pine-needled grass near our tents. This Sasquatch had studied the throw of Roger Clemens; he could have no doubt won prizes from the dunking tank at any town bazaar. When the bombardment stopped not half a minute later, Romp got to his feet, unafraid of another possible projectile, and yelled, "Ba'oosh, my brother! I'm coming to get you. Ba'oosh! Attack, Charlie, attack," and he darted naked into the forest with the aforementioned hoots, spear, and primordial know-how.

Now, in such a predicament, one's trusty neocortex takes a backseat to the simian brain that was our battery for about five million moons. That is to say, one behaves like a lower primate instead of the cognitive human he evolved to be and purportedly is. Instead of taking up firearms, machetes, flashlights, I impulsively darted after Romp into the wilderness with nothing but my idiotic nerve and the trouble-causing chemicals we've dubbed adrenaline. If I hadn't fallen asleep with my boots on I probably would have given chase in my socks. So into the darkness I plunged, my thinking parts no better than oatmeal, my heart in riot, stray twigs stabbing into my shirt, my feet stumbling over various forest floor matter, and my voice beckoning Romp to halt, halt. Of course, I couldn't see where I was thrashing but only followed the foliage-pranging sounds in front of me, Romp's cries and some ungodly snarl I took to be the distress call or battle cry of the Sasquatch we had so upset.

In that thickness the ancient, werewolf moon was about as much help as your decrepit aunt in a motor vehicle accident. Branches and bushes whirred by my hair; my extremities flailed about in mockery of someone trying to run. When I landed on a not-so-trodden footpath I gave chase in a more respectable fashion but still could not see Romp or the thing in retreat, the pulse in my ear like the gut-borne tribal drums Romp had been grooving to around the fire. Shouts and yowls off to my left; then yowls and shouts off to my right; then an irreligious wail right in front of me about fifty yards, Romp in ecstasy or peril, triumphant or defeated. Racing forth toward the twig-snapping, bush-riling ruckus, all I could ponder was the possibility that Romp, not I, would capture the hominid and thus spoil my only chance at regaining Gillian. This was selfish, yes; I should have considered his safety, his flesh being rent by a woolly heap three times his weight. But—every man for himself and et cetera.

The footpath I raced along degenerated into more impenetrable depth as I shouted Romp's name over the insults he and the beast were exchanging. I heeded Romp barking, "Take that, bitch, and that, and that," and then his victim retaliating in a tongue I've been told the Assyrians used, his honor tampered with. But the cacophony seemed to be coming from all around me; I spun and spun, trying to get a bearing. And then—the death yelp of one or the other, a blood-gurgling resignation—and silence. The quivering crutches my legs had become didn't plan on motion for at least a minute or more, and so through the mass in my throat I called out Romp's name and received not a reply, nor could I locate him once my limbs decided to cooperate again. He was, as they say, disappeared. I crouched in the darkness trying to regain control of my lungs, frightened by the sudden midnight hush, and, yes, asking myself once again: *what* in the world are you *doing*?

What would you have done had you been in my boots that night? Trample on through that turf and attempt rescue? Perhaps return to camp and implement one of the satellite phones to dial assistance, park ranger or Smokey the Bear? Maybe curse the asinine impulses that landed you in such a jam? I did indeed return to camp after half an hour of searching for it, and I sat vigil at Romp's ample fire till daybreak with a Beretta nine-millimeter pistol in my hand, petrified that the stinky shag who had made a meal of Romp would soon come to eat me too. I thought about venturing to find the disturbed patch of forest Romp and Bigfoot had used as a wrestling ring; perhaps clues would be had there, sprays of blood on the leaves, a chomped-off ear from one or the other. But dread had parked itself in my guts—too far from home, Gillian no closer to my loins—and I said, "Charlie, take a drive now. Leave this madness. Seek the calm of Buddha or some Zen derivative. Monsters, guns, and men named Romp cause allergic reactions."

Yes, I wanted to estrange myself from all the thunder that sits in the sternum and turns, turns. And I'm here to tell you that that's exactly what Charles Homar decided to do: I abandoned all Romp's gear to the things of the woods and drove away in that beastly SUV toward a Shangri-la I knew not where. I felt mildly yellow for leaving Romp, and shuddered at the thought of telling Friend I had done so, but a person has minimal powers on this earth we've made. What could I have done? I no doubt would have ended up a man-sandwich just like Romp, and my aspirations said nay to that.

Behind the wheel, some indistinct vestige of data long locked inside my headache leaked to the fore, as if on cue: A woman I had once dated and nearly went aboom for, French-kissed the crevices of, pre-Gillian—the very woman I had attempted to tell Friend about—had relocated just outside Seattle the last time I checked, just she and her poodle named Pow. Sandy McDougal: divorced, yes, and infertile, too, but a masterpiece of pith with much wisdom to bestow upon an avant-gardist like me. Maybe I would find a computer and start punching keys, present myself on her porch with a bun-dle of sunflowers and hair combed to the side.

Would she welcome Charles Homar, a mental klutz badly in need of a path and a map? Would she bake me a casserole and tell me I'm an okay human, despite some proof to the con-trary? Think about it. Would *you*?

5. LEGEND HAS IT

HERE'S WHERE MY life story goes haywire and more than a tad willy-nilly (as if): I had a heart harassed, self-esteem booby-trapped and tripped-over, and was much in need of sugar kisses from a certain double-X chromosome there in the Seattle area. So I hightailed it from those ancient woods in Romp's SUV and crept down to the suburbs where I knew Sandy McDougal had set up shop. Never mind that it took me days—days!—to emerge from that greenery, making turns left and right and back again with no regard for circumference and the radii therein, polygons and vertices and whatnot. No matter: I quite enjoyed the scenery and snail's pace, stopping at parks and rest areas to nap in the spacious cargo hold of the SUV, tapping out "Sasquatch Love Song" because I had another installment due and, my editor insisted, Luciferian fans who were hoping I'd fail. Some fans. If I wanted the swag directly deposited into my checking as per our contract, then I'd deliver the manuscript on time, and this I did, trying not to remember my fugitive-cum-castaway status and the fact that I was on the wrong side of the continent if not the law. Trying to get an Internet signal out in those boondocks was like trying to find a truesome Christian on a coed campus.

About Sandy: In addition to needing moderate doses of female attention—any slob in my situation would—my craven self needed counsel, a break from commotion. Sandy happened to be a psychotherapist with advanced degrees in Freudian this and that, knew the alchemy of a moon-man called Jung, had published papers in journals with names like *Cognitive Continental Transubstantiation*. People, I was a frantic insect now at an impasse, my Sasquatch plan botched. If I was going to get Gillian back—I guessed she was still in New Zealand reveling in the spotlight—and calm the clamor beneath my breast, I required the acumen of this gal who once said I was cute, my day-old whiskers western in a Wyatt Earp way.

It took me almost a week to find her—precious time gone astray—me holed up in a motel that put one in mind of the acedia monks suffer from, an Internet signal so lame only a Luddite could love it. With technology supplied by those eggheads at Apple I finally located Sandy M. in just a matter of hours after arriving at an upstanding county library not far from the motel, the well-funded sort that attracts the unemployed and otherwise unambitious. At the doors to the library, some bookworm on welfare recognized me from color photos someone had put on the Web. The forty-year-old Seattle native—a squinting nonathlete in glasses who was also, no doubt, loyal to his mother and the pies she baked him—provided me with the much-needed directions to Sandy's homestead, just twenty minutes east of where I was then standing.

"So, Charles," he said into the sun, "your Gillian found the giant squid in the cool waters near the pole. Her life's passion. When will you be reunited? I'm waiting for that part of the adventure."

"Stranger, you and me both. Right now I am in want of pleasure and a pause from all things giant squid and Gillian. I am withered and just a cha-cha away from wasted, so if you don't mind, step aside and watch me go."

"I read this week's story!" he yelled after me. "How could you have abandoned Romp? That Bigfoot ate him!"

Over my shoulder I showed him a middle finger as I fiddled with the beeping handheld thingie that was supposed to unlock the SUV. I ended up squirming in through the back hatch when the other doors refused—refused!—to open. Some passing teenage joker in a hemp getup said to me, "SUVs kill the environment, pal," to which I replied, "Despots rule the earth, donkey, so write that down and remember it."

Now . . . the most prudent part of me declared that before delivering myself to Sandy's doorstep, I needed to bathe and perhaps dress in threads that were not stained with the rank loam I had rolled through on the Bigfoot expedition just a week earlier. I trekked behind the motel, through unsightly weeds and scrub, to a ghastly Walmart nevertheless looking majestic in the midday sun blaze. The heat was everywhere and outrageous; I longed for an arctic blizzard to chill me into submission and acceptance. Instead, I had the summer and the way it makes a man lonesome and tender. That clothing I planned to purchase had been wrought by orphans in Malaysia; but I needed new duds and could not afford to mime a person with choice or leisure. I also bought a tube of sticky gump to plaster back my hair in a way that might suggest

Clark Gable, and a five-dollar cologne in a plastic bottle that smelled of turpentine or birth fluid. The loinclothéd guy on the box seemed to swear by it.

Understand: in addition to needing Sandy's guidance, I was feeling just a smidgen sexy-like, and this I welcomed as a respite from the fangéd melancholy that had been chortling at me since Gillian had packed up and said bye-bye. I looked up *fairness* in the dictionary and it was not there. Yes, I was a schmuck who entertained himself on Bigfoot expeditions and went in search of long-lost gals who lived in foreign time zones. Fine. Since prison I had acquired a fear of sitting still, as if I might fossilize, the only remnant of me those stony bones speaking to anthropologists, far into the molten future, who would hold me for just a minute before deeming me unworthy of study. I had to keep moving, partially useless though the movement was. Think of those austere Spartans marching off to die at Thermopylae. My DNA and other vital strands chanted *Go!* I figured Sandy McDougal would appreciate my verve and perhaps compliment me, which, truth be known, was all I required at this point: a female compliment. Every man is a walking mouth after milk.

As I strutted before my motel room mirror that day—freshly scrubbed, clothed anew, sporting a suntan the Aztecs would envy—I said aloud, "Charlie, be a gentleman and quote Catholics frequently, perhaps Chesterton or, better yet, Newman"—two British clowns I had perused in college—"but above all stand erect and declare your distance from baboons." With that I sallied from the motel, directions in hand, and did not think of poor Romp devoured by Sasquatch, only of my Gillian in the multiple arms of another organism and the possibility—pray—that we would be reunited before my seed stopped swimming.

Amped up though I was, with deeds to do, I still possessed sound enough mind to know that landing unannounced on the doorstep of a dame unspoken to in several years was not altogether orthodox behavior, and that my spontaneity might be met with flying spittle or else out-and-out indifference. Or perhaps fisticuffs with a new beau not pleased by another man's assignment, or by another man's . . . fill in the blank. Imagine my delight then when finally I found Sandy's quaint suburban Cape—after several lefts and rights down very wrong roads, and several moments of wanting to turn around, abandon my plan as I had abandoned Romp—and she greeted me like I was a delivery boy and she badly in want of what I had—hugs, kisses almost on the lips. For several minutes there on her front porch I explained and she listened: Gillian and the giant squid, our ruined nuptials, my being in Seattle, Romp and Bigfoot in the wilderness, my blood moving liquidly through each limb and digit, and the counsel I had come seeking.

"I read that you were in jail," she said.

"Oh, that. Yes, well."

"You tried to kill Gillian and the giant squid hunter she fell in love with? Murder with a rifle? I mean, Charlie, really."

"Sandy," I said, "I wasn't going to admit all that. But seeing as how you read that installment—well, then, yes, it's true. I've become an ex-con. And must you say *fell in love with*? We don't know that for certain."

"Sorry. But you shouldn't write up your memoirs for that magazine if you don't want anyone to know, Charlie. I've been reading your pieces. You have comma trouble, I think. Plus your syntax is so . . . I don't know . . . *unkind*."

I was simply glad, at this juncture, that Sandy M. didn't mention the time I drove down to Virginia and attempted to kill Marvin Gluck. Perhaps she had missed that one.

"Sandy," I said, "I need leadership and perhaps arsenic. I have come to you because I have no one else. The mistakes I have made are legion. Please help."

Sandy had neither added unwanted pounds nor altered hairstyles; she looked remarkably as she did the last I saw her several years earlier in the ice of Connecticut. Those tight auburn locks still curled down to her shoulders; and her eyes, well—one was still stuck to the wall, like Sartre. No mind: her skin and figure (bosom and buttocks both), good girl's Unitarian voice, and the multiple gigabytes of psychoanalytical data packed up beneath her hat—they compensated for that indolent eye. It felt exhilarating to be that close to her again, as if my soggy will had been dried out and reanimated. The dinnertime sun behind us was about to begin its drop.

"You look really great, Sandy."

"Oh, thanks, Charlie," and she blushed a bit, glanced away. "You're still handsome. I can't believe you're really here."

"I'm here, all right. I've been . . . well, you've read where I've been."

"I thought about you all the time, you know. And I was worried sometimes. You seemed so . . . out of control. That wasn't how I remembered you when we were dating."

I kept looking at my shoes and the bricks beneath them, half afraid that I would start a humiliating weep.

"I needed to talk to someone who knows me."

"I'll help you if I can. But listen, Charlie, right now I have supper inside and someone you must meet. Follow me."

Someone? I must meet? Hmm? But what of my diagram for Gillian's immediate retrieval, and maybe some one-on-one sultry cuddling to jump-start my man-parts? As she led me inside by the wrist I glanced left and noticed that indeed there sat parked in her driveway a testosteroned pickup truck that had recently slogged through some gluish mud. Lord. There was still time to turn around, maybe knock on the wooden door of a monastery, make my persistent state of broke and babeless look deliberate.

Supper was no more than a bucket of chicken and some side dishes from KFC—unromantic, not to mention acid on arteries—and the someone who needed my meeting was—I'm not lying—a Filipino UFO scholar so dwarfish he looked as if he had just climbed out of a test tube. I had no time to take in the house's interior—the décor, the clean or filth of it—but I did have time to put this together: after Sandy introduced Casey Gonzales as the preeminent UFO scholar in all of the Philippines—never mind that being the preeminent *anything* in the Philippines is nothing to light up over a ballpark—I understood that Sandy's hazel summer dress, clanking brace-lets, and crystal pendants were the mystical sort that hippies and weirdos everywhere call their own. Could it be? So this was how she had altered, then: not in weight or hairdo, but in her affiliation with the Great Pyramid of Giza and the vari-ous spins of Orion. Please tell me she did not forsake her hefty intellections in favor of hocus-pocus and awful clothes. The air conditioner in the house droned so well I felt the drips of sweat freezing to my forehead.

"Casey," I fibbed, "a pleasure to meet you. I as well once spotted a flying saucer, but this came from scorned Mrs. Millbury next door, throwing all the dishes out the window. That woman drank obscene quantities of bourbon. Plus took pills."

"Ah, yes," he said, releasing my handshake with those doll's fingers. "Charles Homar, the chronicler and memoirist. You are slimmer than your photo. Malnourished, maybe."

His voice had no evidence of Filipino in it but was, rather, part homosexual, part Houston. He squinted my way as if I were dawn and he newly awakened. His T-shirt and shorts were a matching set made for grade-school boys: they showed a smiling pudgy race car with VROOM printed beneath it.

Sandy said, "Casey is here tracking the recent phenomenon."

We were all seated at this point around the dining room table, the center of which contained a disorganized display of plastic gizmos and other bubble-gum-machine junk, including those green urchin aliens with the exaggeratedly Asian eyes, the kind you've seen twenty-six times too many via the X-filing travails of Fox Mulder and Dana Scully (who was played by actress *Gillian* Anderson. Coincidence?). The bookshelf behind Sandy stood as an affront to the cranial capacity of the averagely educated, all those fluorescent spines published by places called Nebula Press and ET Books and Shock Editions, on subjects such as Atlantis and Easter Island and, for the love of God, *vampires*—and this from a woman with the gall to criticize the punctuation and word order of my prose.

With a mouthful of chicken leg—and listening to the hope fizz from my intestines because I saw that Sandy was goo-goo on pop culture conspiracies—I said, "And what, strange people, would that phenomenon be?"

"The Seattle Lights," he said.

"The Seattle Lights," she said.

And I said, "The Seattle Lights. We're many miles outside of Seattle."

"Well, you know," she said, "the Suburban Seattle Lights doesn't sound as nifty."

Nifty. Right. What had become of the girl-genius who could quote Sigmund in guttural German?

Casey said, "How could you not know of this miraculous event? You a man of reportage."

"Casey," I said, "I report only from the shady corners of a continent called My Heart. Sandy, I'll take those mashed potatoes. Furthermore, science fiction and the supernatural interest me not at all. I am one who's thumbed through *The Principia* and some pages of Kepler. You cannot impress me."

"Are you not a Christian? I believe I read so."

"Honestly, friend, I am having second thoughts about all that. Besides, I don't see your point."

"The perpetual mystery," he said, making circles with his cauterized arms. "The awe. The awesome. The larger-than-thou."

"I still don't follow, little fella. Sandy, I'll have that pepper. And, okay, I hunted Bigfoot last week, but every man is entitled to a lapse. Flying saucers are not up there."

"Sandy begs to differ," he said. "Don't you, Sandy, my dear?"

"Charlie," she said, "I've been visited."

"No, you haven't."

"Oh, I have."

"Oh, she has."

"By whom?" I asked.

"That," and she pointed.

I looked up to the spot where her finger aimed. "The ceiling fan?"

"The Seattle Lights."

"Sandy is an abductee," Casey told me. "The most convincing case I have ever documented in the Philippines or America. A case that would put to shame the scholarship and theories of Mr. Budd Hopkins."

"I know a Hopkins, one Gerard Manley: Victorian poet, Jesuit priest, probable man-lover, wrote of a place called Heaven-Haven, plus cliffs of fall frightful. I wonder if they're related."

"I doubt it," he said. "You didn't seem to hear us: Sandy is an abductee."

"No, she isn't," I said. "She might be lonely and—forgive me, Sandy—newly stupid beyond all measure, but she isn't being abducted. By the way—didn't you once have a poodle named Pow?"

This nearly opened up the floodgates. She said, "Pow has been taken, Charlie. Taken."

"By the dog catcher?"

"And I have marks on my body, Charlie. Inexplicable marks."

"I do, too, Sandy. And so does this hobbit over here. And so does the common person out there walking down the sidewalk. Look, there goes one now."

"You know not of what you speak," he said.

"Aliens don't exist," I told him. "And neither do angels or—"

"But apparently Bigfoot does!" He almost crawled across the table at me.

"I told you I had a lapse. It lasted a day. I'm guessing yours has lasted a lifetime."

Sandy chimed in with, "Casey is a leader in the field of ufology. He's studied crop circles in the Philippines and all over America."

"And I am a man schooled in splotches and what can be done with bleach, plus I am capable of knowing metallurgy and how to sail by stars. I also recite Hamlet. So? Let me repeat: aliens don't vacation on earth."

He squealed, "Then explain the Nazca Lines in Peru, you brute!"

"Pictures to impress their gods. They frolicked upon them drunken and disorderly much like Bacchus. p.s.—don't call me brute."

"Liar!" he said, his face a storm, a baby fist clunking the tabletop. "They are landing strips for aliens! Hellfire on you!"

A tense moment, I had to admit. Sandy looked sad. This here was the difference between the smitten and the smote and I had trouble telling who was whom and which was what.

"People," I said, as calmly as I could, "listen. If space aliens traveled a gazillion miles across the cosmos, I doubt they would need some rocks in the desert to land their airplane. Remove head from ass. Are we out of chicken here?" and I presented the empty bucket.

Sandy said, "Well, explain Roswell, then, Charlie. That was no weather balloon. And wait, I'll get you some more chicken. There's another bucket in the fridge."

"Yes," Casey said, "explain the Roswell incident, then. Blasphemer! Goddamn!"

He was like a Filipino leprechaun unleashed. We watched Sandy leave the dining room.

"Mr. Gonzales," I told him once Sandy had gone to the kitchen, "I suspect you've bamboozled my onetime gal with Bronze Age confabulations. She is clearly brainwashed if not hemlocked. Surrender and withdraw or I'll expose you for the fraud you know you are. I actually did come across in today's paper your quote-expert-unquote comments on the Seattle Lights, and you strike me as someone with the logic of Cotton Mather."

"There's nothing going on here. I don't know what you mean," and he tried to giggle.

"What I see before me are definitions one and two of the word *diddle*. Shall I grab a dictionary?"

He grew quietly irate over there across the table from me, his little face getting more crimson every five seconds, until he couldn't help himself anymore and he yapped out, "You won't win her back. She's mine. Goddamn!"

"I need her counsel and some friendly kisses. I've been to prison, I warn you. My cellmate there was a knave who believed in the Loch Ness Monster, and you saw how I ridiculed him rightly."

"Hellfire!"

"Also, my moral courage is troubled by this chicanery. You have shifty mind-craft afoot, and that cannot stand. I've never seen a brain so altered. A heart, yes. A brain, not at all."

"You won't spoil this for me. Viking! I have an entire year invested in her."

"Not my problem. Here she comes."

Some of my motives felt BCE, indeed; and I was an individual accomplished in zaniness and the finer points of making
messes, true, in addition to being a lothario who could disrupt
entire zip codes, but seeing Sandy in that twisted state of worship, every millimeter of her emitting despair of the doctri-
nal sort—the very wrongdoing which damns that madman
Faustus—and this at the hands of some gremlin mercenary for
the unearthly—it all inspired in me a great deluge of paternal
caring-for. I had to do something; this parasite's sapping of her
mind was unnerving and wrong, and what would become of
my Gillian quest without her feminine know-how? Human
life unfolds between the covers of a comic book.

"Sandra," Casey said when she returned to the table with
more chicken, "Charles here was just struggling to explain
Roswell. Apparently he cannot."

"They're stories told by drunkards, Sandy, by the mytho-
logically minded. The only thing to find out about Roswell is
the bartender's name who served the booze."

"It began with the crashed saucer," she said. "I've read
thousands of pages on this, Charlie. The declassified Air Force
documents included. I'm a bit of a Roswell raconteur, holding
court with the best of them. Isn't that right, Casey?"

"Right you are, my dear. You're out of your league here,
Mr. Homar. Goddamn! Perhaps you should go back to scrawl-
ing your little stories of Gillian and her giant squid."

"Sandra McDougal," I said, "first of all, notify this homun-
culus that if he mentions Gillian's name to me again, I will
do very evil, very bad things to him. Let me repeat: very evil,
very bad things. I am a man. Second, I admire your nerve and
your skin is divine. But what bit the dust in the desert of New

Mexico was a high-altitude spy balloon made to monitor the Russians' nuclear program. The government couldn't admit such top-secret tasks and so they let you jokers believe it was a flying saucer. I've done some research of my own. Thanks for this chicken, by the way. I've always liked it better cold. My father does, too, bless him. Sandy, I quiver for you."

"Why, Charlie?"

"For heaven's sake, listen to you! Swindled by this palooka. And you have a doctorate!"

Watery eyes now. "Come with us tonight, Charlie. Come with us if you don't believe."

"Yes," Casey said. "Come see for yourself. That is, if you aren't too scared of having your pedestrian preconceptions vanquished."

Here's what I should have done just then, considering that the past six months of my life had been fit for a pop-up picture book and I really didn't need a new adventure: I should have risen from the table, bowed like a Renaissance duke, and made my exit trailing thank-yous and good-lucks, so-long-see-you-tomorrows. But no. We human monsters make choices with the minds of worms; good sense lies east, we veer west; trouble sends an invitation, we RSVP the very same day. But—and this is crucial to my development as a higher-thinking primate—I had meant what I said to Gonzales about my morality being rankled by this exploitation, by the taking advantage of a mid-age gal marinating in grievance. Yes, I couldn't have saved myself if you had given me a life vest and drained all the water from the lake I was drowning in, but I had the rather Christic (read: chivalric) urge to come to a lady's rescue. I had my conscience, that underrated organ residing somewhere within the ghouls we are. Watch me work.

So I said, "And where exactly are you going tonight, people?"

"Casey has information that a sighting will happen just before midnight, beyond Hannibal Gorge. It's a holy place. They want something there."

"When I was a child my mother made me promise never to go near a gorge with the name Hannibal."

Casey said, "You see, dear, he doesn't want to be enlightened," and he rose from the table just then, hardly a hair taller than when he was seated. I wondered how he operated that mammoth truck outside, if he had a pint-sized pal who controlled the pedals while he himself stood on the seat and steered. It seemed an excellent way to cause traffic calamities.

He went on, "I won't be insulted by this homicidal loon. Hellfire! Yes, I've been reading your installments for that hopeless weekly. I know you attempted to murder Gillian's ex-lover, and then all that nonsense at the dock, when you tried to sink the ship she was sailing away on with the giant squid hunter. Goddamn! Plus it's unspeakable what you did to Romp, left him to be consumed by Sasquatch. Sandra, dear, I think this character is a danger, to himself and to others. He's hardly credible. I advise caution. Half a million people will be reading about *us* next week if we're not careful. Plus I can tell he harbors prejudice against little people."

I muttered the *m*-word.

"Damn you!"

"Gentlemen, please," said poor Sandy, about to sob.

"I am not amused by your bigotry," he said.

"Sorry, I can't help it, Casey. You offend my concept of what congruity consists of. When I see a beautiful woman on the arm of an unsightly man it turns me angry, makes me question the justice of the cosmos. I want to see the good rewarded and the not good punished or else made very lonesome. Guess which one you are."

"I stopped listening to you several minutes ago," he said, inchworming his way around the table toward the door, and when Sandy asked him where he was retreating to, he replied, "Back to my motel. I must prepare for our excursion tonight. When I return to retrieve you I trust you'll be alone. Mr. Homar," he said, "you might want to mend your impolite ways."

"Imp Gonzales," I said, "I hope you choke."

Really, none of this was pleasant. If only I would have taken the time actually to contemplate my direction and decisions in life instead of rushing haphazard and headlong into the unknown, prompted by passions much older than the Middle Ages. Just stop and breathe and think. But of course not. What now?

WELL, IT COULD have been worse. After telling me that I didn't have to be such a discourteous know-it-all out to besmirch, Sandy insisted on stripping off her summer dress near the lamp in the living room—it fell from her speckled shoulders, she stepped out of its pile in no bra or panties at all—on account of the heat, of course—and further insisted that I inspect her dairy skin for marks of the green or gray invaders. Whole districts inside me went asunder by the sight of her; that body couldn't have been more than sixteen years old, so taut and mostly hairless in the

Penthouse fashion of our day, not to mention her height, hardly five feet tall, which only added to the nymphet formula stalked by Humberts everywhere. Folks? Folks, Charles Homar felt blotto on the longing loose throughout his many nether regions, and I thought, *WWRD?*: What Would Romp Do?

"Sandra," I said, "heaven must be a lonely place without you. All the angels stand erect."

"Look," she said. "Look where they have probed me."

And indeed I did look, dropping to my knees before her Venus-ness, my nose scanning the surface of her lotioned skin, each strawberry freckle a miracle of nature. The marks I discovered were the quotidian sort of any person not mummified in gauze: a scratch here, a pimple there, a tiny red bump I diagnosed as an ingrown hair. See me now on my knees before this shrine: I had her backside cupped in my happy hands and my nose pressed into the dank mound of lips at the center of her. My visions of cunnilingus and copulation were only moderately interrupted by remembrance of Gillian: would some section of me experience the remorse of an infidel? All I had to do was whisper, *Open sesame*, and then delve face-long into her peachy center and then lap, lap myself to health. Technically, it wouldn't have been cheating because, as you know, it was I who had been ambushed by abandonment. Couldn't I have made my home here, she my Circe bringing closure to a quest for Penelope? We'd be so cheerful, stay basic, use baby talk in bed.

Upon us: the perfect example of how quickly fond leads to fondle.

Nose-deep in the center of her, a finger slipping in backside, my erection hard enough to crack glass—a first in God knows how long—I fluttered tongue and lips against tentacle-like labia as Sandy parted thighs for better entry. Her creamy moans! My own! The clean-animal scent of her. The id-driven beasts we are as civilians. Both of her hands in my head of hair, squeezing and pressing. How are you, human person, possibly going to fight off that moment?

And yet, and yet: this was injury to my Gillian quest—if I could locate succor between the thighs of another—but those thighs!—why then my chase? Besides, a gentleman doesn't take advantage of a mixed-up gal recently harpooned by the blarney of a con man. I stopped myself because I once read about gentlemanly manners in an Austen tome. Think, for a moment, how nearly impossible that must have been, what with the lava in me ready to leak.

So, I said to me, *Stand, Charles, and look into the pools of this woman who needs you more than you need her*. So I did, and when I saw the several tears marking mascara paths over her cheekbones, I said, "Sandra, this has got to stop. You aren't being abducted by aliens. That guy has performed feats of malarkey on you. How he has done it I don't know, but I'm certain it's against the law."

She reached down and pulled up her dress, saying, "I thought you'd understand. Maybe you will tonight. Tonight you'll see I'm not mad," and she fell back into the sofa.

"Sandy, listen," I said, and sat myself next to her. "I'm sorry about this. I'm sorry. But I'm your friend, you know that, and I don't want to see you tricked like this. What's going on with you? If you're depressed or dejected or whatever, believe me, I've been there."

That all sounded very reasonable to me.

"We broke up kind of abruptly, you know."

She shielded her eyes with a heavily braceleted wrist and I could not see if teardrops had begun their dropping.

"You got a tenured teaching job out here, Sandy. You told me one day and were gone almost the next. It seemed that way to me, anyway."

"I'm not blaming you. I'm just saying. It was abrupt for me. And reading about you and Gillian—I mean, I was happy for you and all—but it was hard for me. Everything has been hard for me since coming out here."

"Why? You're so successful. I don't get it."

"Successful, yes," she said, and seemed to think a moment. "Come with me," she said, and got up to lead me into her study, a handsome mahogany library where all the real books were shelved—she clicked on the lamp and I saw Kleist to the left of me, Jaspers to the right, some Pushkin dead ahead—and to the wall above her desk, adorned with her various advanced degrees, she waved her arm as if to say, *Ta da!* There hung her PhD from UConn, which was where I had met her when I traveled there one dismal day to give a lecture—to a group of English undergrads with no oomph—called "How to Sound Like You're Mostly Telling the Truth in Your Memoirs"—no one believed me. I met Sandy afterward, had decaffeinated coffee with her, felt hunky-dory and not so doggéd despite some sophomore still with acne having called me "a make-pretend Gay Talese," whatever that meant.

I looked at her degrees, then at her, then back at them, and said, "What?"

"You know what these have done for me? Nothing. Not a gosh darn thing, Charlie."

"I don't see how that's true, Sandy."

She stood with her arms crossed, not eight inches from my own crossed arms, one eye wandering as it was given to do, the other laser-beamed into one of my own.

"I spent eighteen years in college because I wanted to be a scholar and taken seriously. And I came out here for this job, all the way out here, far from my family and friends, where the college promised me a dozen things they didn't deliver."

I asked the whats and whys of one in my position.

"How about the respect and regard that I worked so hard to earn, Charles? How about the piggish male faculty—and they're all male; I was the only female in the entire psychology department—how about them not glancing at my tits when they talked to me, or turning around to see my ass when I passed them? They think that because my right eye wanders I can't see clearly?"

Oh, boy.

"You said *was*? What do you mean, *was*?"

She said, "I quit a few weeks ago."

"Yeah, that's what I thought you meant."

She kicked around her leather swivel armchair and plunked herself down into it as I stood staring at her degrees and attempting to think of a sentence related to helpful. Goethe's name eyeballed me from the undusted spine of a slip-cased *Collected Poems*. German sage: be with me now.

"My career has gone nowhere, Charlie. I haven't been able to publish my dissertation, the journals have been turning down my excerpts. The editors are all men. You have such egos, I swear. Is a giant ego a necessary side effect of having a penis?"

I told her I'd need to look that one up.

"And you know how hard it is to find a guy out here who isn't a jerk?"

"Pretty hard, I'm guessing."

"These people on the West Coast: It's like an earthquake rattled their brains. So, yeah, I miss home and I'm sorry I came out here."

"But you're a powerful and modern woman, Sandra. You can do—"

"Charlie, *please* spare me the Betty Friedan speech. We can hardly vote. All that crap about how far we've come since the fifties—well, that's just what it is: crap. I'm tits and ass to most men *and* women, too, now with all these lesbians. Let's face it. And you know what? I'm fine with that. Just don't pretend that education and political reform have made us equal. Don't have me move across the country as an equal if I'm not. I'd have more respect for those assholes at the college if they admitted that I was just tits and ass to them instead of their pretending that I'm not but treating me that way in secret."

I'm not at all certain what my face was doing at this juncture, so I cannot describe what must have been the riddled look of it.

She said, "I'd like to be banged."

"Pardon?" and I glanced around in hope of seeing a Q-tip that might mop away the crud from my eardrums.

"I want a guy with the guts to tell me he wants to bang me."

At the bottom of my throat was something in the neighborhood of *gulp*. I had never known her to give such shining

endorsements of Hugh Hefner and his mansion. I might have
been panting.

"Sandy, please," I said. "My narratives are PG-rated."

"And that's what's wrong with them, Charles Homar. You
should have listened to Romp."

The noises that came from me then were the dopey kind of
the lobotomized everywhere: *huh* and *hmm* and *err* and *umm*.

"Sandra McDougal," I scolded finally, "we are Democrats
from Connecticut and I will not have you speak that way. We
believe in suffrage, pro-choice, and penicillin, and you, my
friend, are a powerful, dignified woman. You just met some
jerks at a bad campus, that's all."

I knelt at her feet then because it was the humble and
affectionate thing to do. I put my hands on the fabric over her
knees in a nonsexual, some would say brotherly fashion.

"Listen, I'm sorry you've had a shitty time out here, Sandy.
But all this UFO stuff is beneath you. And that guy"—I nodded over my shoulder as if he were still polluting the dining
room—"is such an unspeakable muppet. He's exactly the kind
of guy you're talking about, someone pretending."

"You're wrong about him."

I might have commented that he looked a little as if he had
crawled out from under a mushroom.

"Why can't you open your mind a little? One of the reasons
I loved you was that your mind wasn't in a headlock."

Sound check here: check, check.

"You loved me? When was this?"

I could see her thinking and see her seeing me knowing I
knew she was thinking.

"I never told you that?"

"No, you forgot to tell me that, actually. We were dating for only a few months, Sandra. You never even referred to me as your boyfriend."

"Oh. Well, they were a special few months for me. And yes, I was in love with you."

With I still on my knees and she still in the chair, I felt myself getting tragic. It occurred to me that I hadn't spoken to my parents in a long time.

She said, "And then I left and you found Gillian."

I told her again that I was sorry because I was—the sorriest hombre this side of the Rio Grande. Or *that* side. Whichever. She let me wipe a tear with the bottom of her dress.

"Anyway," she said, "Casey is a sweet guy. He doesn't glance at my tits when I look away."

"That's because he isn't tall enough to see them."

"And you can't say for sure that UFOs haven't been coming here. You don't know that for sure. And I feel it, Charlie. It's like love. I *feel* it's true. Pow has vanished. These marks are all over me. I dream of them coming into my room at night. I have flashbacks of being probed. I have missing time. A textbook case."

(An aside: Studies have shown—is there a more worthless phrase in all of English?—that females are more prone to supernatural belief than males. Who those pollsters and their mothers were is a question open to inquiry. True, I've never seen a male psychic with a tie-dyed doo-rag on his scalp, and also true that women tend to believe in soul mates and wispy guardian angels more than men. However: the studies doing the showing are jury-rigged against womankind, what with their implications that because gals are on average more emotional than guys, they fall for every paranormalist with a Ponzi scheme. Men are more rational than women, the studies show, a conclusion you'd find highly suspect if you were to visit a tailgate party in the parking lot of any American football stadium or, say, the alleyways of Pamplona where the X/Y chromosomal combo enjoys jogging alongside irritated bulls. Ordinary second-graders can see that the stooges in search of Plato's Atlantis, the abominable snowman and his North American cousin, the Loch Ness Monster, and that thing in Lake Champlain dubbed "Champ," the not-so-mysterious mysteries of the Bermuda Triangle, the sneaky messages in the "poetry" of a counterfeit called Nostradamus, and the ghosts that go boo in beat-up mansions—these stooges are by and large *male* stooges. Paul Fuss and Romp and, uhh, me, I suppose, are cases in point. Plus if you were to tune in to one of those Sunday afternoon broadcasts of an evangelical superchurch in Colorado Springs, a spectacle just shy of circus folk, you'd see as many men as women waving their arms in the air above their empty heads and wanting to say, *Sieg heil*. Plus grown boys are the monkeys who make war, not grown girls, and if there is a less rational activity than what happened at the Somme and Antietam, I've never heard of it.)

"Okay, Sandy," I said after some quiet between us. I got to my feet and took her hand. "I understand. Maybe I should go. It was wrong of me just to barge in on you like this."

She sprang up from the armchair as if it had a catapulting contraption hidden in the leather. She held my hand—my left one, if I recall.

"No," she said, "I'm glad you came here. It's great to see

you. But come with us tonight to Hannibal Gorge. It's arrogant to think we have all the answers, Charlie. It's arrogant to ignore the mysteries or think that there're no more mysteries left. And, quite frankly, it's a little boring."

Well. How could Charles Homar argue with that, considering where I'd already been? I was nothing if not *not* boring. Let's lollygag a little more.

But first: a nap never hurt anyone.

JUST PRIOR TO midnight—why must such shenanigans always unfold at midnight?—we stood at the curb as Casey's ludicrous truck grumbled down her street to get us. Normal people all along the block were asleep right now in their probably paid-for homes, strangers to disturbance. In the morning they'd have doughnuts and coffee, put the kiddies on a swing set, let the dog dig a hole in lawn groomed by gringos. Wash the Cadillac. Do cannonballs off the diving board.

Casey was none too happy to find me there, but he donned a pleasant face for Sandy's sake, and on his stereo played the Bruce Springsteen song "4th of July, Asbury Park (Sandy)"—there was the Boss's gravelly voice belting out the chorus. I could not decide if the move was either very slick or very disturbing or perhaps both. We were going to this puzzling place called Hannibal Gorge and I wondered what would have possessed the founders of the ravine to name it after that Carthaginian lunatic fond of elephants and defeating via the Alps the superior wordsmiths of Rome. It was so inky inside the cab of the truck that I could not ascertain how Gonzales reached the pedals. Our faces—one of which was thoroughly bewildered—glowed with the blue hue from the stereo, and everywhere hung the smog of a ninety-nine-cent air freshener that smelled of toilet cleaner.

We forged on into that odd darkness for numerous miles until unlit houses gave way to woods and neither us of could think of a sentence that sounded even remotely Anglo. Sandy hummed a show tune I could not identify and Casey Gonzales switched into four-wheel drive at the mouth of a dirt road pockmarked by what felt like shallow graves. The darkness deepened under the canopies and I was quite certain that if I had to, I would not be able to find my way back to civilization and the lunatic tribe who built it. There at a bend stood the pounded-in wooden sign announcing Hannibal Gorge, and beyond the sign, to the right of the actual gorge, lay a wide-open field with nothing but the infinite heavens and their sparkling jewels above us. The day's oven had died and now the temperature smiled at just under seventy degrees; rappelling down from the truck's door, I inhaled that pristine air and almost hoped for a spacecraft to come hold a convivium, obliterate the silence between us.

Casey obliged by saying, "Here is where we will be visited."

He carried a duffel bag stuffed with God knows what—UFO detection devices he had ordered through the mail and glued together himself—and an empty five-gallon bucket of the sort ice fishermen perch upon, the present use of which I could not guess.

"I can feel them here," Sandy said, her arms out as if she required balance and then a drink to wreck it. "I feel them. They're close."

"Indeed they are, my dear."

"Indeed they aren't," I said. "I don't feel a goddamn thing."

Nothing but the coolish breeze coming from across the field.

"Open your mind to it all, Charlie. Be ready to receive them and they will be yours."

"Sandy," I begged, "porcine Republicans are fond of saying that if you open your mind too much, your brain will fall out, and for once, I agree with them. This shrimp is a fraud and nothing will happen here. He's trying to bed you. It's the oldest impulse on earth and one I know a thing or two about. I was a teenage boy, remember."

Just then, to our left over the gorge, as if on cue to taunt my heretical self, emerged an orange light the size of a Volkswagen bug, circa 1968. It hovered and then glided almost noiselessly toward us, moving rather like a helicopter, I thought, and not a tub of magical tin from the other end of eons or the pages of Ezekiel. I might have said, "Hmmph."

Casey began squealing, "You see! You see! They have returned for you, Sandra!"

I twisted around just then to tell him that the nuts and bolts above us were some kind of prototype helicopter with a mega-light fastened to its belly, and when I did, all I beheld was a crowbar coming to my temple, swung like Reggie Jackson by that errant little scamp. He was standing on the bucket. Even as I fell, in my unconsciousness I somehow had the idea that my search for Gillian was about to be snuffed. This was where love had brought me: head trauma in a far-out field in the Sasquatch state of Washington, cavorting after UFOs with two asylum inmates in a monster truck.

Oh, Gillian, I thought, slinking further into sleep. *I am so far from home, my sweet.*

WHAT SHOULD MY dreams have been that night as I lay slathered in a mix of much-needed sleep and head-bludgeoning black? I neither fled an enemy nor flailed about, but rather rested well in some strong sunlight streaming in through a window I thought was in my college dormitory. And that was my dream: the warmth and calm of a silent sun-filled room, nothing at all for a Freudian to scrutinize and then rehash into a sex-filled mommy/daddy narrative.

I woke to more sunlight on Sandy's sofa, feeling the ache of where Casey's crowbar had bashed my skull, but besides that I was in good shape, I thought, recharged and rather well anointed. Sandy was there at my feet looking maternal and worn, though her tiny smile hinted at the indignity that comes with some revisions of mind.

"You were right," she said over the length of my bereaved body.

Grunts and groans that meant, *Huh?*

"He was conning me. He nearly killed you. And that thing in the sky was a helicopter of some kind. I'm a fool, Charlie."

"Wait. Who was flying the thing?"

"I don't know. A friend of his, maybe. All this smoke and mirrors, for what?"

"Wait. How did we get back home?"

I was still lying down at this point. And the brave dame told me the account of how, after she witnessed Casey batter me, she in turn battered him, so stunned was she by his violence against an old chum. She wrested the crowbar from his toy hands and smacked him upside the face with it, then collected me into the truck—apparently I was semiconscious and able to move only slightly—and we drove that tank home, leaving Casey there in the field with his manufactured light circling above him. She had sat vigil all night watching me snore, hunting Casey Gonzales on the Internet, revising her version of the past six months, all that flirting with the other-worldly. She had never before beheld with her own eyes one man doing bloodshed upon another—sheltered and naïve dar-lings: let them run the world—and apparently the shock of it forced a reckoning. The poor bird betrayed the sorrow of the truly disillusioned, so fraught was her want of an alien influ-ence to descend and pulverize the filth on this blue ball.

And she asked me again, "Why did he do it all, Charlie?"

I moved upright on the sofa and declared, "For you, San-dra. He and I are not all that different, I suppose. I've said it before: a man is not made well. Can I have some Advil?"

There it was on the coffee table; water, too.

"By the way," she said, "I was surfing around last night and came across some information on Gillian. They are set to arrive in Boston by the end of the month. With the living squid."

Okay. Process this now, help me: Gillian, Jacobi, giant squid, Boston, end of the month.

"Sandra," I said, "if it's no bother, we must move on from your crisis to mine. What does this mean? What should I do? I no longer trust my own judgment, which tends to lean towards gunfire and Bigfeet, plus puts me in close proximity to trolls and flying saucers."

"What do you want to do, Charles? I mean really *want* to do."

The Sandra I knew and half loved had returned. That was her old voice: psychotherapeutic.

"I spoke to Friend about it back home and he thought going to New Zealand with pleas and roses was out of the question. But now that they're returning to the land of the brave and the home of the free, or the, you know . . . What? Meet them there?"

"Charlie," she asked, "would this make you your old self again? Because right now you seem a different person to me. All those magazine articles about what you've done. And your poor parents, Charlie. Have you thought of them?"

"I've tried, Sandy. I'm possessed or something. You know the feeling."

A few sniffles here and also the sensation of being a failure for the ages.

"You should go to Gillian, I think, but prepare yourself. You have three weeks. No more knives and guns, please. You must prepare yourself to accept her, because it seems to me that therein lies the problem: you never really accepted the giant squid."

One more sound check. How could this be right? In my patience and adulation for Gillian I never *denied* the slop that is the giant squid—although, true, okay, I didn't exactly embrace the foul tang of it. But then I recalled the Polaroid photo I had taken of myself in Virginia, on my route back from attempting to butcher Gillian's ex-beau: a photo of me beneath a rubber giant squid suspended from the rafters of some bozo's barn, a photo I had shot precisely to show my lady that her sea crea-

ture was not unimportant to me. When I informed Sandy of
this gesture and the impetus behind it, she sighed in a manner
half sympathetic and half disappointed, as if I were a toddler
learning not to touch hot pots. Didn't I get it? A woman of
ideas needs Support, capital S, and Vigor, capital V. A woman
of ambition needs a loyal huckleberry with Fuel, one who
knows about Purpose and Will.

The gist: it was my fault that Gillian discarded me for
Jacobi, because he shared her Passion and I simply Didn't.
Leave it to a psychoanalyst to blame the fiasco and its ensu-
ing escapades on the victim, the maltreated one, he who had
been incarcerated by the penal system and nearly cremated by
pain. But—and this is a massive *but,* not at all like Sandy's—I
do recall my father saying when I was an adolescent: Charlie,
he said, Pay attention to your girl, Charlie, or someone else
surely will. Apparently all the attention I had been paying was
the erroneous kind, not conducive to the perennial coupling of
two snazzy hearts. And so.

When it was time for me to depart that day after more
badinage and bowls of Cheerios, Sandra M. gave me the contact info of someone she wanted me to consult during my
cross-country drive back East—I had decided to commandeer
Romp's SUV for a little while longer; he wouldn't be needing
it in the digestive tract of Sasquatch—since Sandy herself was
rusty on all issues amorous. This man was an academic astronomer, she said, an old colleague in Boulder, Colorado, my fellow marquis who knew how to worship a woman and make it
count. He could enlighten me, she said, teach me tricks.

"Sandra, right now I could use all the enlightenment of
the eighteenth century and then some. I am indebted to you,"

I said, though I thought: *Well, just a little; the epiphany you handed me was miniature and lacking, like all epiphanies.* But it would have to do for now; I was an exiled oaf on diseased soil.

We embraced under the hot morning bulb, me with a Band-Aid on my head where I had bled a little, she in pajamas that looked huggable, and then we both blinked out some minor tears. I thanked her profusely.

"Thank *you*," she said. "Are you sure you don't want to stay here awhile? Move in with me? Give us another shot?"

My face gave the answer.

"I know," she said. "It's ridiculous. Gillian is out there waiting for you. But if the bitch doesn't come to her senses, give me a call. We'll have a perfect life."

Utopias are always hells.

"What are you going to do?" I asked. "What about a job?"

"I'll think about all that later. I'm not worried about it right now. I'm worried about *you*, Charlie. Stay away from people who want to harm you."

And I refrained from telling her that such a thing was not possible in our world. Take a glance around. See the harm? Hear it calling you? Father Hopkins said it best: "There is your world within. There rid the dragons, root out there the sin."

Ahh, the dragons and the sin. Good luck with all that.

6. HELP ME WANDA

TWO SURPRISES FOR Morris Hammerstein, prince astronomer, the day I arrived one week after leaving Sandra McDougal's place (it shouldn't have taken a whole week to lope down to Boulder from Seattle but about halfway there I found a Best Western and slept for three days straight—avoiding moxie and the wanton—then spent another three days meeting a deadline for my uptight editor).

Surprise 1: Charles Homar showed up on his doorstep slipshod and bugged out (three days of sleep had done zero to calm the hound dog I had become, barely bipedal).

And Surprise 2: a lesbian named Jo decided she was in love with his wife, Wanda, and I mean hard-core in love, the kind that straddles destructive lust and causes all the chemicals in the body to swoon, swoon.

I knew that sort of love, and so did he; it was how he felt exactly, even after a decade of marriage. A white man in round glasses, a stick figure with the athletic ability of an amputee,

Hebrew, no less (though nonaffiliated), should thank the spirits daily for his being married to a chocolate champion—his term—like Wanda, and not just for all the lovely stereotypical characteristics of a black woman—the lips, the bust, the butt, lovemaking that is really the rumba or boogaloo—but for the way she called him Honey Ham and rubbed his bony back after a not-so-difficult day teaching astronomy to college freshmen fragrant with what Coors makes. He told me this. We'll get to the Babylonian lesbo in a moment.

So. It was for reasons of chocolate love and female veneration of the general type, and his much-practiced expertise in both, that I arrived at his home at the suggestion of Sandra McDougal, with whom he still exchanged weekly emails on topics ranging from a modern frog named Michel Foucault and his visions of human hanky-panky, to all the dark matter in the universe and how it holds the galaxies in place like God's good magnets. He had heard of me, he said, had read my "irreligious tales" of Gillian and the giant squid—"all that I-obsessive memoirist trash so in fashion, self-expression without self-assertion"—and only because a colleague had given him a subscription to *New Nation Weekly* last Hanukkah. The slick one hundred pages—of political assessments, persnickety film reviews, poems as space filler, fiction by the same six people, some fine cartoons, and, of course, the fanatical personal pieces penned by me—arrived in his miniature barn mailbox every Tuesday to harass him.

"Morris Hammerstein," I said to him that day on his semi-shaded front porch, "I have come seeking lessons on how to woo a certain woman into forever-with-me. I'm told you're the best, a Semitic Casanova with a Negress bride. Please help."

"Very glad to meet you," he said, although he sounded unsure. "Sandra told me you were coming."

A minute or more must have passed as we looked at each other's clothes. I noticed the well-watered plant next to the door, a gardenia, I think.

He said, "Can I ask you a favor?"

I told him to ask away.

"Please don't write about me or my family. We're intensely private here. I just read this week's piece about Sandy and the UFO, and I don't think you were fair to her. She's really not like that at all. That's not Sandy."

"Morris," I told him, "I was there, you weren't. She was put-upon and pathological, and those are just the *p*'s. As for not writing about your family: you have a deal. But as to the English word *fair*: perhaps cut that one from your repertoire. I myself recently looked it up and the *OED* didn't seem to know of its existence."

The way he stared at me and didn't speak: like I was Turkana Boy come back to life with a hand axe for a gift. He had a lovely home, though, precisely what I had always imagined for Gillian and me: a high gable front with three bedrooms, one-car garage, ample driveway, all tucked back in a Christian cul-de-sac. The sky out there loomed large and blue.

"One more thing," I said. "I agree not to write about you and your family if you bless me with the estrogen info I've come to acquire, also knowledge of what Jack and Jill might have discovered on that hill we hear so much about."

"I'll try," he said. "What else can I do? You're here now."

We continued on the porch beneath those mighty Colorado skies, neither of us pleased, but one of us—the gangrened Jehovah's Witness—certain that some sort of discomfort was possible.

"So," he said finally. "You're a writer."

He wouldn't invite me in.

"I've been told my sentences salsa."

"I have a nagging suspicion that only about forty percent of what you write is true. I also think your people all speak alike, or at least you and Friend and Romp."

"Well, Morris," I said, "style can be infectious. Look at blue jeans. I am friends with Friend and Friend is friends with Romp."

"Also, if I may offer another opinion: most of the events in your memoirs occur outside the scope of normal human possibility."

"Normal? What's that? Sounds Mesopotamian. And not a single instance in my chronicles disobeys the laws of physics. I defy you, sir, to find one."

With I on the bottom step of the porch and he on the top step, I realized he was in the perfect position to karate me across the teeth, if that urge should so strike him.

"I don't need to," he said. "Tom Clancy does not disobey the laws of physics, either. Would you care to defend his multiple transgressions against trees?"

Multiple transgressions against trees. I was beginning to adore this fellow.

"My yarns," I said, "are propelled by the mysteries of human longing, which are essentially feminine. Clancy's are propelled by the ego, which is essentially masculine and destructive."

"This from a man with guns. By the way, Mr. Homar, I will not allow guns on my property. I have a child."

"Morris—if I may—be gentle, now. I'm wounded in the soft spots, the spiritual equivalent of what Keith Richards looks like."

Hearty laugh here. He had television teeth.

"Charles—if I may—you weren't even born when *Exile on Main St.* came out."

"But still. I've heard it. Friend is a fan of Mick's lips."

Why couldn't this progress smooth-like, without hindrance and feelings hurt? Why is everything so hard?

"I agreed to help you, Mr. Homar, but as a favor to Sandra. I'm asking you to respect my family."

"As I said, Morris, you have a deal. All I know about women I learned from my own erratic and hellward breast. Plus the huntsman Romp taught me about gals of African origin. Maybe you can tell me if he was right."

"I hope that Romp person was indeed inhaled by a Bigfoot, because I found his insight into black women reprobate. I had to hide that week's issue from Wanda. Her opinions can shake concrete."

Opinions that can shake concrete? Was *he* making fun of me now, too, just as Romp had in my bathroom? And must all academics dress alike? Why the pressed khaki pants, penny loafers, and white button-up shirt (with a pen in the pocket) on a Saturday afternoon?

"Wanda, I take it, is your wife."

"My chocolate champion, if you please, Mr. Homar. But

yes. Come in, and prepare your plasma for voltage, your knees for quaking."

Okay, now I knew he was poking fun at me—who puts *plasma* and *voltage* in the same sentence?—but I had neither the daring nor the wherewithal to begin a row.

"Kind sir," I said, "lead the way."

ON TO THE lesbian named Jo—Wanda's sister's lover—who arrived not five minutes after we had entered the house and began our necessary save-me chat. Wanda's svelte, head-shaved younger sister Shavan liked to roam, dabble, defy expectations with white women: she dressed like a slattern and talked in a voice that made you lean.

Almost immediately upon seeing Wanda that day—this was the first time they had met—Jo couldn't breathe, her heart was performing dangerous feats of acrobatics, and she just stared, stared—like someone recently back from battle who can't stay the blasts. There was a lot of standing around and not speaking. I tied my shoes that didn't need tying. Jo, by the way, as you might have expected, dressed like a GI and spoke in a way that suggested cigars.

Wanda's sex-beckoning dark beauty could eclipse any stage show—in fact Morris had just begun telling me as much, and how a man should go about handling the fray such beauty makes—but he had never before seen it strike a human with paralysis. Wanda dressed summery, was the very incarnation of what you mean by *olfactory*. Her voice sounded the way a velour bathrobe feels.

We were in the kitchen now (nice cabinets and granite

countertops). Jo leaned her beefy frame up against the stove and stood slowly shaking her lesbian haircut as if in disbelief. She attempted to compose herself with yoga breaths.

Shavan asked her what was wrong, and Morris, now at Wanda's side in the kitchen, said, "What's happening around here?"

Their eight-year-old daughter, Mocha—of course they named her Mocha; what else would you have them name their gorgeous gal with skin the color of cardboard: Mocha Hammerstein, it just spills from the tongue in glee—said from behind us, "Daddy, there are strange people in our house."

"Yes, sweetie," he replied. "This is Mr. Homar, don't be rude; he might write awful things about you. And that over there is a lesbian with an issue or two." And then, to Wanda, nodding at Jo, "What's wrong with her?"

She whispered, "Shavan says she's in love."

"Right now? With me?"

"I don't think so, Ham. With me, apparently."

Morris informed her, informed us all, that she had been in the house for only ten minutes.

"Love at first sight," Wanda said.

I said, "I've heard about that in pop songs and on some late-night TV reruns. It's a verifiable occurrence."

Over there by the window Shavan and Jo were whispering to one another like venereal nuns.

"Well, this isn't right, dear," Morris said. "Not right at all. Especially not when we have a guest. Charles Homar is here and he has his pencil and pad in hand."

"The poor thing appears sick," she said.

"Poor thing?" Morris asked. "She's two hundred pounds and has a tattoo on her forearm."

Indeed: the tattoo looked like a cancer splotch.

Morris said, "A poor thing is thin and sickly and shakes in the rain. This is not a poor thing in our kitchen."

"Wanda," I said, "I concur. If you want to see a poor thing, glance my way. I make betterment seem somewhat beside the point."

Some more minutes of the awkward and unusual, of the silent dilly-dally enjoyed by the discomfited. The lesbian and her mental illness she confused with love were interfering with the forecast I had come for.

And then, imagine this: Jo gets hostile with Morris. All he said was, "What seems to be the problem, Jo?" and she snapped, "Don't get in my face, little man."

Yes, she called him little man, in his own home. Never mind that he wasn't even in her face—rather hard from the opposite end of a capacious kitchen. This touched a nerve in him, I could tell, and I would be informed later that he had been picked on psychopathically while he was a youth, Irish and Italian hoodlums named Mikey and Ralph tickled by making him eat mud. Here was where his preoccupation with the cosmos began: while Mikey and Ralph were tying him to a tree with clothesline rope and trying to dump a shovelful of dirt and earthworms into his underwear, he'd point his chin up to the sky and imagine the constellations, the comets burning like bullets, supernovae swirling. It was a meeting of brawn and brain and sadly brawn carried the torch. I felt for him.

"Excuse me?" he said to Jo, in that way that really means, *You must be crazy talking to me like that in my own house*, which was what he should have said.

He had rights, damn it, and I nearly said so, but I was trying, really, not to intrude, just stand in the kitchen with them and watch the misfortune of others, pleased it was not mine for a change.

Wanda said to Morris, "Leave it alone, Ham. Shavan will deal with this."

"Yeah," Jo said, still scowling. "Leave it alone. And just let me talk to Wanda. I want to be alone with her for a minute."

Shavan didn't say anything to that; this perplexed me. She was clearly frightened of this career lesbian, and this perplexed me more: why would you want to befriend or take as a lover someone who frightens you? Nature is clear on this point: fright causes a creature to flee. So did it follow that Shavan was not a creature, or perhaps an anomaly in the animal kingdom? Morris adored his sister-in-law—he told me so—but she was missing the chromosome that permits a person to be foursquare when she needs to.

Wanda looked at Morris and shrugged—such well-defined deltoids—then patted his upper back gingerly; she was calm in times of crisis—that much was clear. Morris told me about the time he had witnessed her exiting a department store inferno as if she were modeling Gucci on a runway. Their photo appeared in the newspaper the next day: behind them were the flames and beside them frantic faces—Morris's included—and there was his Wanda, applying lipstick without a mirror.

"Lunacy," he said now, looking at Jo. "You can't do this. Get control of your chemistry."

"You don't understand," she shouted, and nearly took a step toward him.

Heedless and done in though I was, I was prepared to do battle for this stick-figure astronomer, in defense of middle-class domesticity and American wholesomeness. This was injustice, and Morris had trouble abiding it. The solar system is a finely tuned mechanism; laws govern motion. The solar system does not tolerate abnormalities in fixity; nor could he. Also, a man is not an insect; you cannot step on his head with impunity. I'd been saying this all over the country.

"Jo," Morris continued, "I think you should leave. This isn't natural. We have a guest here and he needs our attention."

She said, "If your guest is the same Charles Homar of those Gillian stories, then he isn't worth your effort. He's a misogynist and homophobe."

And then she turned her glare on me and claimed, "I have certain friends who want you dead."

"Josephine or Joanne," I said, flanked by Morris and Wanda, "you flatter me, really. Stalin wanted certain writers dead, too, but only the best. Some of them turned their own hands against themselves—a chap named Mayakovksy, I've heard, also a good witch named Tsvetaeva—and I'm trying to avoid that. Thus far I've had only minimal success. As for the homophobe remark: I've marched on the lawn of Connecticut's state capital building in Hartford jabbing a handmade sign that said LET ALL THE RED-BLOODED BE FREE TO WED. Keep in mind that the root word of my home state is *connect*. You Sapphic hunchback."

"I'll throttle you," she said, and I think I swallowed the little orb of fear in my gullet.

"Jo," Morris said again, "please remove your oddball self from the premises. I'll have over to our home whomever I please."

"I'm not going anywhere, little man. Let me talk to Wanda, I said," and again another step toward him, toward us.

This lesbian was driven and jittery, here to hobnob and stand ground.

"Okay," Wanda said, "I'll talk to you, Jo. Ham, honey, why don't you go back and continue talking with Mr. Homar about his Gillian and her squid—"

He cut her off here, not something he was wont to do very often—that was obvious—but he did not have run of his lungs and spleen.

"No way," he said. "There will be no talking between you and this man-woman. I've asked her to leave and that is what I expect. The mortgage is in my name. I am a professor of cause and effect, and a student of all that's proper. Children and animals admire me. How am I doing, Charles?"

"Very well," I said. "I like the part about cause and effect."

This was the point at which Jo said she would introduce Morris to the fearsome twins, Ruin and Woe. He asked her if that was a threat and she told him—she told the both of us, actually—that she threatened people daily, was quite skilled at it.

Wanda said, "Ham, let's convene in the living room for one moment, please."

He would not move; his and Jo's eyes were caught in a gravitational field that would have made Newton groan. My own intestines felt the tension and I thought: *This is delaying my personal growth needed to secure mine Gillian.* The sister Shavan shrugged as if to say that this oily unpleasantness upon us was out of her hands. I thought her not admirable in the least.

"Please let's talk a moment in the living room," Wanda said again, and this time she took Morris's elbow with some force and would not be refused.

I followed because, with my highway-numbed brain, what else could I have done? Chatted with the lesbians about Gertrude and Alice, or maybe the newest model of Harley-Davidson chopper?

Mocha was there on the sofa with her ear cocked toward the kitchen, cute little pigtails poking up in question marks. As Wanda consulted with Morris in the corner, I sat on the sofa next to the lass and asked her about how love works in the fourth grade. I believe she said something about Saint Ignatius of Loyola and the spiritual warrior he was, and this somehow made sense to me. (She was, I realized later, the same age and height as Bartholomew when he died.) Mocha was now lacing up the new boxing gloves her mother had bought for her recently in an effort to teach her self-sufficiency and how to punish violently all those who transgress against her dignity. The carpet beneath my sneakers looked shampooed.

"Mo," Wanda said from over there, "please don't bother Mr. Homar. He's riven."

"Wanda," I said, "this is no bother. She speaks sagacity I haven't heard since Connecticut lowered real estate taxes. I believe she'll be president or at least vice."

"Mocha," she said, "Mr. Homar is only being kind. Please go into your room and practice piano. I want to hear your Chopin."

Mocha did not budge but looked over at her mother with those oblong brown eyes that will one day mean cardiac catastrophe to many a hapless male.

"Mo, the next time I ask it will be with the back of my hand, little girl. Put down those boxing gloves and get gone."

Their daughter bolted from the room and Morris looked

like his chest was throbbing for the lamb; her being in danger of physical harm from her normally placid mother was really the fault of this intrusive lesbian in their kitchen. I knew we'd see bloodshed before long. That's what happens.

"Ham," Wanda pleaded, "why don't you and Mr. Homar go out back to the picnic table and you can show him the view of the mountains and talk there?"

"I really don't understand this," he said.

"It might be my fault," I said, falling back into the cushion. "Wherever I go, *sturm und drang* seem to follow and then pitch a tent. Maybe I should leave."

"Nonsense," Morris said. "This isn't your doing, Mr. Homar. Just please give us a moment to clear this up."

Before Wanda's good sense had the chance to reach Morris or me, Jo appeared behind us and said, "Did I hear boxing gloves? Let's put them on, little man."

"I beg your pardon?" Morris said.

"I'll box you for her. We'll settle this."

Settle this? What *this*?

Earth was just then quite possibly caught in the tail of a comet, and as a result our precious normality had been altered. After this day Morris would clearly have to rethink the Milky Way and his puny place in it. This was melee and scandal, very much how he had felt, he said, when Dylan went electric in '66 (a year as unfamiliar to me as are the culinary arts in an igloo, seeing as how I would need another decade entirely to get myself born).

The three nonlesbians in the room glanced at each other and then at the boxing gloves next to me. At least one of those nonlesbians was expecting a reality TV camera crew to bust through the door with declarations of *Ha ha*.

Morris said, "Very well, you bitch. You want to box me, fine."

And he did not hesitate another moment. He reached down quickly to grab the gloves, slapped them into Jo's fleshy middle, and went into the laundry room to retrieve his own gloves—gloves his father had bought for him when he was a freshman in college and still being victimized daily by barbarous Italians and those Irish disgruntled over Britain's meddling with their motherland. Of course, he never did learn to box; the gloves were simply his father's way of saying that he needed to be testosterone-led, more in touch with the sadistic early days of *Homo sapiens*, perhaps searching for that part of him—of you, of me—that was still *Homo erectus*, or *Homo habilis*, or perhaps the jaw-jutting australopithecine that bore us. Shaddai, the Lord's name in the Bible, means, as Dr. Donne put it, "spoyle and violence and depredation." Let's not forget this, people.

I thought Wanda would veto this duel, but, as Shavan laced up the gloves on Jo's hands, Wanda seemed resolved to this inevitability. She stood beside me with crossed arms and pursed lips. No dissuading, no talking-sense-into. Morris, as well, was resolute.

"Darley," he said, handing her the gloves, "assist with my weaponry. I shall smote and slay and be glad for it."

Smote and slay: that's what I'm talking about.

But I don't think it occurred to him that Jo was at least twenty pounds more advanced than he, nor did he seem to be doubting his noodle limbs, nor bothered by the fact that he had obviously never before engaged in fisticuffs with another mortal. True, there was Semite righteousness on his side, Yahweh in his corner, the memory of Israelites fuel for his ire. Plus he had once admired Bruce Lee. This heathen Gentile and disobeyer of the procreative plan didn't stand a chance. Still, I could see his knees were not happy.

"Let me warn you," Jo said to him, "there is judo and pillage in my childhood."

I couldn't help myself; I said, "And Hammerstein has various forms of mathematics, plus the films of martial arts champion Chuck Norris. Mercy is a stranger to his ways."

"You're next," she told me, smacking gloves together. "After him, you're next."

"No, please, I'm sorry."

Wanda laced up Morris's gloves with a fortitude seldom seen in suburbia. This preparation for battery was accompanied by the Chopin coming from their daughter's bedroom; I think it was the "Funeral March"—appropriate and apocalyptic.

Jo licked her lips in anticipation. This lip-licking only served Morris's fury. Keep in mind that all this was happening with speed, too speedily for any of us to assimilate properly; randy Jo had been in their home for only twenty minutes at this time. As far as I knew, this was the way events transpired in other nooks of the universe, at the other end of the black holes Stephen Hawking is always robotting on about.

All four gloves were laced; Morris clapped his together as he had seen countless boxers do.

Wanda said, "You two are going out to play in the backyard. I won't have smashed furniture or shattered vases."

Morris and Jo went out the sliding glass door in the living room, onto the deck, and into the backyard. It took every calorie I had to get my body off the couch. They stopped near Mocha's jungle gym, an elaborate log concoction that looked to me like an invitation to spinal injury. Morris no doubt heard in his noggin the theme song to *Rocky* and maybe the immortal cry, *Yo, Adrian*, as anyone wearing boxing gloves must. The noises coming from him were those the barbarians had uttered as they ravaged a village of weaklings. For some reason I thought of Pancho Villa.

The sisters stood shoulder to shoulder at the sliding screen door, and I stood behind them, still looking, I'm sure, how I felt: dismayed and much bedeviled by the fact that tempests followed me from place to place, that the solid objects I touched seemed to turn very swiftly to shit. Who's the Haitian priestess that pushed pins into the doll of me, and why? One of the sisters smelled of coconut lotion; I brought my nostrils very near their necks in order to know whom.

"Wanda," I said, "pardon me, but I'm curious. Why aren't you stopping this folly?"

"Of all people, you should know, Mr. Homar."

Of course I asked her what in the Sam Hill I was supposed to know.

"When Morris gets to feeling prideful and slighted, nothing in the world can change his mind. I've learned you just have to let him do his thing, what you men always do."

"What we do?"

"Go crazy with overweening love and then get punched for it."

"So you think Morris is going to get punched out there?"

"And how."

"Shavan," I asked, "do you have anything to say for yourself?"

"The fifth," she said, by which she meant, I think, pleading the fifth.

Out back: No more prefight taunts or tough-guy parlance. An imaginary bell rang. Jo's punches were pain, her moves magic. I knew after just twenty seconds or so that Morris was hopeless; I'm not sure he landed even a single blow. The stars and other flashes of light should have made him feel at home, but a guy is never at home when his own blood is pooling in his mouth. It was all he could do to keep his gloves near his face to block her onslaught, never mind retaliate. There was a *whomp* and a *poomph*. Important pieces inside him were getting loosened; others were snapping. I thought I heard a rib pierce his liver. Shavan kept saying "Oh," Wanda "Ouch." Curious neighbors on either side, we saw, had rested their noses on the wooden fences between back lawns.

Morris yelled, "Compassion, care," and Jo responded, "Wreckage, waste."

His only source of self-respect was the fact that he managed to stay vertical for nearly ninety seconds. Indeed, this was how the world ended, not with a bang but a whimper, and I heard poor Morris give that whimper.

Would Jo really win his wife, filch her away from him and his child? Would she go to honor the deal? In just another minute Wanda would rush outside to stop the bludgeoning of Morris's person, and I would run out to help him to his feet, but, blacked out and swollen, he wouldn't see any of it. He wouldn't see Wanda clobber the gal Negress-style, as they do in the ghet-tos of Detroit or Harlem, but he'd cherish her for it always, I'm sure.

Jo's final punch landed evenly on his temple, and as Morris dropped to the ground, the last thing he saw before the blackness was not his wife, but his child in the upstairs window, her round face only slightly traumatized, and rather strangely resolved to the fate of her overzealous father, a fate he himself had commanded. When this was all over, Morris would say to me, "I remember my exact thought at that moment, as I was falling, about to pass out. I hoped my darling child saw the lesson in all this scuffle, and I hoped that later she might be sweet enough to tell me what it was, to tell me the story of love."

BUT—LOVE AND LASTING was *his* story to tell this day; a fraught isolato had driven from Seattle to Boulder to be dished the facts of endorphins that were Morris's to dish. Wanda had thrown out Shavan and Jo while Morris lay recovering on the leather sofa in his library with an ice pack on his face. I sat in the armchair next to him, one leg crossed over the other and very far from the living. A painted portrait of Carl Sagan grinned atheistically above Morris's desk. Wanda, bless her, was just then detraumatizing their child, who no doubt had questions about paternal blackouts and how a man arrives at a place where a butch lesbian batters him on the back lawn.

Morris was the one who had just been despoiled and yet he said he felt pangs of pity for *me*. He was implying, I think, that I looked gaunt and gone, just moments away from a postmodern meltdown.

"Morris," I said, "you have wonderful books here. Why

does leather soothe? Something in our Cro-Magnon past, no doubt. The view through this window is stupendous. What are those?"

They were the Flatirons at Chautauqua Park. He told me this with a speck of pride, as if he had assembled them.

"Lovely. And that was impressive out there, Morris. No Sonny Liston, but still, my admiration swells."

"That," he said—putting aside the ice pack and sitting upright on a sofa that made leather sofa noises—"was lesson number one for you, Charles. Always defend your lady's pride, with dynamism and dash if need be. Have standards, go to battle for them. Let her see. It's sexy and shows your worth."

"Yes," I said. "Dynamism and dash. I know what you mean."

"No, I don't think you do, Charles. You drove to Virginia and to a dock in Maine to commit capital crimes. That's not what I mean. It grounded you in jail for several months and without your prize. Not good."

I would need ibuprofen soon, I could see.

"Why not? That's dynamism and dash, like you say. Defending my gal."

"No, it's desperation and dearth—not the same thing. It defends you and your meager heart, not your lady. Those homicidal excursions had nothing at all to do with Gillian and everything to do with your own grievance. You fail to win her as you failed to keep her because you misunderstand female hormones and what it means to seduce."

"Morris," I said in a yawn, "you confuse me. And I'm looking for clarity, not confusion, of which I own plenty."

"And that's precisely why"—he clapped here—"we're taking a little ride up to the Flatirons at Chautauqua Park, just past the university. Some stellar rock faces where you will be able to look down and see what I mean."

"Please don't get all naturey, Morris. Have you ever tried to read Thoreau? It's like listening to someone with Alzheimer's try to tell you about his high school prom. Nature and I have never really got along. You should have seen me in the woods of Washington chasing after Sasquatch. Plus I hear people in Boulder do draconian yoga, eat granola, subscribe to discordant fitness creeds. And don't you have a headache from the beating you just took?"

"True," he admitted. "Have you read the *Kama Sutra* lately?"

"Vishnu pornography."

"Not at all. A tome about female psychology and how to harness affection from the fairer of us. You should try it, because that's your dilemma, Charles: your relationship with Gillian Lee was all about Charles Homar, regardless of how you loved her and thought you worshipped her."

Christ, not this again. "It's all my fault, I suppose. You sound like Sandy M."

"Let me read you a little line from your first Gillian story," he told me, and stretched over into his stack of magazines to retrieve an old issue of *New Nation Weekly*, the week that contained "Antihero Agonistes," about my unwise trip to Virginia.

"This is a line," he continued, flipping pages, "that you do not realize the importance of and have never come close to mentioning again. It appears about halfway through the essay, comes and goes very quickly, but it's the gist of your trouble and you're too myopic to realize it. Here it is, right here. It reads this way: *And lastly, Gillian and I have never had a single argument (although, yes, there was that one time we agreed to disagree about having children: she said two sounded nice and I said they sounded like smallpox)*."

He slapped shut the pages and eyed me as if I'd just been caught with a hooker in a convent. "What?" I said, and then I said it again.

"*What?* Charles," he declared, "that is the reason Gillian left you. She couldn't give birth to her own children and so you forced her to give birth to the giant squid."

My face was an ink-drawn circle, two dots for eyes and one for a mouth.

"Are you a Romeo or a Winnicott?"

"And that," he said, "is what you neglect to fathom, my friend: a successful husband and lover is both. Didn't you see me here today? Don't you see what I've built? My wife, my child, my home, the way it all harmonizes and thrives. You think that's an accident, a dart thrown in the dark?"

"I must admit," I said, "it's admirable, and mysterious. Love oozes from this house."

"Charlie," he said, leaning forward for some much-needed emphasis, "I've kept Wanda enthralled by keeping her pleasured, and not just with my man-bat and tongue, but with her child—every woman, if she's a woman, wants children. It's the tick of nature. Here, wait here a minute, let me get Wanda. I want her to tell you herself."

He left, I stayed, looked at the Flatirons through the window, wondered if the fall would shatter my skull sufficiently, about the quickest route from hari to kari, and then Morris came back with Wanda, which was fine with me, since readers had complained to my editor that there were too few female characters in my memoirs, as if I had control of that. "This isn't fiction," I had told him, "I can't just invent female characters and drop them into my life," and he said, "Remember that most of the readers in this country are women and unless you're female-friendly you will not sell," but I never could remember it.

So Wanda and Morris stood over me and Morris instructed her to tell me how their marriage thrives. She said, "Well, he's malleable, I suppose. He can subject himself to humiliation when necessary, as you just saw, and stand strong when necessary, as you also just saw. He avoids routine when possible and shares my lust for the hair-raising guitar riffs of Hendrix. We go to concerts and can dance like hedonists with the best of them. He *knows* me, in addition to loving and licking me. That's all."

Was I in Colorado or the Crab Nebula?

"Thank you, Darley," he said, "that's precisely what Mr. Homar needed to hear."

"How's your head?" she asked, touching his arm as Gillian used to touch mine. "I think your hook is broken. It's twisted."

They were so in love I wanted either to applaud or else call a chemist to explain it.

"Morris," I said when Wanda left, "I need to lie down. I drove hundreds of miles to get here, plus I've chased UFOs and Bigfeet, witnessed a lesbian thwack you, and everything else you already know about. And from what I now comprehend I'm a man who lived with a woman for years and failed to know a single strand in her. If I die in my sleep, just dig a hole and dump me in it. I never asked to be born in the first place."

Morris Hammerstein covered me with a colorful blanket, and a minute later I got flattened by the munificent steamroller of sleep, no closer to nirvana than I was when I had arrived—exactly what I had expected all along. Everything Morris had just tried to sell me was a fabrication through and through, swift tricks he had learned from his bullshitting freshmen who couldn't make it to class or hand him papers on time.

Here's what the astronomer should have told the likes of me: *The awful and exquisite truth is that I have not the slightest inkling how I've managed to keep Wanda all this time—absolutely none. Every day I wake up and shake my grateful head in surprise to find her still here with me. Some guys are lucky, I suppose, good-ole-fashioned lucky, and Charles Homar, you simply aren't one of them.*

MORRIS WOULDN'T LET me drive away that afternoon because he believed I wasn't well, so for two days I roved the streets and bike paths of Boulder, Colorado, sleeping on their library sofa both nights after terrific meals with the Hammersteins at their dining room table fit for banquets. Listening to their three-sided cheerful yammer cracked a dam in me: their plans and memories, complaints and compliments, amusements and scowls, sports and academics, all the while passing red potatoes and rice, buttered bread and corn on the cob, sautéed veggies and grilled shrimp (they were vege-quarians)—this was living in a way I had not seen except synthetically at the tables of sitcom actors failing to convey an actual family.

When I was growing up the dinnertime dialogue between my parents and me—especially after Bartholomew's death—

was curtailed by my father's nightly business phone calls: he'd yak and eat while my mother watched sideburned television newscasters and I tried to read *Gulliver's Travels* or *The Invisible Man* or *Robinson Crusoe*: a paperback in one hand, a fork in the other.

So the Hammersteins amounted to a real show for me. Maybe I was just tottered from Morris's suggestion that Gillian had wanted children and I, as flippant and self-concerned as always, had denied her an important piece of the blueprint. Still: I felt salubrious and safe in their dining room and suspected in my cells that this lifestyle was possible. The family-value wonderments I witnessed there! So this is what the GOP is always blathering about (minus the interracial element). Mocha made me promise I'd forswear meat, anything at all that goes *moo* or *bah*, *cluck* or *oink*. She had done a report for school on the holocaust that is the meat industry and was now mailing her allowance to PETA. In gratitude, I gave the gal my word.

And Boulder—here was a town I could die in and be glad: the mountains jutting up just beyond the foothills; Boulder Creek charging down from the canyon; all those young and youngish dwellers, so many of them UC Boulder students, making merry and biking shirtless or in bikini tops, throwing Frisbees near the creek by the library. Shoeless hippies harmonizing with suited professionals; artists and musicians performing on cobblestoned and carless Pearl Street. Boulder Book Store: I roamed the aisles of that singular haven and missed reading, missed my own books alphabetized by subject and century. The altitude: it entered me as if I were perforated straight through, front to back, side to side. The new air, the closer sun, mountains near enough to brush, graffiti and litter nowhere in sight: everyone was so young and beautiful and athletic, joggers and bikers, skateboarders and rock climbers—I had never entered a town like this before and so it appeared to me like a kind of happy hallucination or the mirage of a parched traveler, a place to make a home if a person had a home to make.

On the afternoon of my final day there, I roosted on the stone slab steps of the Boulder Museum of Contemporary Art (BMOCA, I was told) and watched the creek cut through a many-treed patch of land across the street, the bikers on the path pedaling along the creek up to and down from the canyon. I wouldn't say that a small peace had seeped into me during my two days strolling that town in all directions and eating granola, but the tempest turning in the mess of me had calmed a little and I didn't feel either milliseconds from the tears of self-pity or else on the brink of being torpedoed by forces beyond my hold.

At the other end of the steps, ten or twelve feet from me, near the glass door of the museum's entrance, sat a couple smoking and talking, taking stock of their lives as if they were about to make an essential decision. I wasn't trying to listen but for nearly an hour I could hear them. She was a Boulder native and worked at the museum; her father had deserted the family for a younger woman; her mother recently had a mastectomy. He hailed from New Jersey originally, had a father killed in a crash of some kind just a year earlier, and was trying to be a novelist, of all things. I almost broke my reverie to advise him against such a wobbly occupation.

But they were young, in their early twenties, and although

they were speaking about the bad luck that had found them and their families—tallying, it seemed to me—they loved each other. I could tell that not so much by their language or the way their arms touched ever so slightly—hair to hair—but by the way they sat and smoked together: in comprehension, in camaraderie, as if they shared a solid history and had made notable progress away from a goodly amount of pain. A move was on the horizon for them now: they were about to relocate somewhere, begin a new installment of their life together, and I think I heard Boston, but I couldn't be certain because I had Gillian's imminent Boston arrival with the squid trapped in my mind like a body under ice. Why would a couple move away from such a magical place, even for Boston?

If they had sought my instruction just then, what would I have recommended? You youngsters don't have a prayer? Your love will perish as per the designated shelf life of all young love? Or would I have told them thus: Be sweet to one another. Stay in this beauty and brawl against the world's power of pulling apart. Recall Old Testament terminology: *covenant*, *sacred*, *sacrifice*. And mind always that Adam wasn't a schlep fruitily duped by Eve. He turned his back on God because he knew that a paradise without her was no paradise at all.

7. BODIES IN MOTION

THAT ASTRONAUT CALLED Ahab, on the wavy trail of his own white sparkle, once bellowed thus: "All my means are sane, my motive and my object mad." Well, at least he had means, which was more than I could say for my own sick self at this juncture. Send me some signal, Captain; this is your story, too, methinks, your whale replaced by octopi and a girl but with details no less religious and wild. Okay. Something new and not altogether toward was about to happen here; my marrow and other pulpy liquids told me so.

No more than a blot from neck to belt, I had this exchange with myself on Interstate 80, somewhere between Colorado and the East Coast, driving at a slug's speed in hopes of being socked with something reminiscent of a concept or clue:

—So, Charlie, what now, you colossal, colossal incompetent ass?

—Oh, I don't know, just thought I'd mosey my way to Boston to meet Gillian by month's end. You know, get her back. Woo and whatnot.

—Brilliant, brilliant! Bravo!

And that was as far as my dialogue reached. Mostly the radio spoke and sang and I simply shrugged in agreement with whatever pundit or pop song happened to be espousing a view. All that American airport flatness out my window, entire football fields of swaying soy, many hours of miles indistinguishable from the last many and the many more to come. What did people do out there with all their infinite sky, real estate, and John Deere tractors? And those barns half in ruin, half in use? Was I in any position to say that it all appeared a maddening abidance, cut-off and antiquated? You might know the answer to that one.

It took eight days to drive cross-country because I kept collapsing at forty-dollar-a-night motels, cocktailed on the mattress and morphed into vegetation. Employed some credit-card porn when I could not conjure semicolons and commas never mind sentences and paragraphs. Spent much time on the toilet with a malarial Amazonian waterfall, such was the highway's nutrition, the fried and the fast related to food by an f only. My heartburn was so Szechuan I could have drunk from a fire extinguisher. All around me the heat of summer was a blazing fact. Every time I stopped to let the brontosaurus SUV gorge on gasoline—every few hours, it seemed—guilt gnawed me in its molars.

Somewhere in the nil of Ohio my cell phone falsettoed to life—it hadn't rung in ages and I'd forgotten I had the thing, shocked it still had some jingle left in it. Friend was on the line, his voice aloe for poison ivy or some stovetop burn. We exchanged the compulsory opening chitchat of every phone conversation between two chums who haven't talked in untold weeks.

And then he said, "Charlie, you've been stumbling. I'm worried."

"Friend, I've been afraid to call you. I have some sour news about Romp. Sasquatch ate him in the woods and I ran the other way."

"I read that. But don't worry: Romp is in Canada at a nudist colony for Negroes. He's vicar there and thriving. I spoke to him yesterday. He sends his love."

"Oh, thank necromancy, what a relief. I sat six hours on a plane with that man, plus pitched a tent with him. We were close. I've been humiliated, my honor shat on."

"And that's not all, from what I hear. Mom just called me. She's been reading your memoirs every week, Charlie. I've been in Iraq making dead bodies or else I'd have read them myself. What's this I hear about a UFO, a midget, and some Hebraic astronomer battered by a lesbo?"

"Oh, that. Well, Friend, I went in search of wisdom from two separate sources and came out none the better. Morris Hammerstein thinks I should have focused more on Gillian. You know, prostrate myself before her, join her cause. He thinks I should have given her children, become a man who wears an apron. He himself wears an apron. I've seen him."

"That's a negative. He wants to turn you into a female. Charlie, I have one last mission for you, should you choose to accept it."

I was beginning to understand that Friend was to missions what Zeus was to lightning. The manicured rest stop I veered into seemed not a half-bad place to have a conversation.

"Friend, I need your aid, but I've failed you three times already. I believe I am what you call helpless."

"I nearly concur. But you need to be reminded of manhood, of how the hairier of our species keeps appointments. I've been thinking: Jacob Jacobi is nothing if not man, and perhaps sweet Gillian set sail with him because you, alas, were not man enough."

Huh? Me not man enough?

I said, "But I shave my face sometimes and leave the toilet seat up. I grow erect at the sight of feminine products. I resorted to gunfire! What do you mean by this terrible suggestion?"

"Women want muscle and male stubbornness, also square jaws. This I've seen firsthand, and I've heard stories from reliable sources. I want you to steer towards northern New Jersey to see an ally of mine named Richie Lombardo, a virile Italian and human anomaly that will give you lessons. And not those useless quips so glibly given you by the stargazer, but lessons you can use to earn back Gillian and then keep her once you do. Keep in mind that his last name contains the word *bard*."

I mumbled sounds of acquiescence and ache, saw that I was almost out of gas again.

"This is my last resort," he said. "After Richie Lombardo, I have nothing, and perhaps will not again appear in your narratives. Besides, what else were you planning to do? Just show up one afternoon in Boston and beg?"

"Something akin to that, yes."

"Negative. You are going to New Jersey, a town called Ridgewood. Do you copy that?"

"Affirmative. I copy."

But what's that term mean exactly, *copy*? What was I supposed to be replicating?

"And Charlie," he said, "I've been considering something else."

"And what would that be, Friend?"

"The possibility that you shouldn't even try to win back Gillian. Bachelorhood, orgies, multiple ninteen-year-old gals without inhibition or ethic creeds. Girls with bad fathers and talented tongues. Could be quite a rodeo, just the balm you need for a throbbing ego."

"Come again? Not get Gillian back? Did you say orgies?"

A family from Pennsylvania, American Dreamed to the hellacious hilt, exited their SUV several spots in front of me: the mother looked exhausted, the father miserable, the children obnoxious, and the dog indifferent. Where were they going? And why? Did they really require all that plastic junk stuffed in the hatch and strapped to a rack?

"Just think on it, Charlie. You're still fertile, and Gillian is almost past breeding age, her tubes ready to retire. And honestly, I never understood what was so wonderful about that woman anyway. Forgive me that. Richie Lombardo will set you on the proper course. Prepare yourself for revolutions of mind and groin."

This was all a bit overbearing for me: flush my plan to retrieve Gillian? What in the name of Moses had got into Friend? His suggestion seemed Calvinist and pagan both. I had always known he didn't approve of Gillian, but did he really expect me to forgo my heart's hunt? And what would I report on if not my Gillian quest? A publication was relying on me; I had deadlines. A person requires a quest in order to doodle yarns; Odysseus knew that much and more. Fighting battles and fashioning cadavers had obviously turned Friend into a libertine. I suppose that's understandable. We must support our Armed Forces.

And so I let Friend provide me with numerous directions and numbers. I had to check the road atlas to see where in the hell I was and where, gasp, I was going. Apparently ten hours, give or take, separated me from this lady-killer Lombardo, about whom Friend would tell me very little, and this I thought confounding. What awaited me at the end of that highway, where the pavement met New Jersey, and what price passion? All I knew of the Garden State were Bruce Springsteen, Walt Whitman, and a mythical creature going by the name of Jersey Devil. Considering the manner in which my recent days had proceeded, I simply hoped that my newest task would not have me confronting the hornéd and light-of-foot ambiguity others hound through mist.

And so I rolled on for those ten hours, abiding by speed limits to avoid the notice of state troopers intent on tickets or other forms of boredom-inspired butting-in. I was scarcely a hygienic human behind the wheel—my scent feculent and almost damned—stopping for coffee when I required what it does to the brain, for almost-edible items, and for the relief of my bladder in littered weeds. Plus now I had to worry about not being manly. Didn't I take the bona fide manly actions when attempting to thwart Marvin Gluck and the sailing of *The Kraken*, or when I rescued Sandy from mind control?

At one rest stop, as I held my disliked urinating penis, I found myself trying to will it into expanding an inch or two. But what of Gillian's multiple orgasmic splendor, and several times a week at that? Surely only a genuine male product could bring such a lady to those heights of carnal exuberance.

Surely. My Lord, but what if she had been faking it? There was that movie, remember, with the appalling, mousey thespian Meg Ryan and the even more appalling Billy Crystal, the one with that scene where they perched in a diner, she explaining to him how a woman apes orgasm, and for reasons that sounded to me explicable at the time, though I was youngish when I saw it. Christ—I had a potent enough plague upon my house; I didn't need masculine self-esteem issues, too, all that modern malaise that twists a man into a figure from Camus.

At that rest stop, in the backseat of the SUV, I got slain by somnolence and slept for three hours straight with the sounds of mammoth engines snoring around me. For a time I hovered in that peaceful dreamland where nothing at all works properly but everything is okay.

FAST FORWARD THROUGH about ten hours of asphalt, green signage, and the silent ponderings of a hobo polluted by gloom, and you will find me trying to navigate the circles and switchbacks of northern New Jersey's highway system, which appeared to have been planned by elfin pranksters wanting mutilated metal. I was about to ring the bell of yet another stranger but had ceased to care about my obvious frailty. The town of Ridgewood off a highway numbered 17 was one of those upper-middle-class suburban fairy tales we and foreigners daily fall for. I do not subscribe to the cynical, bohemian, anti-bourgeois rants of certain sets and so I found it lovely, a place to live and spread seed, even in my bedraggled state brought on by insomnia, travel, toxic food, and all the you-know-what that defined the yours truly I had turned into. Instead I subscribe to the need of normality and regimen, am not nettled by cosmopolitan objectives, think fondly of naps, backyard cookouts, and family time on the sofa.

That's what Friend failed to grasp: excitement caused me anxiety, stimulation caused me sweat; I wanted tedium and vapidity, a settled-down matrimony that made a man only the tiniest fraction of what he was at eighteen and eager. Traipsing around the continent in search of dispossessed souls to aid me in my campaign was fine to fuel several months' worth of yarns, but sooner or later a seeker must get dull or else risk rapture, must be henpecked and housebound. I believe I was this way, or beginning to be, before Gillian bailed, and I yearned for it again. The exiled in other lands know my feelings precisely.

Just as I was trying to maneuver through (across? over?) New Jersey's psychopathic highway system, I received a distressing call from Morris Hammerstein. I wasn't even going to answer the phone because I didn't recognize the number, but the part of me that was love-rent and rapscallion—that would be all of me—wanted to believe that perhaps Gillian was using someone else's phone to call me and apologize.

"Charlie," he said. "Asshole. You are a very bad man. This week's issue of *New Nation Weekly* arrived an hour ago. You gave me your word you wouldn't write about my family."

"Umm" and "Uhh."

"I will sue, Charlie! You hear me, I will sue!"

"Morris, wait a minute. Do you think you should be disseminating stereotypes? Really."

"I will sue you and that magazine, Charlie."

"For what, Morris?"

"Defamation! Slander!"

This was illegal in the Garden State, driving and talking without a hands-free headset, and that made sense to me because it indeed felt homicidal and suicidal both, trying to scream into the phone, use the blinkers, stay in the lane, and watch out for my exit, the number of which I had forgotten. Hang up and drive before you kill someone, stupid.

"I didn't defame you," I said. "You come off looking quite well. All of you. Not the lesbian, naturally."

"For invasion of privacy, then. For misrepresentation! I don't speak that way, Charlie. No one speaks that way!"

"Yes you do! Yes I do!"

"You can't get away with this, Homar."

His spittle came through the line and wet my ear hole.

"Morris, a long time ago some gents wearing wigs got together and started scribbling in a notebook. They called their ditty the Constitution. There's a bit in it called Freedom of Speech. Look it up. I'm about ready to crash this tank talking to you."

"Good. I hope you crash and get maimed."

"Morris, be a gentleman."

Some huffing and puffing and wanting to blow my house down. Then some silence. A tractor-trailer with a hundred wheels salivated with thoughts of running me over.

Then Morris said, "Charlie, how much do they pay you for those memoirs?"

"It's rude to ask about money, Morris."

"No one is ruder than you, Homar. How much do they pay you?"

"Depends on the word count."

"How much did they pay you for this new one about my family?"

I told him.

"I want it," he said. "You will donate that money to Mocha's college fund and you will be glad to do it. Send me a check, Charlie, and send it right away. If you do it, I won't sue."

"I think this is blackmail, Morris."

"No, you asshole, this is the right thing to do. That money belongs to my child because you used her and us for your own gain. Sandy, by the way, is never speaking to you again."

"Oh, Christ, Morris, you brought Sandy into this?"

"No, Charlie," he said, "*you* brought Sandy into this."

I had to pull off the highway just then to avoid zooming SUVs, each one boated by a shrew on a warpath to the mall, she the sole passenger in a behemoth made to carry a clan. (But so was I, alas.) Horns hollered at me, middle fingers flipped because I was going too slow or else swerving. There, in park on the shoulder of some God-forgotten Jersey freeway, I sat with the phone to my ear fending off an anxiety attack I could feel gathering momentum somewhere inside my sternum. For some reason three *r* words occurred to me in quick succession: *rampage*, *ravage*, *repugnance*. And then I couldn't hold the dam any longer; roughshod cries burst free from me as if they had been fomenting in there since the Iron Age. Some kind of cardiopulmonary event felt possible. Bawling, wailing, unable to ease my disgrace, I sniveled into the phone how sorry I was.

"Forgive me, Morris," I said. "Please forgive me. I'll send you the money for Mocha. I'm so sorry."

"What were you thinking, Homar?"

"I wasn't thinking. I can't think. You saw me. Tell Wanda

how sorry I am. Please. And Sandy, too. I'm a mess, Morris. A chimpanzee without abstract thought or empathy. I mean, I can no longer decipher the gradations between innocence and irony or irony and insult."

A sigh indicating the pitiful joke I was. "Just send the check, Charlie," and he snapped himself gone.

LOMBARDO WAS EXPECTING me; Friend had phoned him many hours earlier. His Colonial home looked out onto a wide front yard trimmed around the edges, the kind that allows a person to love his lawn mower and perhaps polish it, too. Those towering oak trees: ancient scabs. One so angry-looking it seemed ready to say something. That U-shaped blacktop driveway: smooth. The shrubbery: Edenic. The day's weather: eighty-two and sun-filled. My interior: trembling. Why? I'll tell you.

You should have seen Richie Lombardo in his front yard: a six-foot-two mass of hairless, striated muscle, three hundred pounds of rounded granite tanned bronze, one of the most famous bodybuilders in the Northeast, his physique in multiple magazines and on protein products and TV programs, gold and silver trophies adorning the rooms of his dwelling. When he shook my hand I feared he'd detach it from the wrist. And you thought cartoon characters were not real.

He ambled like a being more robot than man, more metal than flesh, his oversized torso twisting on top of his waist because the wings beneath his arms confined him like someone in a body cast. When he greeted me on the walkway, his nearly naked frame blocked out the sun and cooled my face. I had never before beheld in person a thing so freaky and sculpted;

Michelangelo no doubt would have shuddered in approbation. He was simply grotesque, a man misshapen into the mechanical, and yet he was stunning, an item of beauty if you were inclined to see him that way. I had thought there existed only six abdominal muscles, but this creature had eight, four on each side of his stomach, each of them a rectangular wedge of marble. In contrast, my midsection had become a bleached and hirsute mound of dough that maintained finger indentations for twenty seconds or more. His legs nearly defied description: quadriceps that met at his knees and had multiple chiseled parts, split hamstrings that bowed out half a foot, and calves roughly the size of genetically altered cantaloupes. In other words, the legs of a rhinoceros, mobilizing a body that humbled Hellenistic statue and Bowflex Man both.

New Jersey: a state so Martian I half expected to look up and spot six-wheeled rovers parachuting down through a bloodshot troposphere.

"Charlie, babe," Lombardo said, "Friend informed me that we have some necessary work to do. When Friend calls, I answer. He saved my life once in Bosnia, back when I was Special Forces."

I had expected a voice gorge-deep, but his was normal and I daresay pleasant.

"You're the satyr who attacked unsuspecting Eurydice in that field."

"Pardon?"

"Richard," I said, "forgive my mouth ajar. I've never stood before another male undressed so. What are those little shorts made from? Nylon?"

Nylon—stupid me. They were spandex.

"It looks like you have a soda can in there. And forgive me for asking, but is it physiologically sound for one's veins to be the size of electrical cords? I've never seen veins in a human being's pectorals. Plus your nipples are the size of eggs."

He flexed his pecs. "Do you know how much discipline it requires to delete all the water from underneath the skin in order for these veins to wind around the muscle like this? One must be privy to the workings and interactions of potassium, glycogen, and H_2O. Feel me, babe?"

How did he get his grass so green?

"Jesus, you shave your body? The whole thing? It must take days."

"You need to see the muscle definition. Why be shredded like stone if those shreds are covered by hair? You dig?"

"Richard," I said, "I'd rather not dig. I'm confused about why Friend sent me to you, and, to be perfectly honest, I've lately been spending my days in riot and roar, a hoodlum with no home."

"Have you been crying?" he asked.

"Me? Crying? Do I look like a man who cries?"

"You want me to answer that?"

My silence said no for me.

"It's cool, babe. Friend advised me to read your memoirs in order to gather intelligence, diagnose the whole dilemma. You have tight narrative structure and a pretty strong sense of dramatic thrust. But if I could make one, not unimportant suggestion about your erratic prose style—"

"Can you not, Rich? Thanks. I'm afraid of you and my penis has retreated up into my body so that now I am effectively a female."

"Chill, babe. Let's go inside. The real females are waiting. I ordered us a pair of beauties from Madam Chung's House of Superior Entertainment."

Females? Waiting? Madam Chung? To what brand of debauchery and Mother-Nature-fiddling godlessness had Friend sent me? And why was my horror now tinged with a splash of thrill? Dr. Frankenstein or Jekyll no doubt stood just behind the front door gripping a mallet, prepared to perform sacrilege on my own outmoded body. I still had time to turn around and sprint. Why wasn't I?

"Actually, Rich, listen, can we just talk outside in the pleasant sun or nearabouts? I need a relatively calm scene here. I spoke to my editor a few days ago and he said readers are emailing complaints, doubting my hijinks."

"I think you wrote in 'Help Me Wanda' that you needed more females in your stories, and I have two waiting right inside, babe."

"Somehow I have the feeling, Rich, that the women from Madam Chung's House of Superior Entertainment are not the sort of women the average American female reader can bring herself to sympathize with. Plus I shouldn't haul my scourge into your house. I taint all I touch."

"You can't taint me, babe, it's cool. Come on, now, stop the dumb excuses, let's get learnéd."

As I followed Lombardo to the porch I couldn't help but notice—honest: I couldn't help it—that his buttocks were a perfectly level and square slab that did not jiggle as he moved. He was a pink anatomical chart, animated in three dimensions and smelling of tanning oil—you know the smell. This consummate lack of body fat did not appear to me in any way healthful; evolution chose body fat for a specific function, and whatever that function is—warmth, buoyancy, what have you—Richie Lombardo seemed not to need it. Physics took a detour at his form. The bodybuilders of America had gone from a barely registered curiosity one slakes with drugstore magazines to an imposing reality with sound and scent.

It would take me several moments to notice that his walls were festooned with blown-up photographs of him posing onstage during various championship competitions, and this because the only two sights I took in at first were the naked Asian women massaging each other's feet in a block of sunlight on the carpet. Lombardo introduced them as Mimi Squared— he meant, I guessed, that they were both named Mimi—and the two rose to greet me near the front door with tender hugs and kisses slightly French. I simply stood there aghast and impotent. Before me was the destruction we ill-fated all too often greet as stimulation.

"Sorry," I said, "I haven't brushed my teeth," but it didn't bother them.

They looked nearly identical and could have been twins except that one had itsy-bitsy breasts pointed upward and the other had itsy-bitsy breasts pointed outward. Pubic hair: pencil-line strips. Body fat: zero. Lips: pink pillows recently fluffed. Height: in the low five-foot range. Weight: light as air and love. Plus they smelled of some island fruit one longs to crack open and suck the flavorful sap from.

"Mimi Squared," Lombardo said to me. "Descendants of the Huns and other Mongoloid virtuosos. Schooled in submission and the art of orgasm. The yellow horde has insight we Caucasoids only dream of. They can walk across hot coals while playing violin."

I palm-knocked on my sideways head in order to clear whatever blockage was distorting his sentences.

"Huh?" I said. "What?"

"Chinamen, both of them, although Mimi to the left has some Japanese shogun in her distant past. You should see her wield a steak knife. Also meat eaters, as were all mongrels."

Palm-knocked the other way this time.

"I don't think I follow, Rich. Can you speak more slowly, perhaps pause a long time between each word?"

"Carnivorous, I say, like our ancestors on the African savanna. Buddhist and Confucian, respectively. Fluent in four languages apiece, plus as many in the martial arts."

"I'm sorry, really, but I'm still stuck on that yellow horde comment. Did you say *yellow horde*?"

"Sure did, babe. Asians are my bag, but what we're about to teach you can be applied to any of the races, even Native Americans and the Inuit tribes, although they are much harder to bend."

I took a step back here, toward the door.

"Richard," I said, "I am from New England, which, as I'm sure you know, means I'm a Democrat. We believe in equal rights and the liberation of women. They are not objects to be bent. What I see before me is sexual enslavement and a degradation most foul. Wait here, I'm calling the police. My morality, what little of it remains, is offended."

I think I had a hand raised in the air, finger pointed upward, at heaven.

"No it isn't," he said.

"But still, it's the proper thing to say and the expected reaction at a time like this. I smell slavery and traces of sodomy."

"You should cut it out," Mimi the First said. "Don't judge us, wimp. Just cut it out."

And Mimi the Second said, "Right. Either you've arrived for illumination and good old-fashioned fun, as your friend Friend said you were in need of, or you have no desire to rid yourself of the shackles civilization has fastened to you. Which one will it be, Mr. Homar: the nature that begot you or the cell society has slammed you into?"

I must have looked at Lombardo with an expression that indicated mystification and disgrace, because he said, "Mimi on the left graduated from Yale, and Mimi on the right published a study with the University of Chicago Press called *Sexual Fantasia from Caesar to Sade*. I have copies on my shelf. You're free to take one. Both women were born and raised in Manhattan in the 1980s, by the way, which might account for much."

Hmm. Let me think here. What possibly could I have said just then? My options were not many and so, unhappily, this was what came out of my mouth: "Uhh, Sade was an ogre with no compassionate feeling for humanity."

One of the Mimis—I was already confusing them—the one with the outward-pointing teats—countered with, "That's an egregious miscalculation, and a clichéd one at that. Sade was a comedian and fantasist forcing a hypocritical society to see that its own laws of morality are paper thin. Also let's not forget Wilhem Reich and his theory of orgone: sexual adventure is the only guarantee of mental health."

"Yes," I said, "and let's not forget that Herr Reich landed in prison for fraudulent claims."

I had read that somewhere but wasn't exactly sure it was true.

"So," she said, "you have something in common with Reich, then, you ex-con. Come down, Charlie. You look so silly up there."

Yes, your leading actor and chronicler actually glanced about to see where he had to climb down from; and then her meaning spanked me true and the real blushing began. I knew she was making superior sense just then, sure, but it struck me as a shade difficult to take her seriously with those candy-corn nipples vibrating on the ends of her little teats. Plus she had sat spread-eagled on the carpet and so her hairless packed mound of genitalia was aimed right at me.

Is this the burlesque Friend had in mind for me? What good, people, could possibly come from this exchange? None, right? These gals made a gent remember maelstrom and mayday.

"Really, Rich," I said. "Did you have to give them my memoirs to read?"

"They've been here all morning, Charlie. They were curious. Those memoirs are public property, babe."

"Okay," I said, on the sofa now, "what's the meaning here, Lombardo? What does Friend want you to do for me? I need to recline. It's not every day I commune with a gargantuan superhero and his two Asiatic scholar-slaves."

"You want some water or something?" a Mimi asked. "You look faint."

Lombardo sat on the sofa opposite me, the slaves in the middle.

"What are you thinking right this very second?" he asked.

"I'm thinking: I can't explain where I am or even begin to connect it with anything. I'm willing to acknowledge absurdity and randomness but I believe I prefer Bigfoot and UFOs to the likes of you three. And really, Rich, you know what the saying-makers say about situations that seem too good to be true."

"What do you mean?"

"I mean two gorgeous courtesans who just happen to be Ivy League scholars? Are you kidding? Who's going to believe this?"

"Why does anyone have to believe it? And nothing is too good to be true if you have the cash to pay for it. These girls are a thousand bucks an hour, babe."

One of the Mimis said, "But worth every nickel."

"Charlie," Lombardo said, "if you'd come off your high horse and cut the crap for just one second, you'd see that Friend wants to help you. I've known Friend since way back and I've never seen him care for a buddy the way he does for you. He feels terrible for sending you to that dock with his gun and then you sitting in prison for three months."

"Richard," I said, "if you're trying to infuse my narrative with a shot of sentimentality, please refrain. My readers recoil from bathos. Plus I don't know how to refute that. It makes me look bad."

"Friend thinks you need to sever the cable attached to this Gillian. I have to agree. Not a healthy union."

"Oh, and this is healthy?" I asked, gesturing, it seemed, to the house around us, but I didn't mean his house was unhealthy. "You look like you're about to burst from anabolic injectables, your skin is tanned a color that does not exist in nature, and you grease this grotto of sin with the paid-for lust juice of two Asian Eves. Plus you pray to false idols—look at all these photos of yourself."

"Affirmative," he said, "and that's what we want for you, babe, self-esteem included. Take out your pad and begin taking notes, because you're not going back to Gillian. That way of life isn't working out for you, in case you haven't noticed. Look at yourself. I promised Friend I would fix you and that's exactly what I intend to do. You're gonna get muscles and eat raw meat with me."

"No can do, Rich. I promised a little girl I wouldn't support the slaughter of animals and that's exactly what *I* intend to do—or *not* to do, you know, *not* support it, I mean."

He squinted me a look that spoke first of troglodyte righteousness and second of the vegetarian sissy I was trying to be. Some pieces in me quaked; whether they were bones or tendons I could not tell. I imagined myself bleeding, perhaps planted in the backyard by his tremendous arms. Behind his head above the sofa was an obscenely large photograph of himself flexing so hard it looked as if his skin might unzip. The two Mimis kneaded each other on the carpet not six inches from my shoes, four eyes heating me with glances of confusion, perplexed by my elephantine idiocy. And yes, I'll admit it: I didn't gallop from the room because—come on, people—I had two vulvas and four breasts making promises and professing poetry. The mammal in us will have its say.

"All right, then, Richard," I continued, "say again that part about my becoming like you. I'm feeling some minor movement in me."

"Yeah, babe, that's more like it. Follow us downstairs. Come, ladies, let's get bacchic with Charlie Homar."

. . .

WE FOUR WENT through the kitchen—a gleaming off-white cleanliness for which his housekeeper deserves a green card or at least a raise—and descended the basement stairs into another gleaming, intensely lit expanse that contained his home gymnasium of professional weight-lifting equipment. The walls were ten-foot mirrors throwing around fluorescent light and nudity, the floor a blue rubber pad on which sat multiple machines for exercising one's back, shoulders, quads, biceps. The space smelled of pristine perfection. A long row of dumbbells was lined up against one wall like metal soldiers, silver weights from twenty-pound lollipops to two-hundred-pound bombs. There in one corner sat a squat rack and bench-press station; there in another sat metal triangles that held his Olympic plates with the circumference of truck tires; and in yet another corner, that reliable contraption any gym fiend knows as a Smith machine, a barbell attached to the sides of the structure with oiled cylinders. And then there were places to perform chin-ups, sit-ups, T-bar rows; a pulley machine for triceps and the devil knows what else. Plus more framed photos of him posing onstage and creepy cartoon images of Asian banshees in coitus.

"It's so warm and dry down here," I said. "My basement is like a rain forest."

"Climate control," he said. "That's pivotal for weight lifting and lovemaking."

One of the Mimis opened a door next to the bathroom and revealed a sun-strewn room with but a king-sized mattress on the carpet.

"This is our launchpad," she said.

My face must have asked the relevant questions.

"Launchpad," she said. "Use your dreams. You wrote in one of your essays that every person wants to be a spaceman, and so this is how we do it. In fact, when you wrote that line you were referring to sex with Gillian. We aren't that different after all, are we, Charlie?"

"No, Mimi, my darling, I suppose not. Well, you know, in some ways. I still have remnants of a moral center."

The other Mimi—upward-pointing teats—said, "Every time I hear you mention morality it makes me want to puke. You attempted to kill several people. Plus Morris Hammerstein asked you specifically not to write about his family, and just today you ran that very story about his wife and kids. You called his wife a chocolate champion? Are you serious?"

"*He* did! *I* didn't! *He* did."

She said, "And you named their daughter *Mocha*, for crying out loud? You know how offensive that is?"

"Wait, *they* named her that! *They* did. I just reported on it. People are entitled to their language."

The other Mimi said, "I doubt they named her Mocha. Her name is probably Mary or Marge."

"What's wrong with *Mocha*?" I asked. "What? Ever have a mocha latte? It's delicious!"

She said, "And every last lesbian in the land is going to boycott you, I hope you know."

"But *I* didn't tell Morris to fight that lesbian! Guys, I'm a victim here. Come on. Let's be friends."

"Richie," she continued, "I might suspend my Buddhist restraint and smack this dope. How do you think he's going to characterize *us* for next week's installment? As a couple of chinky, hypersexed, preverbal prostitutes."

"You're not preverbal!" I said.

"Let's chill, baby love," Lombardo told her. "Charlie is damaged and lacking perspective. We need to show him affection now, not violence. Be like Bambi."

Vigorously I nodded to show my support for this view.

"He doesn't mean any of that morality garbage anyway," she said. "He's saying it only because it's what his readers want to hear, because he wants to be the loftier character among all of us."

"Not true," I said, "not true. I can write anything I want, any version of events, any at all. Why would I be saying this now if I didn't actually believe it? I could tell you three what *you* want to hear right now, and then just alter my dialogue before publication to paint myself as Mr. Moral. You see? It must be genuine."

She was already busy with a tube of lubricant, lathering her backside and the other Mimi's, too. Lombardo was seated splayed on the shoulder-press machine, pumping himself up in preparation for their (our?) launch in the next room. I thought that by changing the subject to bodybuilding I might buy myself some time, figure out how I'd flee from what would certainly be the mortifying experience of copulating with these three cranks. The unholy bulge in Lombardo's spandex had increased from a soda can to a twelve-inch semolina bread loaf. My T-shirt was damp and getting damper.

"So, Richard, tell me now, how does one achieve your physique?"

"First: be born with the genetics of a freak. Without those, you cannot advance. Second: become a scientist and turn your body into a project. Drugs are key, babe. I am supplied with the finest chemicals science has invented. They're over there, on top of the cabinet. I like to keep them in plain view for motivation."

He pointed to the scores of ampoules, syringes, and pill bottles, and explained. Those to the left were mass-building magic, oil-based drugs: Sustanon 250, Deca-Durabolin, Anadrol, Dianabol, and so forth. Those to the right were precontest cutting drugs and diuretics, all of them water-based: Winstrol-V was the best. It burned as it went in, babe. Also, locked in the cabinet was GH, growth hormone, extracted from the pituitary glands of the dead. Only the architects at Los Alamos would understand that shit—it's like going from uranium to plutonium—it builds a better blast. He said I wasn't ready for that intel.

"I should say not," and for some reason I uttered that line with an Englishman's accent—Devonshire, say. I was also just then looking for somewhere to sit down but was terrified that if I sat on a muscle machine I might be expected to make the weights rise.

"You must train like a rabid animal, with spit and sweat and blood and screams. Muscle doesn't want to grow, so you must shock your system out of stasis. Only a handful of champions in the world can train like this. Heavy weight and low reps build mass; light weight and high reps make rips. Diet is key: I consume eight thousand calories per day, most of it from fat and protein. The misunderstanding is that fat causes fat. It does not: carbohydrates cause fat. I'll tell you one thing, Charlie: Gillian would never have left me."

If Lombardo had been another mortal—that gnome from the Philippines, maybe, Casey Gonzales—I would have retaliated with kung fu and perhaps, given the conversation, sadism, too.

But I could say only, "Okay, that stabbed me in the chest vicinity, a place already bombed to dusty rubble by kamikaze pilots. Must you? I mean, please, be kind, Richard."

"I'm talking about manhood here, babe. Look at me"—he was still pumping up his basketball deltoids on the shoulder-press machine—"I am what the Greeks imagined. I am Achilles and Atlas, Hercules and Adonis. Look behind you at the two Mimis pleasuring each other on the bed"—and by Jove, they were, with tongues flapping—"and tell me you don't want to be us. Those girls, and my other girls, will not abandon me, not while I give them pure, mainlined manliness—"

"You're *paying* them."

"That's not the point. I pay them but simultaneously *deny* myself to them in any other way. That's the key to human sexuality, Charlie, what Sade—not Freud, mind you—understood above all: the forbidden. You weren't forbidden to Gillian—a husband is not forbidden—but the squid hunter was. Get many girls and forget about the one. Matrimony is not in nature."

"Neither are porcelain toilets but I quite prefer them to squatting on sticks."

The mention of porcelain toilets made his face crinkle into a remark that meant: *What kind of cretin mentions a toilet at a time like this?*

"I'm talking about the emotional element, Rich. Aren't you forgetting that? Human beings aren't androids. It's all I can do to give emotional attention to one woman, never mind two or six or twelve. Plus your manliness is artificial, injected not inspired. And by the way, we're turning into mouthpieces here for the views of an author, which is exactly how Sade wrote, which is to say, execrably."

"Everyone's a mouthpiece for something or other," he said, "even if only himself. You lost me with that talk of emotions a minute ago, but I will agree that humans aren't androids. They are, however, animals, and let me tell you a little scientific fact, because, as you know, I am a scientist."

And here's the fact Lombardo so graciously passed me: If a male bull is housed in a pen—or penned in a house—with a female in heat, he will fornicate once or twice with her, but no more. He's not tired, nor has the female affronted his bullness; he has merely lost interest. Now, if you introduce a different female in heat, the bull will get keyed up and pleased once again and fornicate several more times. But then his bullness will lose interest again, and the process has to be repeated. If you try to reintroduce that first female back into the pen, even with eyeliner, a scarf, and a spray of perfume, the genius bull knows, he cannot be conned, and so he ignores her. The same is true for horses and goats and other barnyard beings with nothing else to do but stand around and piss in dirt.

Lombardo said, "I'm talking about the need for variety that permeates all of nature, us included. Please respond, babe, go ahead."

It was surprising I could pay attention to Lombardo's theories, what with the slurps, mutters, and assortment of moans emanating from Mimi Squared. I doubted any progress could have been made had I told Lombardo that a man is not a bull—

well, most—and that during my tenure with Gillian I never for a flash lusted after another lady. He would have no doubt replied that I was not a real man, then—my sole quandary and the reason I had mislaid Gillian in the first place. Charles Homar the tennis player: I anticipated Lombardo's little green projectiles of anti-logic and was somewhat proud of myself for doing so and keeping mum. Devil knows how hard it was.

Still, I needed a way out of this pickle or else it would be proven to me just what a remorseful display of sexuality I really was. Lombardo's pink eggplant would have made my own member look like a clitoris or smaller, and I was hesitant even to ponder how those two maenads would devour me in a ritual of vampirism and vice. Whatever vestiges of excitement I had felt thirty minutes earlier had evaporated and been replaced by an exhaustion and sudden dread of vagina. Perhaps they were right: I was not a real man, but an article far behind or else off to the side.

And then it fell into my head from on high, the perfect diversion, the question that could put the kibosh on this humiliating exercise, a ritual of late—although, yes, I knew also that it might get me wounded irreparably.

"Richard," I said, "don't you think this whole bodybuilding lifestyle is a little . . . you know . . . *gay?*"

He let the machine smash down, eyeballed me in the mirror (I was sitting behind him on a padded bench), stood very deliberately, with peacock threat, turned ever so slowly, latched eyes with mine, and asked, "What did you say?"

"You know. Bodybuilding. It's kind of . . . gay."

"Gay as in stupid or gay as in homosexual?"

"Yeah, that's right."

"That's right what? Which one?"

"Homosexual. Did you know, Rich, that Sade would have his valet bugger him? That crazy Sade. Maybe he lifted weights, too."

If a look could raise the dead, happy Lazarus would have jumped up through the floor.

"You have about one minute to explain yourself, Charles. Because, among the significant differences between you and me, one is that you've only attempted to kill a man, while I myself have massacred many. Start talking."

I sat back and crossed my legs, woman-like.

"Well, it's nothing, really, I was just sitting here thinking as you worked out. You know, how similar a bodybuilder is to the average young female in summer: hairless, suntanned, obsessed with the body and with food, always looking in the mirror, yearning for the esteem and attention of men. I mean, all that time spent with nearly naked men in the gym and onstage. I can imagine it now, the gym life: a clique of hairless men in spandex harpooning each other's buttocks with needles, massaging the painful cramps out of each other's deltoids and quads, positioning each other into poses before the mirror, lying naked in the tanning bed, showering each other with compliments on muscle shape and density. It just all seems so, well, so *femmy*."

Surely this was the point at which Lombardo would demand I vacate the premises in a jiffy for insulting his muscled machismo, perhaps head-slap me and call me ingrate, maybe faggot, then say I'm lucky to be leaving on two legs that are not fractured compound-wise. He stood looking at me with a countenance that affirmed ambiguity outright. His straight line of a mouth, I saw, was starting to spread into a smile.

"Oh no you don't, Homar. Friend warned me that you might try some misbehavior in order to get out of being schooled. You almost had me there for a minute. Homosexuals! Ha! As if! Okay, now, stop the silliness, Mimi Squared is waiting for us," and here he peeled down his spandex panties and made me eye-to-eye with his eel, which, if I remember rightly, winked at me.

What magus would I beckon now? I felt so drained. Months of skirmish seemed just then to catch up with me and harden like concrete in my skeleton. I felt the pressing need to get monastic, take a vow, wear a robe. Our species swam laps in a cesspool and I needed pause, maybe a month-long siesta under a goose-down quilt in an Andes mountain town, tended to by kindly Sherpas. My T-shirt had gone from damp to wet; a fever rose from my feet to my cheeks. In several seconds I would be sobbing. Again.

"Richard," I said, "can I use your bathroom? I need to, you know, soap my scrotum."

"By all means, babe. It's behind you. Then undress and join us. When we're done I'm giving you a workout routine and a diet for victors. Soon you'll be happy again, the word *Gillian* just an ancient grunt on the tongue of *Neanderthalis*."

With a locked door and water hissing from the spigot, I studied my face in that bathroom mirror and imagined my skull through the blanched and unmoisturized skin around it. My hair lay tousled and desperate for a trim—I looked like an American Christ—my teeth needed scouring, and a shave was overdue by a fortnight or more. I wet my face five or eight times and, propped up on the vanity with elbows locked, watched the drops dribble from the edge of my nose and disappear into the puddle at the drain.

Some diabolical and depressed force had seeped into my being and demanded attention. It was a wonder my legs would work. Into the mirror my mouth admonished my face, "Charlie, go home now and find refuge. Sleep a long time, begin to pray. Remember the first century, fight off this flu."

I had a two-hour drive back to my condo in Connecticut, and for the first time in four months Gillian was not pushing unduly against my cerebellum or breastplate. Illness of any ilk can be corrective if one is willing to be corrected or else surrender. That's what I was doing now, giving up and going home, perhaps never again to see Gillian Lee, a possibility with which I was, oddly, quite all right. Charles Homar had had enough. Ten years to Ithaca is far too many.

When I came out of the bathroom that day—a splash transformed and still feeling faint—I saw that Lombardo and his Twins Attila had begun their sortie without me and, alas, didn't seem to recall that I was present or care about the fact that I knew I would be fine on the earth from now on. Their saliva and body-fluid fest was in full swing, and I won't describe the sight in case children come across these pages, but you can shift your own imagination into action and conjure for yourself the right-side-up and upside-down of what they were doing, and then, if you really want accuracy, add a pinch of depravity to your picture and imagine Vlad the Impaler making love to a couple of captured Ottoman gals.

I left that palace and did not glance back lest I be turned to salt . . . or something worse.

8. INTERLUDE

WHISPER THIS (slowly, in earnest): Why do we do the things we do? How can we make sense of our lives in the belly of this madness? Do we suffer so much for wealth and renown, for the love of a boy or a girl or God? All this emptiness, within and without, and we here with a shovel between two nothings, trying to fill, and fill. Our silent Savior's broken body: in *that* believe? How? Which way? Is it *each* way? But we can't *hold* it. So in the lifetime of our discontent we worship one another and then wither when left. The paralytic on the corner will tell you: he longs for his legs. He used to feel such comfort when he shouted insults at the Lord, and the Lord, as patient as the grave (*is* the grave), said back: *Oh, child, you just don't understand.* Meaning he one day might. Which he won't.

On Interstate 84, somewhere between Richie Lombardo's Jersey pad and my Connecticut condo, my mother called to tell me that my father was gone, had died in the nighttime from a heart that said *No*, from a god that said *Come.* My thoughts— nay, my *emotions*, those niggling products of serotonin and dopamine run amok—were not with him, his spirit stuck to the ferryman now, boating from here across to Hades, but with *her*, my mother, this woman alone now, because dying means nothing to the dead. I said the words you say: *I'm coming; it's okay; don't worry; I'll take care of everything; he's in a better place; I'm sorry I've been out of touch; I'm sorry.*

She was only slightly weepy with me on the phone, nor could I weep—not now—and this despite Sigmund's certain claim that the death of the father is the single most monumental event in a man's life. I could not think of him on ice in the morgue, or in the hearse en route to the funeral home for a bodyful of ethanol and formaldehyde, because all I could see was my mother alone in that house, perhaps on the sofa knitting something no one would ever wear. Did she have bridge partners? Had she ever played bridge before? And what, exactly, is bridge? I've never thought to inquire.

Lashing up the highway in an SUV that was not mine (did the thing have insurance?), rushing to be at the side of a mother I was not worthy of and had not spoken to in weeks or seen in months, not even after the Maine authorities deemed me releasable from jail, my Gillian-inspired jaunt came down on me as ridiculous, I a dervish in rags wrapped around an outdated eros that squealed volumes about the lamebrained ass I was. Commonly selfish is what I'm saying and how I felt. The remorse was like the immolation of my entrails. I needed a shower and a massage. Maybe a haircut or an enema. (Replace that *a* with a *y* and I already owned enough of those, real and imaginary.) That truck must have had an astute autopilot because I remember nothing of the last fifty miles home.

My mother was roosted at the kitchen table, swaddled

by her two sisters, my obese aunties, experts in gluttony with beehived hairdos straight out of *Grease*, one of whom had once uninvited me to a Christmas meal because she said my memoirs were the work of Baal or else a roustabout recently concussed. (Always the aunts who cause the most trouble in a family. I told that aunt to relocate to Colorado Springs where the evangelical rabble would be gladsome to have her. "New England," I said, "doesn't want you.")

On this day both aunts creaked to their feet and hemmed me in with snivels and "Oh, Charlies" and "He was a good man," and I espied my mom through their fleshy smothers. She was still sitting with a mug of coffee, smiling half a smile to show me that she was relieved I had arrived. I went to her and held her and didn't say anything, her shampoo more fragrant than grapefruit. Both aunts began whimpering behind us.

"You've lost weight," she said.

"Yes. Prison and cross-country travel."

Aunt Chris had prepared a baked ziti and Aunt Pat had smacked together a lasagna. They attempted to spoon-feed me. Neither was Italian but both had married Italian men and liked to pretend, which was precisely how they had inflated to unlovable fatsos the blubber of whom could light the lamps of an Inuit family for a winter's spell. Their dresses looked chaotically cut from curtains.

My mother and I went out back and took a seat in the sunbeams at a picnic table my father had purchased from Home Depot even though I told him I could build one for half the cost. ("You couldn't build a table with Legos," he said, and just to prove him wrong I built my own with Friend's help and the thing now sits splintered and unused in a backyard it takes up half the square footage of.)

"You've been busy," she said. "You and your monsters."

How did she manage to look so unafflicted and health-ful when my father and her sisters were the very snapshots of human debris? Her pink and white running shoes were fresh from the mall.

And how should that conversation have gone exactly? Some souped-up suburban realism is what it was, with lines like, "Are you doing okay, Mom?" and "Will you be all right with money?" Someone said something about Bartholomew—ahh, the dead kid brother as literary trope—and I think I might have accused my father of not really liking me, to which my mother probably said that he wasn't the Great Santini. I had accidentally abandoned my sunglasses on Richie Lombardo's sofa that morning; the lambent world injured my eyes and made me squint. My mother, however, appeared as if she had been born in sunlight. The grass around us needed mowing; the shed could have used sanding and a new coat of paint; insistent weeds sprouted from between the cracks in the patio. (And never mind that the patio should not have had cracks in it to begin with, if only my father had listened to me and hired the skilled mason Friend had recommended instead of the career con man he had chosen at random from the yellow pages. Any info or advice that came from me was immediately discarded, damned.)

There was a lot of quiet and looking at our fingernails and trying not to turn this exchange into a commercial for Alzheimer's medication. Civil accusations here and there about fatherhood and being a son. The self-reproach in my guts going sha-zam. And then that inevitable primetime line from one or the other of us, so scripted for a scene like this you can smell it from the outset: *What do you want from me?* It was as if the sun had been instructed to laser a strait through my cranium. Look, look at the frolicsome squirrels in the shade; they seem so . . . *saved*. There used to be a cabbage-loving bunny rabbit somewhere around here. And then more quiet between us, hanging there like a drape. "The silence of those infinite spaces terrifies me," said Monsieur Pascal. And so they do.

Our bourgeois banter ended with her saying, "Cut the grass," and me replying, "You read my mind."

BOREDOM INTERWOVEN WITH dread, and all I could wish for was Gillian there at my arm to make the abominable viewing and funeral less agonizing, and not because of morbidity or malaise but because having to endure alone the obligatory kindnesses of the supposed-to-be bereaved is an appalling penance. Gillian could have shaken some hands for me, forced some smiles and niceties, even told the multiple strangers from my family's past to move along, move along, now, the line is long. (Ignore, obviously, that bit in the last episode about how I reconciled myself to Gillian's absence and decided I didn't need her anymore, et cetera. Sometimes a man needs to say a thing to hear how stupid it sounds.)

The whole day and a half before the viewing, and after I mowed the lawn, I slept nearly slaughtered in my boyhood bed: the dreams of rhapsody once dreamed there! (Although, not true, actually: the only dreams I can recall are the usual whitewashed ones that don't interest me enough to describe them for you, reader, who will be interested even less because you no doubt know that dreams, contrary to the opinions of an eyeglassed Austrian analyst on cocaine, don't mean a goddamn thing; so the next time you're reading a writer who finds it necessary to give you a meaningful dream sequence, especially in italics, consider that gimmickry a license to skim or else to drop the scribe entirely.)

I was overcome with another exhaustion that felt bulimic, my body emptied out and ready to vaporize. Somewhere from the subterranean kingdom of sleep I could hear voices down the hall, the front door open and close, a laugh, a sob, and perhaps a song. I like to believe my mother checked in on me as I reposed—lay in repose—for an entire earth rotation. Perhaps she put a palm to my forehead and pecked my cheek. The only time I rose from bed was to fill out a personal check for Morris Hammerstein—in the memo line I wrote, *For Mocha*—and then I slouched to the street corner, fed the envelope to a blue box.

Charles Agonistes, I was too lethargic, lachrymose to drive the six minutes to my condo to get into a proper-fitting suit and tie, and so I wore one of my father's getups, a size too big and stained at the knee, but who, really, was going to give a shit? You know how a wake goes: you've been to a dozen. My father's was like every one of those, except this time *I* was the one suffering there in the front row—up and down, up and down, hello how are you, hello how are you, thank you for coming, thanks very much, yes thank you, I know I need a haircut. Cousins crawled out from different corners of town; my father's former business colleagues materialized. You wouldn't have believed the amount of bad polyester in that room, outfits worn only thrice a lifetime. From my chair I could see Dad's nose stabbing up from the coffin's ruffled cavern; it could have been anyone in there. But it wasn't anyone, was it? It was him, he, my father.

I never was a good enough son.

Mom seemed like Hera there at the casket, more or less divine and absolutely in control, wearing navy blue instead of black. Not every death rings in a festival of slobber, especially when the dead is a sixty-year-old misanthrope, and for this, at least, I was relieved.

But it occurred to me (in a flash, as the sayers say), as I watched my Hera mama greeting the party crashers: What if she's pleased that my father is gone? What if she's planning to live, really live, now that the unhealthy hater-of-life is about to join the worms? What if—gasp—she already has a lover picked out, someone who resembles, say, pre-plastic-surgery Kenny Rogers, white beard and potbelly and all? Could this be the reason I had not seen her weeping? Was there a Carnival cruise in her immediate future? A ribbed old-lady one-piece bathing suit?

I should have been considering how zig leads to zag, but I tell you, as those imitation mourners filed in and out for two loathsome hours, all I could fathom was my mother with glasses of martinis, beneath disco lights, at the business end of a dance partner who knew the hop and twirl.

As for my father: the mortician had sewn his mouth into a hint of a grin, which was comical considering that he hadn't smiled in twenty years or more. The skin of his face: a Halloween mask. His hair: combed aslope in a Cary Grant do that never would have occurred to him. What did they do with his blood after they siphoned it from him? I supposed they dumped it down the drain. I stood at the coffin after almost everyone had gone, hands deep in pockets—one had a hole—head cocked as if at a bookstore, and I began feeling shamed for not feeling shamed, for faulty tear ducts, heart like a sewer. What was wrong with me? Why couldn't I improve, be full time first-rate?

There in the hallway—all marble floors and Greekish statues on pedestals—waiting for me in a brown slippish dress only about fifty percent appropriate for a wake, stood tiny Mindy Sirento, my first girlfriend from freshman year of high school. We had swapped virginities at fifteen years old, she too young to take pleasure in it, me too young to tell topsy from turvy. I had seen her earlier at the casket and was grateful when she vamoosed out the side door without needing to come offer me blah-blah. Her mother had perished of lung cancer soon after we had begun dating, and Mindy's response was to turn herself, yes, into a professional cigarette smoker. So that's what her face looked like now on top of the adolescent acne ruts: it looked like tobacco.

From what I had heard with one ear over the years, she was divorced now, a regular in rehab, had a daughter somewhere. And she had come to my father's wake why? When I stepped into the hallway she clicked over to me in heels, my name on her tongue, and soon we were embracing. Her perfume and hairspray: made by Marlboro. Her lithe five-foot frame: it seemed my body recalled the hills and valleys of it.

"Charlie," she said, touching my beard, "you look like a junkie."

"And I feel all jungly."

Come, she insisted, outside to smoke, my wrist in her grip, that body a stranger to me for the past eighteen years. Was she going to make me *talk*? Did she want an update on two decades? I had the feeling she needed to borrow money. I stopped at the bathroom and said I'd meet her in a minute, and when she went out back by weeds and trees to choke down a cigarette, I escaped through the front door, all around me the evening like a bruise. Aside from the obvious—acid baths and iron maidens—what's more uncomfortable than being pinned under an obtuse conversation by someone you knew in high school, before you were actually you?

Later that night, after the last of the hangers-on departed from our house and the free food they had come for—unabashed chubbies almost every one of them, devouring piles of potato salad and oblongs of garlic bread—my mother and I stood in the now-hushed dimly lit kitchen. The aluminum buffet trays of leftover food sat stacked on the stove, bags of bread in the corner, wine bottles making a city on the countertop.

I said, "Well, the worst is almost behind us. After the funeral tomorrow the worst of it will be done."

"For you, yes."

And I told her then of my vision: of her happy and dancing, living out the last thirty years of her life with a pre-plastic-surgery Kenny Rogers.

"You're a dreamer, dear."

She made a move to put the cleaned dishes back in the cupboard, but then thought better of it and instead sat at the island counter, pulling off earrings and rings.

"Now's your turn to get spicy," I said.

"You need a haircut and shave, Charles. Father Henry will think you're homeless tomorrow at the funeral."

I loosened the tie still snug around my neck, the very tie, I wouldn't remember until much later, that Gillian had bought for darling Dad on one of his ungrateful birthdays.

"Did you see your cousin Sammy tonight at the wake? He looks drug-addicted."

Nothing important, I could see, was going to get talked about. How much suburban realism can a family take? And who had the energy?

"Was that Mindy I saw? Mindy what's-her-name? Your first girlfriend?"

I grinned. What could I do?

"Her acne never cleared up."

She left me alone in a kitchen I had eaten in perhaps twelve thousand times. I couldn't decide whether to sit, stand, or squat. And then I realized—because apparently I had been incapable of a realization prior to this moment—that I hadn't eaten anything with nutrients since dinner with the Hammersteins in Colorado ten days earlier. What I felt then was more than a sudden hunger after weeks or months of living like a slob. Think of a termite let loose in a lumberyard: I assailed the baked ziti, lasagna—not the beef slices—cold vegetable medley, and buttered Italian bread with the can-do outlook of a goblin intent on regurgitation, and then drank an ungodly amount of merlot (you ever seen a milk-drunk newborn with a dangling head and those stars in his eyes? that was me) so that the sensation I finally went to bed with—crabbing sideways down a too-narrow hallway—came close to what a Brahmin must feel on the verge of Vedic bliss.

During the night, hours or minutes or perhaps mere seconds after I lay on my boyhood bed, I was awakened by what I heard in my furry wine-sleep as a moan or groan, from down the hall in the direction of my mother's room. I did what one does upon hearing said moan or groan in bed in the nighttime: I lay cadaver-still and listened hard for another. When I thought I heard one I tiptoed to the door and peered down the dark hall; my mother's own bedroom door was ajar, an almighty moonlight knifing through the crack.

Why I crawled down the carpeted hallway, nearly on my stomach in a covert commando mode, instead of walking upright like a respectable biped, I cannot say exactly, but my guess is that I was aware—on some level I am not frequently in touch with—that I perchance might be confronted with a display too repellent for words. Such as what, for example? I didn't know: my mother in sorceress garb trying to converse with the spirits; my mother on her mattress with a battery-operated pleasure utensil; my mother counting prescription pills to determine how many she would require to discontinue her respiratory function.

But what I saw was altogether different: my mother standing at the window, pondering the moon, embracing my father's bathrobe, her mouth and nose pressed into the collar, she and the bathrobe swaying, ever so slightly, as if to the music of a slow dance.

AT THE FUNERAL the following day—just as cinematic as any funeral you've ever seen on the big screen or bedroom tube: heavy sun and vast grass, deep grave and rows of stone, black duds and women in bonnets, teardrops into kerchiefs and roses on the casket—Father Henry delivered a predictably maudlin eulogy chockablock with proclamations of what Christ wants, knowledge he knows by way of personal interaction with humankind's white-robéd savior and all-around model of handsomeness. Adenoidal and lethal on logic, Father Henry had gotten too old for this. It was like listening to Jack the Ripper stutter through a sermon about the civic rights of sex workers. I was this close to pulling his plug and dishing the requiem myself, a little dirge I had rehearsed just in case: *Avoid the eventual*, I would have proclaimed. *Be neither ho-hum nor humdrum.*

But I couldn't do it because my mother and her navy-blue dress never would have forgiven me. As Father Henry nattered on about Christ's notion of eternal reward and made sentences about my father that were not true, at my side my mother nodded in agreement or esteem. I could not knock from my memory the picture of her swaying in the moonlight with my father's bathrobe. When the northbound coal train blasted along at the rear of the cemetery, the engine's rumble squashed the priest's voice for a minute or more.

The giant gravestone before us—a tri-stone? what's it called?—bore the names of my father to the right, my mother to the left, and Bartholomew dead-center, his ten-year-old body a corpse for nearly twice that long. My father didn't include me in the family plot. I was just a teenager when he had to choose this stone; even then he must have felt that I was not worthy of our bunch, that I was an embarrassment and blight. Why? What could a teenage boy have done to his father to earn such ire? Be born beneath the wrong alignment of stars? Or was he protecting me, thinking it an ugly omen for a teenager to see his name in a cemetery so many decades before his own demise (barring unforeseen car crashes and such)? Which was the truth? And why did it even matter anymore? He was erased now, there in that ten-grand crate before me, the mahogany of it lustrous in a late morning sunbeam.

Father Henry said *Amen*, I said *Amen* much too loud, the director of the funeral home concluded the service in her very sensitive voice to invite the attendees back to the chapel "for a meal the family has prepared in memory of their beloved"— I'd prepared no such thing—and then people began dispersing this way and that.

A moment later I saw him emerge from the back of the group as if a phantom from movie fog: Friend, freshly arrived from Iraq or Afghanistan or wherever he had been putting bullet holes into the enemies of America. I nearly hugged him, wanted to weep on his clavicle. His six-foot frame looked very Gucci in a pin-striped black suit and tie; his beard was gone, his hair peach fuzz, and the cologne he wore was last Christmas's Calvin Klein special at Macy's.

"Friend," I said, double-pumping his handshake. "You're here."

And then we embraced, two Comanche warriors meeting again on a mountain path somewhere in, say, Oregon.

"I'm sorry about your dad, Charlie."

"He didn't like you, Friend."

"But I liked him. And he was your dad, no matter what. You can't change that."

"How did you get here so fast? When we spoke last week you were still over there, somewhere," and I gestured right to indicate a different hemisphere.

He said he had hitched a ride aboard a Navy transport plane with a bunch of banged-up dudes coming home to convalesce, most missing limbs and other parts of import. Then he reached into a pocket and came out with an extra pair of shades, dark and bug-eye stylish, and he put them, tenderly, onto my face. My eyes felt okay for the first time in two days.

I said, "It means a lot that you're here."

"Charlie," he said, "you're the only friend I got. Which reminds me: you can stop calling me Friend in your stories. I'd be honored if you'd use my name again."

"Groot! You're back! All right."

Just as we were about to begin the catching-up that needed catching, Father Henry wobbled over saying, "Mr. Groot, Mr. Groot, I don't believe I see you in Sunday Mass anymore."

"If you'll excuse me, Father, I must offer my condolences to Charlie's mother," and Groot left me standing by the grave with him.

"Father," I said, "have you ever noticed that you're like so much toxic material on some people?"

The heat and his lard: he could barely breathe.

"Will you be coming to the meal at the hall of our church, Charles?"

A fat kid on the playground, he tried to dry his face and neck with a handkerchief, but he leaked faster than he mopped.

"Father, listen, I was thinking. We should have a Grand Inquisitor scene right now. I can play Ivan and you can be Alyosha. It's the perfect place for it. Think of the gravity it'll inject into this part of my story."

More labored breathing and his bulging eyeballs. He begged my pardon. His bulbous nose, not unlike Karl Malden's, twitched as if anticipating a sneeze. And he simply stared at me, unable to settle on the meaning of my English.

Just then, Groot sidled up beside me and inquired about the topic of our dialogue.

Father Henry said, "Charles wants a Grand Inquisitor scene to spice up his memoirs."

"Always a bad idea to rip off Fyodor," Groot said.

I said, "Are you kidding? I've been ripping off everybody from the Sumerians to the Beats, with lengthy stops in ninth century BC Greece and sixteenth century Spain."

"Charles," Father Henry said, "I've been meaning to tell you: you rather indicted me in that essay of yours, about Marvin Gluck. I never said you should kill him, dear boy."

"You kind of did. Anyway, no Grand Inquisitor scene for us?"

Across the cemetery I saw my mother get into the funeral home's limousine, and before she ducked down into the car she glanced about her left and right trying to spot her wayward son and wondering, no doubt, why he was not joining her in the limo to attend a costly buffet lunch cooked for ninety percent strangers and their ninety-eight percent ingratitude.

"Mr. Groot, please tell your friend Charles that I'm not about to stand beneath this sun and converse about the facts of Catholicism with someone who clearly believes them to be fictions. Especially not when a buffet lunch awaits."

Groot said, "That's just like your memoirs, Charlie: the tomfoolery between the fictions and the facts."

He exhumed from his jacket pocket a pouch of chewing tobacco.

"That'll do, Groot, thanks. There is no fiction in my memoirs."

Then I told the priest, he who had baptized me naked and confirmed me clothed, that now was the perfect time to make Catholicism once again a literary affair. I mentioned the long list of Catholics who knew as much: Flannery O'Connor and Walker Percy, Evelyn Waugh and Graham Greene, to say nothing of Cardinal Newman. I think I even ventured to say Dante and the good Father Hopkins.

"That doesn't sound like a long list to me," Father Henry said, clutching his Book to a boob.

"No, true," I said, "but it's an important one."

"Ms. O'Connor believed absolutely," he said. "I scoff at your accusation that she did not."

"Tobacco?" Groot said, offering the pouch of peace to both me and the priest.

"Groot, the only people I've seen chewing on that slop are marauders from the world of Sergio Leone."

"Them and me," he said. "Don't judge, Charlie, lest ye be judged. Besides, I'm starving."

"Well said, Mr. Groot. I concur. If you can convince your friend here to stop fooling about, we can all enjoy a delicious meal back at the church. I'm leaving now, Charles. Mend yourself."

"Goddamn it," I said, just Groot and me now at my father's open grave. "That was supposed to be a big scene."

We watched Father's Henry's luxury sedan wind its way out of the cemetery and into the street. The license plate said GOWGOD, the w indicating either *with* or *waterboard*, depending on how you feel about *w*'s.

"Charlie," he said, "I hope you don't mind me saying this, but you don't seem very . . . aggrievéd."

"No, I am. I'm aggrievéd."

"Oh, good. Because if you ask me, old buddy, you don't need a Grand Inquisitor scene right now. You need to come to terms with your father's death."

"What's that mean, *come to terms with*?"

"It means forgive him, stupid. Stop being pissed. He lived the only way he knew how, which is what we do as human-oids. He was such a jackass to you because he couldn't get close and risk losing another one. See?"

"Lame."

"No, buddy, not lame. The opposite of false."

That chewing tobacco was going to create stains dark enough to make Crest cringe.

"So, what are you saying?" I asked.

"I'm saying have a scene at this grave, yes, but just you and him."

"No way, pal. No talking-to-tombstone scenes. Forget it."

Nothing but silence and sunlight for a minute or more.

"I'm just glad you're back," I told him. "I know it's not yet noon, but if I don't get inebriated in the next half hour I might dwell on all the bolts and screws that fasten hurly to burly."

"Charlie," he said, "my thoughts precisely. Where's the beer?"

"My place. You still have a key?"

"That I do."

"I'll meet you there in five."

"Won't your mother miss you at the luncheon?"

Kindhearted Groot: always thinking about moms and dads.

"She'll be occupied with the tens of others. Plus I don't think she's loving me very much right now. She believes my ramshackle soul needs a makeover. I should stay out of her path."

Groot departed spitting mud-colored gunk onto the grass, and I was finally alone with my father's body. Over yonder sat the gravedigger on his tractor, pulling slowly on a cigarette, waiting for me to leave so he could commence with his casket-covering duties and maybe use his metal detector to comb the area for dropped jewelry.

I thought: *Thy soul shall find itself alone / 'Mid dark thoughts of the grey tomb-stone.*

And then: *Cry. Come on, Charles, there's your father in that coffin—now cry. Cry for him. You can do it. Just remember when you were a boy and he would take you places . . . but wait, where did he ever take you? Didn't he take you to Fenway Park for a Red Sox game when you were eight or nine? No, that was Bartholomew he took, just before his diagnosis. Well, then, think about how he would come to your Little League baseball games and take you and Groot out for ice-cream cones to the Dairy Queen on Main Street. Wrong again: that was Groot's dad. Didn't he take you fishing or something on the bank of the Millstone River? (Groot's uncle.) Or maybe hiking across some mountains in New Hampshire? (You and your college roommate.) Well, at least he came to your college graduation, remember? Wrong: he couldn't find a parking spot near enough to the ceremony and so stayed in*

the car in a handicap space next to the entrance of the field, arguing
with an associate on his car phone. Well, what about the time . . .

There weren't any, none that I could recall. But what I did
remember was this: the plenty of times I should have been a
more caring son. Nothing causes guilt like a coffin. And we
offspring everywhere are a plague upon our makers.

9. THE MISSIVE AS MISSILE

WARPED BEYOND NORMAL civilian standards and need-ing gentle reprieve from gals and dads and my migrant task of exploring hither and yon, tit for tat, I, Charles Homar, driving home from the cemetery in order to meet Groot and drink beer before noon, imagined said-and-done and doing thus: climbing into bed after so many months of obnoxious muddle and staying asleep for seven days, maybe more. Sweat out diverse toxins of the soul-clobbering sort, eat nothing, dream of Gregorian chants and their peaceful reach, and feel, even in blackout, a recupera-tion occurring, a restoration hard and right and, I would hope, irreversible. A man—yes, I was a man still; Rich Lombardo and the Twins of Twat, not to mention dead Dad, had done noth-ing to turn me away from that info—can take only so much pandemonium before the cells get sick and call for nourishment. You can read about Victorian heroines in brick-like novels who suffer similar bedridden stints, usually after witnessing their hoped-for beau kiss the gloved hand of some other dame. The zombie in me would amble to the toilet and sip from the faucet when needed, and would snooze again before my body was back in bed: the bed Gillian and I had shared for what seemed epochs, her scent still rubbed into the sheets but having no ill effect upon my gaping slumber or the unruffled dreams therein. How a person goes from a flipped-out dope to an indifferent slouch would be alchemy I could not speak of, though I'd thank some deities for the emotional nullity that had taken control and made me yawn. Sometimes, folks, sickness is a blessing.

Then I'd wake after seven days, the mattress wet halfway through, and feel a cannibal's hunger for meat and bone. In a bathrobe and slippers I'd haunt through my condo in this newly rested state that would be, I imagined, what coma patients experience upon rising from their own drawn-out naps: phantasms with purpose. Maybe such sleep would erase my recently established apathy and I'd wake with commanding Gillian urges undulating inside me. My specter in the mirror would look emaciated, yes, and my hair—I couldn't think upon it—but I would have flowing inside my torso and limbs a tranquillity known to certain saints or Franciscan friars. I'd never mind the mountain of mail on the counter, all those bills and fan or nonfan letters; never mind, too, the shriveled fruit in the fridge, or the sepulcher silence of those rooms—the sun would shine in scattered lanes through the sliding glass door and make all my chromosomes at ease. I'd feel simply grateful that before she had scrammed, Gillian, with her computer prowess, had set up all of our bills to be automatically deducted each month from my checking account: voilà. Otherwise, I would have arrived home from prison and then from scampering around the nation only to find dead electric and water, gas and phone, my house no better than a hut in Zimba-

bwe. I'd have practical, citizen-like thoughts just then, my first
in heaven knows how long, and this, I reckoned, would speak
well for my recovery and possible success as a person.

And then my transformative shower, the first in ages: I
would recline in the tub and let the strong stream cuff me for
half an hour at least. This tub and I had seen upset, sure: first
on the day Gillian had split and I sat in a frosty pond attempting to control my temp, and then on the evening Romp lathered here with his lizard loose and quizzed me on Bigfoot lore.
But that was there, way behind, and here I would be now,
peering frontward to . . . what? Be a Celt, worship rocks? I
wouldn't be able to say or even venture a prudent guess, and it
wouldn't matter all that much because I'd savor the calm that
had crept into me and set up camp. Another long nap would
be in the cards.

Here's what else occurred to me during my several-minute
drive back to my condo, thoughts via my incidents with Sandra McDougal, Morris Hammerstein, and Rich Lombardo:
most advice means zilch on this orb, and most men and women
stumble along to an internal tune that offers no nexus even
to half-thawed logic; we will do what we will do and allow
our unwanted saga to play out in whatever way it will, hoping
for a conquest without any discernible way to achieve it. You
might commune with others for whom this is consummately
untrue, those who know how to absorb advice and fuel appe-
tite and then turn it into triumph—the heroes from the history
of civilization are cases in point, Shackleton and so forth. But I
was me and not them, in this moment and not heroic. We have
no answers to the bile boiling in the hearts of others because
we have no answers to our own. But we delight in talking

and declaring *Do that* and *Do this*, when some major circumstances will have their way regardless of what we do or do not do. This sounds like predetermination or something parallel to the funk of fortune, I know, but all I mean to say is that a human being is an oblivious ape in the grip of nonsense, which is exactly what Sandra, Morris, Lombardo, and even Groot imparted to me: nonsense. They should have simply shut up and said good luck over a bowl of soup. There never had been any valid method for me to win back Gillian. Surrender felt so soothing.

BUT OH, CHARLES, you, speak not too soon or consign to stone any hasty worldview . . . I've prattled of Providence before: the animal that he or she or it is had some more to say to already beleaguered me, altering my calm and dumping in front of me some more mud to wade through. Pulling into my driveway, I saw Groot on the front porch, and on his lap a yellow package with, I saw as I advanced, transcontinental stickers slapped about it diagonally. The organ in my skull went *hmm* and *err*, and when I reached out to retrieve the rectangular heft he was handing, I saw the addressee it was intended for—yours truly—and the terra from which it had traveled: New Zealand. Yes, that terra and my new terror, the very place where Gillian and Jacobi had hit land with the first-ever living giant squid. Lord above. Groot: flabbergasted. Me: vexed. The both of us looked absurd in our funeral duds.

Try to grasp what my inner middle parts were up to during that minute or more I held the package as if it were a meteorite with a message for me: think of the clicks and clacks a broken machine makes. How long had it been sitting there on the porch? Throughout my father's viewing and funeral? During my exploits with the Hammersteins and Lombardo? As I chased flying saucers with Sandy or Sasquatch with Romp? What data did it contain, and how did that data relate to my new decision to be inactive, Benedictine? I much preferred to ask these questions rather than tear into the package and glimpse my new fate, whatever it was, whence-ever it came. It also occurred to me that this could be the scam of some rapscallion intent on raking up the bottom of me, alarming my quiet and causing fret. I was accustomed to getting missives and emails from readers of all stripes both pissed and pleased—had some lunatic been reading my chronicles of Gillian and the squid and, in his or her evilness, decided to disrupt the newfangled me who wanted to be left in peace? Say it isn't so.

And say, maybe, that this in my mortal grip wasn't actually a package from Gillian Lee, notifying me of the life-altering and astral. Where would my ninny self find the mettle to slash it open and examine its contents?

"Groot," I said, "I am holding a package, as you can see, possibly from Gillian. Fear and other uncouth emotions prevent me from reading it. Once again, please advise."

"I guess we're not getting drunk now," and he spit tobacco into my mulch.

"Affirmative," I said.

The sunshine was on his buzz cut and I saw the silver grays here and there throughout his blond, indication that the two of us were not curlicued lads anymore. But hadn't we been nine-year-old boys just the other day, biking all over town, bubble gum and SuperBalls in the cave of Ali Baba, fishing poles down by the river, snow forts in winter and such? Where lived the Gorgon who snatched it from us so suddenly, and who paid her to pilfer?

"Charlie, I've been a failure with advice, an inadequate pal. Only a prostitute could cheer us up, preferably a Samoan tart accomplished in maternal coddling."

"Groot," I told him, "you've been a damned fine buddy. Don't torment yourself over my staggering. We have a new mission upon us and I need your input."

Me, the doofus: I kept feeling the package in my hands as if I could determine its weight and thereby its meaning.

"We don't have to open it, Charlie. We can just drop it in the trash and get drunk like planned. We don't have to describe this part of the day at all. Leave it out of your memoirs."

(An aside: Readers had been chiding me over email to describe more, to be more responsive to stimuli and thus more exact in my written descriptions of how phenomena look and sound and smell. They seem to think that shoe size and ear shape matter; but honestly, I'd rather omit the uselessly precise details and just tell what happened action-wise. I don't believe shrewd old Sophocles ever reveals Oedipus's brand of toga or the Aegean green of his eyeballs.)

For many minutes we two sat and stood there on my front porch in benumbed quiet, looking over each other's shoes and waiting, I think, for cerebral something-or-other.

"Well," he said, "let me see again said package. Is anything inside ticking?"

"A bomb?" I asked.

"I rule out nothing. If I'm not thorough in the field, it could mean my ass and the asses of those in my charge. God is thorough, too, from what I hear, although evidence for that is scant."

"Nothing is ticking," I said, and finally led him inside to the kitchen table—our third such meeting at this table—and to think, when I ordered the thing on sale years ago from an IKEA catalogue—just prior to Gillian's moving in to turn my emptiness full—I did not imagine that dialogues so distressed and dour would take place around it. Who does?

"There it sits," said I, and pointed to the manila beige of the package giving off vibes from the tabletop.

"Are you serious? You really want to open this package?"

He looked over to the fridge, wanting beer and not this thing we were doing.

"Well, half serious anyway. I find that being half of anything is often sufficient. Let us proceed."

He said, "Shit. All right," and loosened his tie. "It's from New Zealand for sure," bending over the table to inspect it. "And it's surely addressed to you. There's your name, see?"

"Yes, thank you, Groot."

I stood behind him, peering over his shoulder, just in case the package emotion-exploded and got me messy—messi*er*.

"It's a manuscript of some kind," he said. "What about the beer?"

"Please focus. I'm coiled in anticipation here."

With that, Groot whipped out a butterfly knife from his jacket pocket, flapped it about swiftly, and with the alacrity of a TV chef he sliced into the manila to reveal a rubber-banded mass of pages. I could see immediately that they were written on in Gillian's exquisite cursive, handwriting in ink that could have won awards; it was as recognizable to me as her teeth and wide tuft of pubic hair. If you gave me six hundred English words on a scroll of papyrus, each one handwritten by a different human or dexterous chimp, I could tell you in thirty seconds or less which word was penned by Gillian.

That, people, is the definition of love. Try it sometime.

Groot had the document in hand at the table; I stood several yards from him, my nucleus all jolt and jounce, and after some breathing I was able to ask him the contents of what he held before him.

"A letter," he said, "of length and ardent."

Gasp. "A letter?" Gulp. "About?"

"Well," he said, fanning through the pages, "it looks . . . as if . . . it's a register of what occurred on the squid-hunting voyage. Assiduously detailed, from what I can tell. Divine penmanship. Narration, exposition, dialogue. Melvillean through and through."

Melvillean. Oh, no. I was privy to those potboilers.

I asked, "What's this mean? Where am I?" and began taking slow steps backward.

"On a threshold, apparently. This may be a speedy analysis, but from what I know of the world, the female of our species doesn't indulge in a journal this voluminous, and then share said journal with her estranged lover, unless that female intends to come together with that lover."

My face must have uttered *My God* because Groot said, "Yes. My God, indeed. It'll take you two hours to read this thing."

The bottom half of my body decided to sit at this point, right there on the hardwood floor, in an avenue of sunlight cutting in from the sliding glass door. Think of how far that sunlight had traveled to find me there in the kitchen. Something concussed from the region around my spleen.

"I cannot read that record, Groot. Moses came down from Mount Sinai aged about sixty years. Look at my limbs: they are each a-tremor."

"Yes, I see your point. Then I shall read it to you. I read to a group of Iraqi schoolchildren last month in Baghdad. They seemed to think me a talented rhymester."

"That's touching," I said, and watched Groot sit at the infamous kitchen table and ready himself with throat-clearing and seat-shifting for some oration of the Arabian variety.

And so prepare now, people, for my summary of Gillian's mesmeric account of high-seas rollicking and scientific stratagem, as told to me by my friend Groot (formerly-known-as-Friend-formerly-known-as-Groot), as told to him by Gillian Lee (formerly-known-as-the-about-to-be-Gillian-Homar), in her own steady hand. After this you, too, will be thinking thoughts celestial and unsullied, most of which have to do with reunification, some of which with the sempiternal. Brace yourself.

ONCE UPON A time, about four months earlier (not too long after Charles had returned from Virginia on a murder mission), a fair and at times not-so-fair maiden named Gillian Lee set sail aboard a vessel called *The Kraken* in order to become the only individual ever to detain a living giant squid, a magisterial (although some would say abysmal) cephalopod dubbed in Latin *Architeuthis* (pronounced, remember, Ark-i-tooth-iss), forty feet of slippery skin cruising in the unreachable depths of its oceanic home. The maiden felt electrified and nearly ablaze by this possibility; a decade of want and wish had materialized in the form of Jacob Jacobi, celebrated squid hunter who had appeared on PBS television and fielded questions from Charlie Rose and his civilized hair. As everyone knows, this means he was an expert. The maiden Gillian could not pinpoint the precise moment she became so enamored of the obdurate cephalopod, but guesses that her life's dream to capture it has its origin in her father's reading aloud to her *Twenty Thousand Leagues Under the Sea* when she was five years old. Of course: her father; big surprise (even though this maiden's suitor had published in an essay the "fact" that the maiden had no grave Big Daddy issues; the jackass should have known that every maiden on earth has grave Big Daddy issues).

Also, there was this: Marvin Gluck's suicide had put her in touch with mortality, the Reaper Grim most of us spend our lives pretending does not exist or else is too busy to care about certain voters. Round and round goes the clock; if she did not pursue her trophy now, when? A woman does not have an ETA on the Reaper Grim's coming by her home with his rusted scythe in one hand and a contract in the other. Would she have accomplished her goals? Would she have journeyed and asserted?

Gillian Lee was not capable of spotting the oddity of her life's pursuit; she felt remarkably at home pondering the giant mollusk's gnashing beak and two feeding tentacles; whether it swims headfirst or tailfirst (you can't tell its head from its ass, which should be a clue as to its intelligence); whether it hunts in packs or in James Dean fashion: she pondered everything about this ammonia-scented outrage (it uses ammonia sacs to remain buoyant), which might or might not change colors in order to communicate with squid brethren. She wondered, *What does it munch on? How does it breed? It is ferocious or docile?* (Charles Homar had similar questions for certain members of society.) She harbored only some remorse for the asperity of her decision to leave with Jacobi, and for the melancholy and rut she cast upon her fiancé by doing so. A woman must be resolute when it comes to her dream. If she favored an invertebrate over the sometimes-vertebrate called Charles, well, then, she didn't pick her passion: her passion picked her (this sounded to Charles like hogwash, a whole lot of mystical gibberish). How could she make him understand and see? She feared she couldn't. This class of passion had chosen but few mortals since the time of Aristotle, who himself had written of the squid and called it "teuthos." (Did everyone have something to say about this swimming heap of gunk?)

The morning she set off from the dock in Maine for the oceans of Newfoundland, New Zealand, and Antarctica, the weather rained gray (as Charles himself was well aware; he was there at that very dock trying to sink the ship with a rifle). Gillian whimpered as the vessel pulled from port; she stood on the stern and watched as a police boat fished Charles Homar from the bay he had plunged into for reasons that evaded everyone. But her whimpering was brief; she had a job to do now, preparations to put forth belowdecks, coordinates to check and coffee to make, plus literature to consult: the papers of Frederick Aldrich, giant squid pioneer; the seminal theses of Gilbert Voss from the University of Miami; the singular designs of Professor Japetus Steenstrup, Danish marvel; stories by that kook H. G. Wells, who called the colossal cephalopod *Haploteuthis ferox*, meaning (Charles thought) one unruly bitch of a squid; the section in *Dr. No* where Bond, James Bond, battles the multiple arms trying to wring him; and, of course, the Arthur Clarke novel *The Deep Range*, which was where Jacobi had stolen the idea of bringing a pen aboard his ship to house the giant squid.

At first the maiden felt an integral part of the team, even though she was but the only female aboard: she manned the sonar and satellite equipment and checked for fathoms and the other data Captain Nemo told her to check for. She was a teuthologist, was she not? True, she had acquired no degrees and published no papers, but she had push and knowledge far exceeding the typical laywoman. The men considered her input as the kibitzers gathered round the computerized map and charted trajectories, possible feeding routes, and anything else chartable. So what if they asked her to make another pot of coffee? Someone had to do it, and heaven knows she herself had become addicted to the bean. In the letters Jacobi had been exchanging with Gillian before their departure (those clandestine letters were still a source of wallop for Charles), he assured her that she would be needed on this hunt, that her contributions would be valued, even above those of his enthusiastic grad students and henchmen who wanted nothing else than to please him.

Sometime during the end of the first two weeks at sea, the maiden began to suspect that Jacob Jacobi believed in the rights of others to gratify him but in very little else. Once or twice in the kitchen, the back of his hand brushed against her buttocks (the mention of these buttocks caused a torrent of lust to whirl up inside our narrator). During their chats about the migratory patterns of *Architeuthis*, Gillian caught him peering down into her cleavage (sacred nadir!), or else fixating on her lips, or trying to catch a whiff of her scent, hearing nothing of her own carefully considered ideas. One evening during a medium-level serious storm, while the men were on deck tending to ropes and tarps, to satellite dishes and mechanical winches, some yelling, "Batten the hatches," Jacobi ordered Gillian below lest her prettiness be fouled. Well, he was a man, wasn't he? But he had promised equality, goodwill, an absence of distortion, disguise.

And then, alas, one evening during their third week, in the mid-Atlantic en route to England to stop for supplies, after an un-Italian meal of meatballs and pasta, Gillian had overheard this dialogue between Jacobi and one of his more vestigial goons (and for some reason Groot decided to recite the following in a pirate's brogue):

"So, Cappin, are ye pokin' our fair lady? She be a piece, Cappin."

"Aye, so yer cappin is, matey. Me own squid plumbs her salty depths."

"I knew ye were a-knowin' her in the biblical way, Cappin. I see the way she looks at ye."

"Aye, mate, so 'tis. A feller needs a fair lady 'long for such a voyage so his loins might be eased."

"Shiver me timbers!"

"Aye, matey."

"She yaks a bit much, Cappin. You know how they say 'bout women and tykes: seen not h'ard. She be an ornery lass, Cappin. Perhoops she be on her monthly vis'tor."

"Aye, but what a pair of teats, matey!"

"Aye, indeed, Cappin! Arrrr."

Jacobi was—shocker—a pervert.

For Gillian, hearing this conversation was like being jerked back into the Dark Ages; she contemplated mutiny, sensed a miasma rising off the sea to engulf the ship; she wished pain and rankle upon Jacobi, a death slow and malodorous, his body desecrated. Were all men infected with a sexual pestilence of the sort that permitted them to crave nothing else within earshot of a female? ("No in thunder!" Charles shouted.) She had thought only adolescent boys concocted fiction of boning girls in order to impress their fellow jocks on the football field. Apparently not, and this news flash jarred her into a kind of disquiet that made her long to hop overboard and paddle home. How could she have been so delusional, so utterly trusting of someone she knew only through a book and some correspondence (all of it an insult to the lumber industry, Charles thought)?

Her choices were not many; they would soon be in England—after a squidless trek up and down the real estate of Newfoundland—where she could go AWOL if she wanted, but that seemed an insult to her every squid-related wish. Like any given heroine from a special-effected action movie, she opted to stay and fight, perhaps saying to herself, "Every woman dies, not every woman really lives," and this in the fake Scottish twang of that twit Mel Gibson in *Braveheart*. Meanwhile, she pondered the miscellaneous among us, how smart turns to dumb, and valor to some other substance they haven't named yet. A week or so later they were motoring along the northern coast of New Zealand—the jagged green hills and toothéd white rock in coves like a photo of what you want bliss to be—the ship abuzz with male/female unpleasantness of the sort that has beset us every day since climbing down from our arboreal beds. But Gillian Lee felt convinced that *Architeuthis* awaited her in those ice-cubed waters of Antarctica, not the temperate tides of where they were. In fact, it was she who suggested to Jacobi that, according to her research, the giant squid was not likely to be caught anywhere along the equator this time of year: they must venture south into the frigid midnight blue. His response: first to guffaw, pat her on the shoulder as if she were a witty youth, and claim that *his* research indicated New Zealand; and second, to consult some computers, change his mind, and pretend that Antarctica had been his target all along, that he had been merely testing her predatory aptitude and giant squid know-how. What could she do? She must inter this resentment and wrath and stay lighted on the goal; all else fell ancillary to *Architeuthis,* including her pride, self-respect, and the liberties of cerebral women everywhere.

When Jacobi invited himself to her cabin one night after the others had tucked in, she told him thus: "Come to my cabin and you'll find scissors in your zipper." (From his spot on the kitchen floor Charles chanted, "Hurray" and "You go, girl.") The maiden Gillian shook off the fatigue from weeks of seafaring and dealing with common cretinous male misbehavior. She took up a journal, continued to work the sonar equipment and satellite system; she studied her papers and volumes, brewed coffee for herself and shared none with the others. And yes, yes, she thought often of her separated suitor, her male Penelope waiting, the warm goodness and special center of him, so unlike these gangsters making comments about her menstrual cycle and mammary glands. (The separated suitor ordered Groot to read that part twice more and then he spanked himself across both cheeks to make sure he was not daydreaming. *You mean* hope? he thought. *You mean* me?)

When they reached the Antarctic Ocean, Jacobi's draft called for reinforced nylon nets once the sonar revealed an organism of proper girth swimming at the known knots. Gillian assured him that this was asinine, an idea straight out of prehistory: dragging nets once a signal was found would only scoop up every piece of ocean riffraff they were not looking for. Did she have a better idea? he wondered. Yes, in fact she did: they must trawl with deep sea lines, maybe two thousand meters long or longer, each one outfitted with thousands of baited hooks. They had come prepared with such equipment and bait, why not use it now? For the love of Christ.

"I'll call the shots on this ship, little lady. You just sit pretty and make sure we can see your thong panties sticking out of your pants."

Gillian Lee had never gone Joe Frazier on another person before, but once she began left-jabbing and right-hooking, she found it quite natural indeed: Jacobi's potbelly and overall fire-hydrant physique prevented him from even raising his hands in time to fend off her waylay. Little lady? As she punched his face overmuch, his eyes went startled and starved like those you see on vagabond Afghan herders in the pages of *Smithsonian* magazine. He collapsed to the deck bleeding from both lips and nostrils, whimpering promises of better conduct, Christian and commendable. Soon his eye sockets would swell and he'd need six ounces of raw mackerel just to see again. The ruffians standing sentry on the tower did not cheer, but neither did they rush to Jacobi's rescue; Gillian pointed at them as if to say, *You're next, scum. If you don't watch it, you're next.*

And then, in the most phallic moment she had ever known, she grabbed the twelve-gauge pistol-grip shotgun from the top of a nearby crate, pumped a shell into the chamber, and fired a shot into the air above them. Jacobi whimpered as if in Pampers; the ruffians on the tower ducked as people tend to do around gunfire. The look just then in Jacobi's swelling eyes declared his astonishment that a woman would resort first to fisticuffs and then to wielding a firearm with intent to rend.

"You think you buckaroos are the only ones who know how to use a gun? You forget I was raised in Virginia? My daddy taught me to shoot, and I *will* shoot the next bastard who disrespects me, who thinks I'll model some thong."

(Charles cheered from his spot on the floor.)

Jacobi corrected his crooked conduct and began deferring to Gillian as if she were a bonneted big sister. Two weeks later, they spotted the signal they were searching for, in Antarctica's Ross Sea—an endless expanse of ice sheets over blue water, air gelid enough to rearrange your particles—and at the precise longitude/latitude that Gillian had predicted it would come. The baited lines were lowered and trawling began; a medium-level electric hum permeated the boat and Gillian felt it down to her toenails. (Charles wondered aloud if she still painted them a pinkish orange in homage to *Architeuthis*.) They trawled for days like that, tense with expectancy and hope, until finally the computers went beep, the underwater cameras went flash, the trawl poles bowed, and the ship buckled . . . and when they raised the lines it emerged from the black morning water writhing and pissed, eyes like black gym balls, forty-five feet of piscatorial grandeur, nearly a ton of tentacles and body glistening in the faintest reaches of the rising sun, much redder than she had ever thought possible, yes, devil-red, the odor a crushing ammonia wake-up, and, God in heaven, how Gillian Lee stared and cried as the creature splashed on the surface and snapped its massive beak. Birth was like that, people; our maiden had given birth and the chemicals free in her blood now were the chemicals of love. She knew it, *she knew it*, knew it would be here in these icy pits of ocean, mating in the comfortable cold, hiding from its archenemy the sperm whale, feeding on smaller species of squid and damn near anything else it saw. Jacobi had wanted to priss about unproductively in the waters of southern New Zealand; they'd still be there now, scratching their asses, devoid of this glory.

And what a glory it was! They swung the crane and lowered the giant squid onto the deck, where it slipped and wriggled and slipped some more, and they battled to disentangle it from the hooks and lines, careful not to get snagged by a suction-cupped apparatus and become shredded breakfast wagging in the razor beak of this beauty. The length and heft of it—Gillian simply could not believe her eyes blinking fast in the mist and spray. She would have been ecstatic with a specimen half this weight; the body alone was the size of a Cadillac, the pimp-preferred kind from the seventies. Secured now with nylon ropes around its arms and enormous helmet of a tail, the squid lay placid and panting. The coral sun had floated up well past the horizon and the grad students began clicking photos in celebration. Someone called for champagne, another for caviar. Jacobi took to the controls and the trapdoor on which *Architeuthis* lay slowly parted under either side of the deck until the prize finally splashed down into the oversized holding tank and everybody cheered *Ahhh*. Gillian bellowed through tears by herself.

They radioed the Earth and Oceanic Research Institute at the Auckland University of Technology, and Jacobi told his colleagues there to burn the record books and perhaps have a sirloin ready when he arrived, medium rare, mashed potatoes, too. Gillian spent all her time now belowdecks in front of the pen's glass face, watching in wonder, in an awe unfelt since the Old Testament: the Battle of Jericho, say. She tapped on the glass and tried communicating with it—no, with *her*—and then she dumped buckets of live fish in through the tank's top and watched it nosh, the whip-like swiftness of those two feeding tentacles, what a divine exhibit of evolution. Her shaky hand scratched scores of notes, numbers, and diagrams into her tear-dotted journal.

At port, *The Kraken* received a regal greeting: scientists and professors, newspaper reporters and TV anchors, politicians and police-folk alike; and almost immediately Gillian witnessed what was going to happen in the next several weeks of media zeal and scientific nudging-into: Jacobi would take credit for all of it. Her photo would appear in some articles, yes, but not her name, and not the truth that it was *she* who had located it, *her* study and wisdom, *her* love. An identical tragedy of justice happened to that unlucky woman—see, we can't even remember her name—who had codiscovered the double helix of DNA and then got trampled into obscurity as those two felons, Watson and Crick, took all the bows. The most unforgivable fact of Gillian's sad story: once they moved *Architeuthis* from the holding pen of the ship to a more suitable tank of study at the institute, she was not permitted anywhere

near the observatory. Someone had implemented Pentagon-
like security around the maiden's squid and then treated her
as an interfering bystander. Jacobi would not pick up his cell
phone when she dialed him from her hotel room.

And that was where Gillian Lee sat now: in her hotel room,
penning this telltale missive to her divided suitor in hope of
finding Christic forgiveness and devotion not extinguished by
the foam of offense and time. Jacobi had fled with the squid
and without Gillian to the New England Aquarium in Boston a week before the writing of this letter; he had numerous
million-dollar deals in motion—with the aquarium, with the
Discovery Channel, with a New York publisher, with well-
endowed universities. After a week holed up in her hotel room,
Gillian Lee herself had hatched a plan two-thirds vengeance,
one-third virtue. Would Charles Homar meet her in Boston to
help bring to fruition this necessary revenge? Would he pardon her passion-fueled desertion and know that she had never
allowed another male near her tender center? Would he?

Some verbatim from the last two pages of Gillian's letter:

I DON'T KNOW how you can possibly forgive me, Charlie. I'll
have to fight to forgive myself. As I've sat here in this hotel room
for the past week I've been flooded with guilt, feeling stupid. I
know I've made a goddamn fool of myself. I've tried to explain in
this letter how I brought myself to do what I did, but there might
not be any adequate explanation. I would have called or emailed
but I needed to sit down and write it all out longhand, the whole
sordid story, in the hope that I might reveal something to myself.
I told you at the dock before I left that I didn't want to turn into

my mother, give up an obsession in order to be domesticated, and I still feel that: I don't ever want to be my mother. Who does? What causes me the greatest sorrow is that I didn't include you in my dream, that I didn't consider doing this together, inviting you along. Part of me has always felt that you thought my passion for the squid was ridiculous. In fact, you hinted at this a few times in your memoirs. I'm not blaming you, Charlie. I'm just trying to say that in my mind I had very firm reasons for doing what I did, and doing it without you. I see now that those reasons were wrong. I could have had our life together *and* the quest for the squid. But when Jacobi came along I was so overcome by the possibility of realizing this dream that I suppose I wasn't thinking with my brain. I'm asking you to join me in Boston to help me regain what is rightfully mine, the creature *I* found, the acclaim *I* earned. I know I have no right to ask you this, but I'm asking anyway because I don't have anyone else. I never stopped loving you, Charlie. Believe that.

BREATHE NOW. BLINK. There Groot sits at the kitchen table, Gillian's record read, her request requested. Clear your vision. Sit up straight. Pay attention. And so I did, but it was a strenuous task to coerce my lungs into cooperation; for the past five minutes or more a vertigo had been braiding up through my brain. My tongue secreted glue and so I stumbled to the faucet and drank with greed and slosh. Groot, with infinite patience, remained silent, simply stared. I had no notice of sunlight, of trees, of atmosphere and air—I'm sure they were all there, just outside my window.

And then I felt them approaching, rising, rolling: the tears that had been built up since my father's death, warm and trembly, tight in my head. I bent over the sink and let those tears gush from my nose and mouth, tremendous cries that shook my kidneys and lungs and pieces of intestine. This went on for more minutes than was manly. Groot had sense enough to leave me be, not offer aspartame platitudes. Empty now, I stood erect and still, the window before me revealing a backyard in disarray—there was the picnic table we had built—and after many more minutes of silence I said in my new-man's voice, "Groot, pack your bags. We have business bloody and long overdue in Boston."

10. RUMBLE ON THE WATERFRONT

GATHER 'ROUND, NOW. We go forth hexed, a little crest-fallen but well intentioned toward an ending always in progress, or maybe just a continuation from that to this, from there to hereabouts, defying the reaper by courting constant motion, shunning seclusion, inventing love, and then needing to see that invention light up, spin, sparkle.

How debased I felt now for having wanted to suspend my quest for Gillian, abandon my aims in favor of what I could do with Webster's idea of *laze* and *loaf*. How unworthy. I had bungled along in a creamy fog of dashed romance, yes, and snubbed reality for that jocund green light at the end of Gillian's dock. Okay. Weary indeed it made me, helter-skelter all over this grand nation, from Virginia to Maine, even to prison, then from Bigfoot's woods to Sandy McDougal to Morris Hammerstein to Richie Lombardo and the Dildo Duo. In cowardice I had wanted to choose retreat and rest, not realizing that such a choice was tantamount to comatose or else turning to ash. My father's death didn't help, not a bit.

Those were my harebrained views in the passenger's seat of Groot's Ford Bronco—a red thing unfashionable and angry, murder on the ozone—the two of us on Interstate 84 trucking northeast through Hartford. We were, indeed, on our way to meet my Gillian, she who would swab the sewage of me, she who was due to arrive the next morning at Logan International piping with rage and planning a retribution only a fifth century Greek could appreciate. Orestes, say. Groot had seen fit to bundle in the back firearms and a combustible cache I was too enervated to inspect. He said he could tell from Gillian's dispatch that we would need them during our palaver with Jacobi, that my gal had .50-caliber bullets and grenade shrapnel on her mind, all the holy cow and tallyho you can count. Me: I was thinking of rose petals and no more nights alone, of never again uttering the terms *affliction* and *avalanche*, and of what Hansel did for that nymphet Gretel. Still stunned by this epic turnabout and the fact that Gillian had come to her senses and wanted me back, I shook off cumber and looked to the other side of my offal. Heavens above.

As Groot motored on in Neal Cassady mode, I read Gillian's letter myself, tried to ignore Mick Jagger's throat, and perspired with a fusion of disbelief and glee. We were children unhinged, not nearly adult, reaching for an apogee that might disintegrate as soon as we grabbed it. Adults, I've been told, do not thrive on frenzy; they go to work, avoid the preposterous. I did not consider what lunacy Gillian wanted us to perform at the New England Aquarium, only what she would think of my hair and complexion and clothes, how we would embrace and smooch upon first seeing each other after so long a spell, and the ease allowed to my ulcerated self. Groot, I could see, wanted a warpath gory enough to satisfy some slighted Iroquois, just itching to shoot someone, his countenance stern and of singular purpose, amped up as if on amphetamines. The love I felt for him just then puffed within me and almost pushed out tears. Our entire twenty-five-year friendship had been cloudless. What a pal. I felt just faintly less remorseful than Judas for saddling him with this glut and lade, but what could I do? We were both actors for a begetter who could not think more fondly of his project. Promethean players, our stolen fire inward and hotter than equatorial Africa.

"Gilgamesh and Sir Gawain and King Arthur," Groot said after a swath of silence. "Robin Hood and Van Helsing. Also the Americans Luke Skywalker and Rambo. Let's get zippy."

"What makes Luke Skywalker American, pray tell?"

"His accent, for one. His California looks, for two. Also his propensity for humdinger and making merry. Need I continue?"

"Please, no."

"Here, put this on," he said, and tossed into my lap a piece of black fabric with two holes cut into it.

"What's this?"

"Your Lone Ranger mask. I have one, too."

"Groot," I said, "I'm not wearing a Lone Ranger mask and neither are you."

"We need to hide our identities. Plus, you know, I'm the Lone Ranger."

"No," I said. "You're not."

Back at my condo we had changed out of our funeral clothes and were now donning inconspicuous summer duds, he in frayed cut-off jeans and a Rolling Stones T-shirt, and

I looking—should I even say?—aggressively adorable in a pinkish polo shirt and pressed khaki shorts. Groot found it necessary to wear his combat boots, I my flip-flops.

With trees and rock faces blurring by outside our windows, Groot informed me thus: "Goethe once wrote that the secret to life is living."

"Leave it to Goethe. That's like saying that the secret to fish is fishing."

I fiddled with the vents so the cool air would come my way and leave me smelling unlike sleaze.

"Hey," he said, "let's stop for some belly-timber, a burger or hot dog or something made in a laboratory. By the way, how are you feeling right about now? I'm guessing your head's in a storm."

"I feel strange, yes."

"We didn't even say goodbye to your mother, ya know."

"I know, thanks. Let's stay focused here. Those guns in the back make me nervous. It's like I'm forever in an ad for the NRA."

Mick Jagger squalled through the speakers with his philosophy of satisfaction for the maniacal among us. What was his point exactly? Groot asked why the guns caused me fright.

"Oh, I don't know, Groot, maybe because I sat in prison for a while because of a gun and, oh, let me see, they *kill people*."

"Precisely. People might need some killing. You remember that movie we loved as teenagers, the one with Christian Slater, before his career went into the crapper, called *True Romance*? His character said, *It's better to have a gun and not need it than need a gun and not have it*."

"That *is* logic hard to argue with," I said.

"Just trust me, Charlie. A gun in the hand of the right individual makes living a more easeful affair."

My father's coffin was right then being lowered into the ground. The scenery outside my window, rocks and trees and houses on a hill, went by me *swish, swish*. Far off down in a valley I spotted, for just two seconds, a large dog sprinting after . . . what? A fox? Freedom? The earth felt tilted. Mack trucks growled everywhere.

"Hi-Ho Silver!" Groot said, and I think I sneezed.

Our lunch break: for those emailers who like to criticize my quote paucity of socioeconomic insight unquote—apparently I was not Balzacian, too self-consumed and solipsistic to pay any heed to issues larger than my own sacked heart—let me say thus: What a depressing rest stop it was, just south of Boston on Route 90, all those overweight and half-asleep consumers jamming lard into their pie-holes, their Nosferatu tanks swigging gasoline, most of them hideously dressed and far from pretty, buying plastic trinkets, oblivious to the Lilliputian migrant Latinos dancing behind mops and rags wet with toxic soap. The place was sadness personified, screwing with my high.

"Groot," I said, "hear me out: I feel mephitic. I'd rather consort with criminals than witness this American ugliness."

Samaritan that he is, Groot stuck a five-dollar bill into the grip of a pregnant sixteen-year-old with bloodshot eyes, washing windows with one hand, holding her belly with the other.

"Let your child be among the killers and not the killed," he said.

She rejoined with a face that called many questions, only a few of which applied to the molecules of this world.

No time to tarry, we chowed our lunch in the truck doing eighty-five into Boston. The midday summer sun took no prisoners, and in my abdomen a jangle indicating anxiety. My inner monologue consisted of: *Breathe, think*, and then back again. But think what? Wasn't thinking for those who hadn't already gone down the rabbit hole with Alice? Groot had made reservations for the night at a hotel he said came highly recommended by someone he had met in Bolivia. He was determined to arrive this evening, not the following morning, because he needed—*needed*—to perform surveillance on the aquarium, on Jacobi's vessel docked in the harbor, before Gillian arrived to disclose her plan to us. Every time he spoke her sacred name my enzymes went a little bonkers, and in my mind were the lines of the immortal Longfellow (lines, for some reason, that my father had been happy to recite when I was a child with no notion of tomorrow): *"Let us, then, be up and doing, / With a heart for any fate; / Still achieving, still pursuing, / Learn to labour and to wait."*

Up and doing. Ah, yes Henry, but the labor and waiting are over now, dear friend, and tomorrow is mine only mark.

WELL, NOT COMPLETELY over, I guessed, because I still had to wait at this tumbledown hotel Groot had found for us—a small manse really, circa 1810—outside Central Square in Cambridge, across the river from Boston, just blocks from those snobbed prodigies at Harvard who sat devising ways either to improve or further waste the world. The hotel occupied a quarter of a block on a residential, spruce-lined street that did not feel even a centimeter urban. It had taken us twenty tense min-

utes and several wrong turns to find the dump after we got off
the Mass Pike. And what did the sign read, the one wired to
the iron gate of the hotel's entrance? It read: CAMBRIDGEPORT
HAUNTED MANSION.

"Groot, what is this?" I asked as we pulled into the horse-
shoe drive.

"It's our hotel. Nice character, right? And history. Lots of
culture."

"What's with the haunted business?"

"That's nothing. Don't worry about it. I have guns. It's
cheap, that's the main thing. Plus we need a garrison set back
from the frontlines in order to consider our tactics safely, without the chance of breached security by one of Jacobi's infantry."

How could I have responded to that? With what wisecrack
would I have retorted? The multiple pink folds of his brain
simply didn't whistle like yours and mine. Give him a subject,
any subject, and he's happy to oraculate.

As we unloaded our duffel bags, the proprietor came
through the front door and down the splintered steps to greet
us. This proprietor wasn't a back-bent old geezer in round
specs carrying a leather-bound copy of the *Malleus Malefi-
carum*, an appearance that might have been better for business.
Rather, she was a twenty-something blond almost-beauty in
painted-on running shorts, sandals, and a Red Sox T-shirt to
boot, plus two eyebrows it took hours every week to perfect.

She said, "Welcome to our haunted hotel. I'm Candy."

"You certainly are," Groot said, giving her his hand, clicking on his mojo. "My name is No Man and this is Charles
Homar, memoirist of no small fame. Maybe you've heard of
him. He's a pupil of the difference between want and need,

plus cares about the path between slaughter and salvation. When you get a chance, ask him about the word *chasmal*."

"Pleased to meet you gentlemen," she said, her voice lathered in Massachusetts-cum-Kennedy. "Charles Homar of the giant squid stories?"

"One and the same," Groot said.

"Wow. I've been following your journey, Mr. Homar."

Circumstance had rendered my tongue useless. I just stared and perhaps drooled. I was in this thing whole hog now, wasn't I? So much to celebrate, and me standing there a spiritual syphilitic, mangled mental-wise from too much tumble.

"Candy," Groot said, "forgive Mr. Homar. He's contemplating cognitive dissonance. We must be shown to our rooms anon to drop our bags. Night is coming on, no time perchance to dream, for I have some quick dealings on the waterfront."

"I hope you gentlemen don't mind, but there's a TV crew here tonight filming an episode of *Haunted Nation*. They have equipment set up," and she jabbed over her shoulder with a lovely little thumb.

"Huh?" I said. "What?"

The sun was everywhere, even this late in the day. Where was my UV protection?

Candy said, "It'll be good for business, I hope. Our ghosts have been especially active these last few weeks. You know, with the Red Sox finally winning the Series."

Groot said, "Your shades and shade hunters won't perturb us in the least, my girl."

"Excuse me," I said, and put down my duffel bag. "Pardon me," I repeated, and mashed my eyes. "I'm sorry, but this is simply a piling-on of the absurdity. I don't have the room in my narrative for ghosts. Plus I'm belletristic and can't write Stephen King litter about sprites."

"Charlie," Groot said, "as your longtime friend, I advise you never again to use the word *belletristic*."

"Okay, fine, but you see my point."

"I do not. Your namesake sang about ghosts and so did Big Willy from Stratford-upon-Avon. Also Dickens. I was forced to read their ejaculations at the Naval Academy and I'm glad I now have cause to drop their names."

"Gillian is coming tomorrow," I said. "We have vengeance to spread. I am right now, Groot, the very incarnation of unease. I cannot take a round with the unsettled souls of this hotel. So please. No more."

You should have seen that ludicrous manse/motel looming over us.

"No more?" he asked. "What does that mean? We came here for more, Charlie. Always more. What are you saying?"

Candy said to me, "We'd be delighted if you wrote about us in one of your memoirs, Mr. Homar. We subscribe to *New Nation Weekly* here."

I counted to ten as I had been once taught to do by a tranquilized someone on Oprah Winfrey's sofa.

"Let me say this real slow so everyone understands. I. Am. Not. Writing. About. Ghosts. Next thing you know I'll be writing about vampires, my narratives no better than the Anne Rice tripe clogging bookstore shelves. Plus a TV crew is here. There's albatross aplenty on my shoulders. I know that in some circles I am considered a tribute to the inadequacies of the prefrontal cortex, but I'm trying to change all that."

Groot made *what the fuck?* faces.

"Candy," he said, "would you excuse Charlie and me for just one second, please? Thanks so much, dear," and he put his arm around my shoulders to guide me to the far end of the wraparound porch. "Buddy, you and I both know that spirits don't flit through these rooms. Believe me, if ghosts existed, I would have played poker with a few by now, considering all the people I've sent from this world. And, if you don't mind my saying so, you've already written about Bigfoot and UFOs, plus a midget and a bodybuilder, and ghosts really fall into the same category, don't you think? Plus we have no time to waste looking for other quarters. Let's malinger no more."

I protested much: "Not the same thing. Sasquatch is natural and so are midgets and bodybuilders. Well, you know, not *natural*, but of this world, at least. Sort of."

Candy was all eavesdrop, inching closer on the porch.

Groot said, "People like to read about ghosts. Think of your readers. I have to go now. Unwind. And don't deflower Candy, because I plan to do that myself later. That gal is walking Viagra, all filly and no frump."

"Viagra, Groot? You're thirty-three."

"And a fan of modern science, Charlie. It's a swell day," and here he sniffed the air as if pleasantness itself had become gaseous.

"Well," he said, "I mean weather-wise, not, you know, funeral-wise, this morning and all."

He made haste to the aquarium to conduct his necessary surveillance—he knew Boston well partly because after 9/11 he had undertaken some shady national security business there, the finer points of which resulted in dead jihadists—and left me on the wooden steps with Candy, two duffel bags in my

hands, the glow of daylight about an hour from death. Four
dingbats stood in the foyer with their array of machines: a
camera guy with his camera, a lighting gal with her lights, and
the two ghost hunters themselves, both of them overweight
underachievers in their mid-thirties, the dweeby breed imagined fairly as staying up for six straight days dueling it out over
Dungeons and Dragons, nothing but Doritos and orange soda
for sustenance. Faithful to form, they even wore those dorky
black Velcro sneakers you can get for fifteen bucks at one of
Warren Buffett's many stores. The lighting gal could have
been half attractive if she gave up sweets for a month, traded
black for more summery shades, did something definitive with
that hair. The three gents, however: hopeless.

"People," I said in the lobby, "I am going up to my room
to have quiet time and contemplation before my muse arrives
in the morning. Like a shaman before ritual, I must cleanse
myself with purity of thought, also a nap. I have toiled untold
months for what is coming to me tomorrow. If anyone disturbs
me, there shall be some fairly hot hell to pay."

"We are demonologists," one of the ghost hunters said,
"and quite at home in hell."

So. He wished to draw first blood, eh?

"Buddy," I said, "if you woke up this morning feeling
brave, I promise that you will go to bed tonight feeling broken.
I have no patience for your paranormal eccentricities. Step
aside and shut your hole. Ghosts aren't real."

"Mr. Homar," Candy said, "I think you'll find your mind a
little changed after a night in our hotel."

She seemed so *serious*; I could have pinched her cheek.

"That's right," said the pudgier of the two ghost hunters,

the one with the ayatollah cloud of beard poofing down from his chin. "We've caught crazy orbs on the infrared camera and voices on the Dictaphone. We have the facts. This place has reported activity for nearly two hundred years."

"I as well have reported activity from the brouhaha that is my heart, and the spook's name there is Gillian. I repeat: shut your hole and stand aside."

But he didn't.

"This isn't a joke. We're professionals. You don't know the facts, bub. We do. The first owners of this house had a little boy who died suddenly of typhoid fever. He left the world too soon and is still here, not in peace."

"Guy," I began, "my little brother left the world too soon also and was pleased to leave it, never once coming back to say boo. He's a sluggard in the grave and glad for it. Also, if you call me *bub* one more time your overweight relatives will be visiting you in traction. I do the manly thing when I can."

"That's funny," said a ghost hunter, the heretofore silent one, "you had no problem believing in the supernatural when Gillian left. You said that in your second piece, remember, that you were willing to consult witches and magicians to get her back. Am I wrong?"

See me there thinking for six or eight seconds, a duffel bag still in each hand and five faces wanting my version of an answer.

"I was in the clutch of rumpus," I said, "not nearly responsible for my hunch. Must everyone quote my words back to me? Ghosts aren't real."

"Oh, I see," said a ghost hunter, although I'm not sure which one, since both were bomb sites of acne, split ends, and feral facial hair. "Now that your quest is accomplished, now that you've won back Gillian, you can no longer relate to those who still seek, who are still fired by passion."

"Number one: please realize, Gillian is not officially attained. Many hijinks can still ensue and cause hoopla with my heart. Number two: my object was always of this world, flesh and the blood beneath it. If you ever thought for one millisecond that you and I were alike, you should sue your doctor for declaring your brain undamaged."

An ambulance siren wailed by out front and I thought: *Come and get me*.

"Right," his partner said, "we'll just conveniently forget that you chased Bigfoot."

"Hello," I said, "Bigfoot is supposedly quite natural; nothing about him defies physics. And if you've been reading my yarns, you know that I ridiculed my prison mate for his Loch Ness Monster love affair. Ghosts are for those storytellers too bored with their lives."

"Yeah," he snickered, "ghosts and giant squids."

The flesh beneath his chin wobbled, like that thing on a turkey.

"You know, if you geeks would clean yourselves up and get an exercise program, you might be able to find females who'd be willing to date you, then you wouldn't have to invest so much energy in fantasies."

"I have a girlfriend," the cameraman declared, his voice too husky for his noodle limbs.

"Where is she?" I asked.

"She doesn't live here."

"Of course she doesn't. She doesn't live here. As in, she

doesn't live, does not exist, just like the Caspers you're running after in this hotel."

All of them: "Nunt-uh" and "You're crazy" and "Cut it out."

"Name the parts of female genitalia and how each differs from the other. Go ahead."

I waited while they glanced at each other, then at their sneakers, then at their equipment, then at the lone female, poor girl, holding the lamp. She instinctively crossed one leg over the other as if to lock her thighs together. She might have boasted of fleshiness through her hindquarters but she still had curves enough to make any half-man half-want copulation with her. A bottom not unlike my Gillian's.

"Well," I continued, "tell me if the clitoris is at the top of the vulva or at the bottom. Tell me if the labia are on the inside of the vagina or on the outside. Go ahead, tell me."

"How do we know Gillian exists?" one said. "She could be a figment of your imagination, all fiction," and the others helpfully added, "Yeah" and "That's right."

"Lord in heaven," I said, dropping the bags, "please send help," and I plunked myself down on the first step, too besieged to ascend the staircase.

I believed I looked as if I might weep again. The day had begun with the ghost of my father at his funeral and wanted to end with more apparitions. Why was no one offering me a glass of Cambridge tap water? And where was my mother just then? I studied my watch and guessed that she was back home by now, the after-funeral feast long finished, just her and a bath and Kenny Rogers on the radio.

No one wanted to speak now. Candy leaned against the desk in the lobby that seemed delighted to announce con-

CIERGE; one specter-stalking ass wandered into the sitting room to touch a sofa that looked older than Adam; and down the hall I could see the kitchen, the cupboards of which no doubt contained cobwebs in place of comestibles.

"Okay, look," I said to everyone. "I apologize for being so . . . what's the word . . ."

"Unkind?" the lighting gal offered. "Rude?"

"Yes, unkind and rude, I'm sorry. But please understand that I am under loads of pressure here. It's the ninth inning with bases loaded and I'm at the plate."

"What's the score?" she said.

That's me with the corkscrew face, asking her what in the world she could mean by such a question.

"The amount of stress you would feel in your baseball analogy would depend upon the score. Unless your team is down by four runs or less, you wouldn't be under any pressure at the plate, depending of course how late in the ninth inning we are talking here. If you're down by four you can tie the game with a home run. If you're down by three or less you can win. Anything other than those scenarios and you have no real pressure to speak of."

She leaned on her tripod lamp as if it bestowed upon her powers of win and sway.

"Even the *girls* are baseball fanatics in this city? What is *wrong* with you people?"

Candy said, "Mr. Homar, if I may change the subject for a second. Just so you know, visitors here have photographed ghosts, and also reported feeling faint, almost to the point of dizziness. Also inexplicable cool drafts. These have been documented since the 1800s."

"Candy," I said, "you are really too sweet for my foulness

right now, so forgive me, for am I agitated and excited both, more nervous than a newborn. Ghosts on film: the film is faulty and what you're seeing is an effect of light. As for dizziness: check the radon and carbon monoxide levels in your basement. As for inexplicable cool drafts: these ancient mansions were oddly constructed with poor insulators. Replace the windows and your drafts will vanish. As I am about to do right now. Excuse me, please."

She handed me the key and pointed up the circular staircase to the second floor where room number 13 awaited me. Room 13, I thought, the rascals—but to prove that I had no investment in bunk, I said nothing about it, only grinned and bowed the bow of a tuxedoed gentleman, all the while noticing those work-of-art brows arching over her eyes. Candy returned behind the concierge's counter and I started up those cavernous stairs, whereupon reaching the first landing I heard this exchange between a ghost hunter and Candy:

"Can we begin setting up our equipment on the second level?" he asked.

"Sure," she said, "let me just make sure the rooms are ready for Mr. Lombardo and Mr. Romp."

Put yourself in my skin at that moment. Can you feel it stretching over my bones and tissue like cellophane?

I hurled myself back down the stairs saying, "Excuse me, pardon me, what did you just say?"

Candy repeated her sentence and I said, "Lombardo and Romp? They're coming here? How? Why? What?"

"Mr. Groot reserved a suite for each of them and said they would arrive later this evening."

"But I don't have room for them here!"

"We have plenty of room, Mr. Homar. We have no other tenants tonight, except for the TV crew."

"No, I mean I have no room in the finale of my narrative. They'll crowd my reunion. My life is no longer about bedlam, only the blithe. Have you forgotten I'm meeting Gillian tomorrow? I need contemplation time. A shave and a haircut wouldn't hurt, either."

Candy suggested that I talk over this tantrum with Groot and so I found my phone, stepped out onto the wraparound porch, and got him on the line.

"Groot," I said, "we are moving beyond the absurd and into the slapstick. This cannot stand."

"First of all," he said, "God is a slapstick artist. Take a look around. Also, how is chasing Sasquatch through the jungle not slapstick? Second, if Gillian has in mind what I think she does, we will need Romp's cunning and Richie's creature strength. I'm doing this for you, Charlie. Besides, your readers miss Romp and Richie. Some have told me so."

"We can't just reintroduce characters because my readers miss them. And I'm not so sure they do. More important: I don't miss them. Characters must propel the narrative forward to its conclusion or else they're merely set pieces. I have to be concerned with my own development at this point, and those two nimrods have nothing more to add."

Rainbowed pedestrians passed on the sidewalk: what were *their* lives like?

"None of us really develops in life, Charlie. We only pretend to while every day satisfying our animal needs, going from want to hurt to want. I'm at the waterfront now, behind enemy lines. Work needs doing. *Hasta la bye-bye.*"

If he hadn't hung up so suddenly I would have injured him with name-calling: Nincompoop and slut. Maoist, maybe. Now that darkness had dropped, the four-member ghost-hunting crew was at turns giddy with excitement and firm with a faux-seriousness. I passed them in the second-floor hallway in front of my room and reminded them that I would be meditating in preparation for Gillian, to bollix me not, the hellish payment and the rest that would ensue. I'd be sitting cross-leggéd and straight-backed, perhaps my palms upward in case clues or pennies fell from heaven. Candy dashed around being meticulous and I asked her if she had any haircutting skills.

"I don't know about skills," she said, "but I used to cut my boyfriend's hair in college. Of course, that was with an electric trimmer. He was on the swim team."

"That will have to do. I can't meet Gillian tomorrow looking like this."

"I like the Jesus Christ/Charles Manson look on you," she said, her face suddenly fierce with a heat I could not account for. "Shoulder-length hair and a beard. It's sexy. Of course, you know Christ was one sexy motherfucker. He protects me in this place."

I had been making a habit of cleaning out my ears with my pinkies, and now was another time. Candy then let fly with a broadside of foul language that would have been welcome at any full-court game of Harlem basketball: F'n Jesus this, and Mother-f'n Moses that, and blank-sucking Paul, and blank-licking Mary Magdalene. Was she ill? It was like watching a rose wilt on time-lapse photography.

"Okay, then, Candy, thank you, dear, I'll be retiring to my room now."

Her fingers found my elbow.

"But Mr. Homar, I wanted to ask you, if you don't mind. I really am a big fan of your memoirs, and I've always wanted to write a book myself."

"Oh, Lord."

"What?"

The lighting gal wedged herself between us, in a hurry, and I pretended to be interested in her jean shorts.

"What?" Candy asked again. "Why did you say, *Oh, Lord?*"

"I said that out loud?"

I did, she confirmed.

"Candy, look, it's like this: I've always wanted to be a fighter pilot but that doesn't mean I'll buy a plane."

Usually that fighter pilot line sends them packing. Not sweet Candy.

"No, seriously," she said. "I have this book in mind, a novel, about a young woman who runs a haunted hotel and how she befriends the ghosts that live there."

"Precious," I said, "there are too many stories in America. The world doesn't need another book. And you really don't want to be a writer. Trust me."

The door to my room was right there: I could've reached over to touch it. I dangled the key between two fingers to show her how close I was to some much-needed sloth.

"But I do," she said. "I do want to be a writer."

"No, no, choose something else. I hear basket weaving is a hoot, also badminton."

"But *you* chose writing, why can't I?"

Those eyes like lozenges looked ready to water; freckles began disappearing beneath a blush.

"You think I *chose* this? To sit alone in a room, pounding keys for a pittance? You think I *like* to write? Darling, I didn't choose this. If it hadn't chosen me when I wasn't paying attention I would have preferred a life in the rodeo or else a race car. Anything but this time-consuming and head-scratching nuisance full of rejection and debt."

"But it's art, Mr. Homar."

"It's what?" I asked.

"Art."

"What is *that*?"

Her expression just then hollered animus and letdown.

"Mr. Homar," she said, "you're influenza."

And me, the moron, I replied with *thank you* because I thought she might have said *influential*.

SAFE BEHIND THE door of my antique-scented bedroom—the paintings and lamps of which were the spooky kitsch from *Scooby-Doo!*—I plunked onto an unyielding bed and attempted purification, although, truth be told, I had little idea what that meant. All I knew was that I felt donned in a snowsuit and lobster claws, a clumsy outlaw with a lot of back-and-forth to account for, a friend to human strength and weakness both, petrified of love and odium and doubting the Big Bang because it had the discourtesy to blow before I was born. She was flying back to me now, yes—right at that moment she sat buckled in an airliner over an Atlantic Ocean that had given birth to the giant squid and swallowed many a man without a burp—but would she leave me again, sometime and somehow? And was there any system in place to prevent it? Should your Charles Homar trust the damsel, walk on eggshells and risk more coronary cataclysm? Or shuck such worry of possible rupture and lunge back in, a high-diver undeterred? Yes, I was having a moment here, one of hesitation and ambivalence I've heard some heroes are prone to, and one essential to the development I lay pondering. I quantum, she cosmic.

Also, how was I going to allow this drama to conclude? Because, despite my perky nerves, I was feeling emboldened, capable of taking over and dictating the outcome, never mind what Gillian, Groot, and those caddish colossi, Romp and Richie, envisioned. Could I allow a *Wild Bunch* shoot-out at the dock, holes in boats and heads? Could I stand by and watch revenge and revolt get their due? Really, now, hadn't we seen our fair share of high blood sugar? It was my responsibility to facilitate an ending both realistic and not too unlawful, which I knew might prove difficult in my off-kilter condition. She loves me, she loves me not. She needs me, she needs me not. She won't do it again, she will do it again. Would I day in, day out be walking on eggshells?

There I lay on the bed for several hours, searching my innermost groves for something that could be called a solution, while those spirit-chasing dimwits banged about in the hallway trying to set up their spooky green cameras in order to film the dust they would later dub the ghost. The yawns came but not the sleep. This was iron deficiency or else chronic fatigue syndrome. What a morose sight: a traveler trying to nap and chastising himself for failure at it. Sometime during my indeli-

cate teen years I had picked up the notion that sleep equals
health, that sleep can fend off disease and debacle. People often
told me I did not look my thirty-odd years; this youthfulness
and brown hair-shine I attributed to a lifetime of naps and a
solid nine hours every night. That regimen had gone kaput
ever since Gillian left, and many times since then I expected a
cancer to come clobber me about the cells. Bartholomew had
never slept well, not before he got sick, not after.

Always a little depressive, "always a little in love with
death," as Eugene O'Neill has it—(always the playwrights
and poets who go loopy; memoirists and novelists are a saner
set)—I began taking ambitious naps around the time of Bart's
diagnosis. After eventful and uneventful high school days: a
nap. Before stomping boozily through town with Groot on a
Friday night: a nap. Saturday and Sunday mornings: a nap
not long after waking. Half of my college years and adult-
hood: napped away. About sleep I was a fascist, though lacking a flag. Even the lightest snowfall could produce in me an
urge for hibernation only a grizzly could appreciate the might
of. If New England's temperature sank into single digits, as it
is glad to do each winter—forget it: you wouldn't see me for a
week. Windy rain or sleet? Good night. Some people, I know,
call this depression. I call it exasperation. The nation seemed
less full of outburst after a midday slumber. Certain problems
had a way of correcting themselves while a body lay uncon-
scious. Either that or you can wake with the requisite restful-
ness in order to tackle sideways whatever trouble had come.
Going to jail had panicked me not because of the dropped-
soap sodomy you hear so much about, but because of the

noisiness you don't. My father, naturally, called me derelict
and bum, but by the time those insults started in high school
I had stopped hearing most of what left his mouth. When
I discovered that Gillian, too, was a napper, I knew I had a
booty Blackbeard himself would boat the globe for. Among
what I missed the most: ashen afternoons bandaged in goose-
down, flanneled limbs entwined, frost on the windows, and
the world far away.

But now, too wired to let sleep heal and press reset, I
dropped to the floor to pump out two minutes of push-ups for
my flagging pecs, precisely what Sylvester Stallone would have
done prior to some patriotic combat he did not want but would
later be rewarded for. Then back on the bed I finally fell asleep
in the dark, the fatigue in my flanks and femurs able to anchor
a yacht, and in my head an array of Ozian characters irking
earnest Dorothy.

All set to have a dream about something salty, I heard
through the darkness those four ghost-hunting comics pitter-
pattering outside my door, saying frantically, "It went in here,"
just before clanging into my room with green and red lights
iridescent left and right.

"Major readings," one was saying, and the other said,
"There it is, by the bed."

I had sat up by this time, not exactly with a jolt but jolty.
Career nappers will tell you: few events on earth are as murder-
inducing as an interrupted snooze.

"It's me by the bed," I told them. "You waifs. Groot has
handguns and flashlights packed in his duffel bag there. Don't
make me unzip it."

"The boy-specter is in this room," the first said. "And that's not all: he spoke to us out there. He has a name, Mr. Homar. He called himself . . . Bart. Does that name mean anything to you?"

Okay, I thought, *now it's personal*.

"Am I on camera right now? Are you filming me? Because I don't want any documentation of my gunfire, which, as you know, I have attempted to inflict upon other mortals in the past. If you're trying to hoodwink me by saying my little brother's name, try again. You got his name from one of my memoirs, you louse."

They said, almost in unison, "Nunt-uh" and "No way" and "We would never."

"I am sharp now, gentlemen, and have had my fill of randomness, I warn you. I can sniff out heresy like a parson on Inquisition payroll. Gillian's return has bolstered me with acuity. I suggest you restore the power and cut the central air."

I had fished out the flashlight from Groot's duffel bag and was shining it point-blank in their grizzled mugs. Doors banged shut down the hall and then we heard a vaporous groaning worthy of Béla Lugosi. Soon, no doubt, chains would clank.

"Explain *that*," a ghost hunter said into my flashlight.

"No doubt Candy putting on a good show."

"I'm right here, Mr. Homar," she said, and my flashlight found her there behind the cameraman.

This was fracture and interference, not at all what I wanted on hiatus from the harsh. The ghost-boy's groans amplified to a pestering pitch and I felt in need of an amulet, a crucifix, or maybe just some water mumbled over in Latin by the Pope. Then I remembered: I had a gun, even better.

When the Hardy Boys saw me snatch it from Groot's bag and load the first round into the chamber, one of them insisted poetically that "the dead don't feel lead."

"But I do," the lighting gal said, "and I'm not getting shot tonight by a trigger-happy memoirist. Either the gun goes or I go."

"Excuse me," I said, "but unless I'm mistaken, demons are trying to abuse us. Have you not seen *The Exorcist*? A gun would have solved that little fix before your fingers got grimy from the popcorn. You can find comfort in Misters Smith and Wesson. Groot does."

More boos and whines on the second floor and the TV crew whizzed out to interview the source of them. Candy followed but not before asking me to remove all handguns from the premises. I accused her of un-American attitudes and she remarked, "I don't give a flying fuck, get rid of the gun," more language that did not become her decent prairieland looks. Now I felt bad about not giving her the writing advice she had come seeking from me. She would no doubt fiddle with my bill, charge me for room service I did not receive.

Just as I was about to follow them down the hall to confront the afterlife, my cell phone lit up in the dark with a ring-a-ling. I unflipped it and said, "Groot, I'm kind of busy here. I'm about to beat some brat's ghost with either superior invective or else hollow-tipped bullets."

"Charlie," he said, "you'll have to save that lampoon for another time. We have a situation here."

"Define *situation* please."

"Oxford's?"

"Groot," I said, "please tell me that you did not, through

some tremendously good luck, overhear Jacobi and a museum lackey talking about their plan and are thus privy to important information that can affect the plotting in our favor. That's *so* nineteenth century."

"Negative. I'm standing at the harbor with Gillian, Romp, and Richie. Her plane landed this evening, not tomorrow morning. We screwed up the timing, which isn't all that surprising, seeing as how the timing in this whole narrative is screwball at best."

I guessed I wasn't responding effectively, because he said, "Do you copy, Charlie? Are you there?"

More reticence on my part. And some breathing that sounded wrong.

"Do you read me?" he shouted.

"I'm sorry," I said, "can you please repeat that sentence with Gillian's name in it?"

"She's here. Right now. With me. At the harbor by the aquarium. Operation Payback begins tonight. Romp and Richie are ready; they just arrived from the airport. Red Team is a go. We need Blue Team here pronto. Get the bags and hail a cab."

Why was *I* the Blue Team? For several long seconds I held out the lighted phone at arm's length as if I were a Clovis hunter who had just stumbled upon it during an unsuccessful mastodon raid. My bladder and sweat glands declared their primacy; some bones in my shoulders and feet vibrated and, I think, spoke. In my midintestinal section howled a din the damned have described as central to mayhem.

I stood there several weeks apart from the person I was

just a minute ago. Gillian one day early? Romp and Richie already at the pier? And my name was what? What about my zip code? Did it have five numbers like all other zip codes in America? My telephone number, too. Who *chose* those digits? Why did physicists have such difficulty bringing together the quantum and the cosmic, creating the Unified Theory that even Einstein could not crack? I had other questions at that instant, all of which had to do with the embryo I once was and the left-right-left that turned it into the six-foot contemplative lug I now was. I had half an urge to click on the tube, find a documentary, see how freighters and planes go down in the Bermuda Triangle, watch the contest between PhDs who blame rogue waves or methane gas and pot smokers who blame a portal to different dimensions.

But, negative. In the next instant I was scramming through the dark, down the stairs, with both bags in hand, saying, "Stand clear" and "Step aside," to the TV crew and Candy. They were half Kabuki, half befuddlement trying to detain an invisible spirit who, I imagined, was cackling cruelly, maybe mooning them.

Now that's me there, out in the midsummer night, the stars winking at heroes worthy of the wink, in the middle of the road trying to seize a cab and not being able to do so for five blocks or more. Once in the backseat I said to the cannabis-addled Rastafarian behind the wheel, "Brother, I have a one-hundred-dollar bill on me that would be mighty pleased if you broke laws to deliver me upon the aquarium's steps in a hurry. This, as you can see, is serious. I believe I'm about to be married."

"I be married, too, mun. Me have one wife on Pluto and another be on Mars."

"Brother," I said, "you speak my tongue. Now drive."

WHAT MORE WAS there for me to ruminate on? Very little, right? Action only now, and a few choice words for my fellow actors. The Rastafarian with multiple wives somewhere in the solar system had broken not only laws but also a world record for taxicab speed and its resultant property damage. I hurried around to the left side of the aquarium—out of breath already, vision a little blurred from ecstasy and expectation—and stopped short when I spotted the four of them on the pier, the water, boats, and various nighttime twinkles their backdrop. This next bit might have happened in *Gone with the Wind* but certainly in some other saccharine shows; in any case, you'll recognize it: the lovers behold each other from afar for the first time in too long; they let go what they're holding—I Groot's duffel bag, Gillian her backpack—and wide-eyed they begin to step closer. The steps become a jog and soon the jog a sprint, ending midway in a kissing crash—crashing kiss?—replete with snivels, the music a crescendo of violins and other tools at John Williams's disposal.

Gillian's familiar scent stabbed through my numbness and turned the faucet on full blast. Our embrace was like being mashed by the giant squid itself: we had trouble with our lungs. The clearing away of tears, the penetrating gaze into each other's eyeballs, her avowal of "my husband," mine of "my wife," apologies and forgiveness all around. Her hair was chopped off nearly to the root; I understand women do this when undergoing upheaval. I ran my hands over it and cupped her face, a face that had launched only a single ship, sure, but one that sent the juices gushing down to my lap in a blast.

It's one of the world's unjust gags: to wait for a darling someone for a spate of time, and when that someone is finally in your squeeze, life goes wavy, gets surreal, so that you can't adequately ascertain the second-by-second unfolding—you're a goldfish trying to lip-read the idiot tapping on the glass.

"Charlie," she said, sobbing.

"If only you knew where I've been, Gill. I've had quite the time. Please pinch me. Here," I said, holding out my arm, "give a pinch."

"Groot told me about your dad. I'm sorry, Charlie. I'm so sorry," and she wept some more onto my polo shirt.

After the weeping she mashed my mouth again furiously with hers, my hands wrapping around her back to cup first one gluteus and then the other, the buns I had for so long gone without, those objects of my dirty dreams I half enjoyed the horror of. More eye gazing and lip adhesion; more sentences with words like *progress* and *righteousness*, plus the phrase *never again*. Behind us: Groot, Romp, and Richie applauding, Richie swiping at his cheeks with a T-shirt sleeve.

We were the motliest five in Massachusetts.

Groot ended this well-known scene with reminders of our mission, Operation Payback, Red Team, Blue Team, all that. I didn't even have to hear the proposal; I knew what Gillian wanted: for us to release *Architeuthis* back into the wild, thus depriving Jacobi of his fortune while granting the creature its freedom. The squid was still in the holding tank belowdecks on *The Kraken*, just down to our right, in clear sight. The aquarium bigwigs were scrambling through bank accounts and the reddish tape in order to secure for the animal permanent digs inside the building. Now was the time to attack, to cause jailbreak and plunder. Something similar had happened in the Hollywood kids' flick *Free Willy*, remember, when the intrepid young protagonist risks it all to return that unsightly killer whale back to the sea. Also, Mickey Rourke liberated all the animals from the pet store at the end of *Rumble Fish*. Gillian and I had watched those films together and gone through a box of tissues doing it, so I had known since reading her letter that she wanted this release and not, as Groot had thought, to nuke the aquarium and everyone in it.

"Come hither all," I said. "Groot, please take off the Lone Ranger mask. You look ludicrous. Romp, it's good to see you. Glad Bigfoot did not have you for supper. How're the Canadian Negroes treating you?"

"I'm a French Cathar cleric: I do the diggy with my flock. They call me confessor."

"All righty then. Richie, good to see you, too. Very pleased to know you left the twins, Mimi and Mimi, ensnared in each other's legs at home. Now, I appreciate your coming here to help execute Operation Payback, but there won't be an operation tonight or any other night."

Huhs and *Whats* and *How comes*, the kind you hear in a stadium crowd when the running back fumbles.

Gillian said, "What do you mean, Charlie?"

A sweat-cooling Christian breeze rose off the water and up my shorts, where it brushed my gonads.

"People? This is how I develop here, people: by taking charge of this situation in a sensible fashion, by choosing order over chaos, by pushing instead of being pulled. I'm asserting my will."

"Oh, no," Romp said, "that dude has got to pay. I've come armed with the sacraments and I'm ready to climb aboard that ship. The African in me knows a thing or two about hegemony, not to mention theodicy."

"And I planned to jump into the tank naked and swim around with the squid," Richie said. "I'll throw some henchmen overboard. Blacken some eyes. It'll make an awesome scene."

"And Groot?" I asked. "I suppose you planned to snipe those people on the deck of the ship and then perhaps plant explosives? You wanted to kill some sons of bitches? Does that sound sane to you?"

My sweetheart said, "Jacobi can't get away with what he did to me."

"If we rescue and release the squid it'll be a loss for Jacobi, yes, but also for science, Gill. You know it needs to be studied. I'm putting an end to chaos and walking away from here, hand in hand with you."

"That's anticlimactic," Groot said.

"Yeah, babe," Richie said, "just a bit."

"Exquisitely gimp," Romp added.

"We should vote on it," Groot said. "Charlie dotes over democracy, is a fan of Pericles. Everyone in favor of chaos and vengeance, raise a hand."

They three raised their hands but Gillian and I did not.

Groot said, "Three to two in favor of carnage. The ayes have it. Carnage it is."

A minute of silence here while we five studied each other

as if meeting for the first time. And in a way it *was* the first time, because this moment would wipe away much of what had come before and alter almost all of what would come after.

"So," Groot said, "carnage, then? We're all ready for the finale."

"No, I think Charlie's right," Gillian said. "She needs to be studied," and she held my waist ever so tight.

An awkward silence and contorted, disappointed faces in every direction for another minute or more.

"Well, can't we at least kill Jacobi?" Romp said. "Leave the squid, but kill that knave? I flew all the way here from Canada for this scene."

"That's an idea," Groot said. "Richie can tear his arms out from their sockets."

"Gentlemen," I said, "do what you will. But I and my wife-to-be are heading back to the hotel. We have some catching up to do, copulation among ghosts. Let's rendezvous there later so we can make merry with abundant booze."

"Sounds wonderful," she said, and I could see in her eyes that she was drained, had aged while enduring her ordeal.

We indeed went back to our haunted bedroom then and feasted on each other for hours, her body steak for a starving man. Everything within me was newly born, tears dangling from my nose tip as I thrust in and out, gently here, fiercely there, lapping her up from toe to ear with a lengthy sojourn between her thighs, the ghosts of the hotel commingling above the bed, grinning down upon us, recalling that life-affirming glee and wanting it to last. Gillian sobbed some more over the death of my father and the heartache her wrongheadedness had battered me with. She felt better after an hour's nap.

Groot, Romp, and Richie returned to the haunted hotel, Candy broke out the beer and bottles of booze, the ghost hunters joined us at the table and chairs out back, and we all of us imbibed in the summer eve until jolly and forgetful. After Gillian and I had left the aquarium earlier, the three guys remained and loitered about, an itch within them that needed ointment, and when they spotted Jacobi emerging from the aquarium offices Groot seized him, got him in a headlock, and passed him over to Richie, who then shoulder-pressed the fat bastard clean above his head before tossing him over the railing into seaweeded water. We all raised our glasses and cheered after Groot relayed this wonderful story.

"How did you know it was him?" Gillian asked. "You had never seen him before."

"Your lover has superior powers of description," Groot said, "I remembered that mustachio from one of Charlie's memoirs. Plus that sinister, smug look on his mouth meant it could be only him," and we all laughed the laugh of contented creatures.

And then back to our bedroom for more lovemaking, inebriated and reckless. Our son, I'm proud to confess in these very pages, was conceived that night; perhaps we were abetted by those spirits, maybe even Bartholomew among them— our son does resemble my little brother. Our wedding would have to wait but one more week, in our own humble Connecticut town. What couldn't wait, however, were our plans, the blueprint for our future, every diagram of which included *Architeuthis*. Jacobi's specimen he stole from Gillian would die in captivity within a month after our night at the harbor, and although its death caused Gillian a monsoon of mucus and tears, I convinced her that this was her new opportunity to catch an even larger beast. It would be hers alone, with no headline-filching fraud to dampen her glory. Soon we'd trade our condo, our cars, and our life savings for a ship and equipment, and spend our seasons out there among immense blue, with our son named Archy suntanned at the stern, we three a story to share, one of us sutured and saved, those monsters still alive, yes, but in memory, memory alone.

ACKNOWLEDGMENTS

Heartfelt thanks to:

Bob Weil, my Maxwell Perkins, who found half a novel and made it whole.

Philip Marino for his incalculable insight and support.

Steve Almond for showing the way with fire and love.

Ed Minus for twenty years of teaching.

Lorin Rees for meals and deals.

The editors and readers who made a difference: Mitch Wieland, Steven Church, Erin Gay, Jane Jones, Todd Zuniga, Christopher Schelling, and Matthew Mahoney.

Bill Pierce, Chris Walsh, Tom DeMarchi, Julianna Baggott, and John Stazinski for encouragement when it mattered, for being the scribes and pals they are.

The committed staff at W. W. Norton, the best in the business.

Katie, my bride, and Ethan, my boy, for *being here*.

ABOUT THE AUTHOR

WILLIAM GIRALDI teaches at Boston University and is Senior Fiction Editor for *AGNI*. His nonfiction and fiction have appeared in *Harper's, The New York Times Book Review, Georgia Review, Bookforum, Southern Review, The Believer, Kenyon Review, Yale Review, American Scholar, TriQuarterly,* and *Salmagundi.* Giraldi lives in Boston with his wife and son.